ZARA DUSK

Scar

To all the people out there who sometimes suspect they're a little bit nasty

Contents

Scarla

Nausea blooms in my belly, and I fear that I'm waking up with more alcohol in my veins than blood.

Man, I hope I had a killer night because I feel like crap. I don't remember where I went and can't even open my eyes. All I can manage is lying still and trying to recall where I am.

My pillow is as hard as Hades. I wiggle my head back and forth slightly to figure it out, but the only message filtering through my brain is that it's unyielding. Uncomfortable. My whole body is stiff with cold, and the points where my shoulder blades and ass meet the mattress are painful.

This bed sucks.

Nothing like the squish-into-a-cloud mattress that I sleep on at Malanox castle. I've grown so accustomed to the spongy bed and cushy life that I can't handle a night on a dodgy bed.

I must be back in the city under the mountain... but even grogum stalk mattresses shouldn't feel this crap. Man, I'm getting soft.

I draw a deep breath, trying to garner the energy to open my eyes.

Between fluttering lids, I make out stone all around me. I'm used to sleeping under tons of rock—I grew up in the Undercity, so claustrophobia doesn't affect me. But this is unlike any cavern I've seen before. A single sconce holds a torch of flaming blubber-soaked frost wood, showing individual paving stones lining the floor and the patch of wall I can see.

I sit bolt upright. This ain't the Undercity. There, every cavern was formed through natural processes or, some say, through the Maker's will. Large caverns and tiny crevices, interconnected by mazes of tunnels.

But this room is manmade, crafted by human sweat. Tool marks are etched into the stone where some poor bugger has carved the rock to his will. Green slime grows in the deepest crevices.

Crossing my legs, I blink several times, trying to figure it out. My brain is still foggy from whatever I drank last night. The air is dank and close, untouched by even the faintest breeze.

I brush away an imaginary strand of copper hair, then remember I cut it all off. My tousled locks are short and curve around my ears like a boy. Well, that was the idea, but my hair is as disobedient as the rest of me, and I can feel it sticking out in crazy directions.

Memories filter back. I chopped off my hair in disguise to go to the dawn market without risk of being discovered by my enemy.

Another wave of nausea has me tipping to the side, retching, but nothing comes out.

My amazing I-am-a-servant disguise didn't work. Obviously. A memory assaults me of a hand clamping over my mouth and a foul-smelling rag pressed against my nose.

I leap to my feet, adrenaline coursing through me, suddenly on high alert. I'm not suffering from a hangover, I'm feeling the after-effects of being drugged. Drugged and kidnapped. Shit.

2

I need to figure out where I am, confirm who captured me, and escape.

I'm sick of being kidnapped by males. First, the Margrave of Malanox took me to his castle, and now one of his asshole angel friends has done it again. Probably. Angel VanDyke is at the top of my suspect list.

Anger tiptoes warily down my spine, warring with my drug hangover. On balance, my rage wins out, and my feet begin moving, pacing out the perimeter of my cell.

My dungeon is quite big, and the corners furthest from the sconce's flickering flames disappear into darkness. I need to know everything about this place if I'm going to escape, so I count my steps, which echo dully.

I'm pleased that my captor hasn't stolen my precious ox-hide boots. These were given to me by my mother before she died and allow me to stand on frozen tundra or burning ashes without destroying the soles of my feet. They are my most valuable possession—I guess the asswipes who took me didn't notice them. Or they were under orders not to molest me.

I stop in my tracks and quickly pat myself down. I'm still wearing the servant garb I thought was such an excellent disguise. A light-brown, coarse-woven dress with a white apron around the waist.

Usually, I'd rather swallow a skitter beetle than wear a dress. Straitjackets for women, designed to keep us in our place. Every time I put one on, I feel helpless, vulnerable, and weaker than the weather. You know you're in trouble when even a strong wind can defeat you. Plus, the damn things are cumbersome—heavy, voluminous, and damn restrictive in a fight. I prefer my shirt and pants.

I resume pacing my cell to figure out its dimensions. Twenty paces by twenty-five, a perfect rectangle—unlike anything you would find in the Undercity. Yet another reminder that I am far from home.

It's hard for me to know where home is these days. My heart clenches when I think of my dad, sleeping and working in the Undercity, and I want to be by his side. After all, he's already been abandoned by my mother and sister, although he would classify it differently.

Death isn't abandonment. His words play through my mind. Even absent, he tries to calm me down.

My sense of familial duty ties me to my father and the Undercity. But I really want to be in Malanox Castle by Zaden's side.

My body squeezes at the thought of Zaden. I have no words to describe our relationship. Sexual, definitely, but it isn't that easy. Sure, he's the hottest male in the Maker-be-damned universe, as far as I can tell, but it's more complicated than just lust.

The emotional side of our relationship is fraught with difficulties. After all, he did kidnap me and threaten to keep me prisoner until I die. But, on the other hand, he rescued me from Leo, who I'd considered my best friend before his stinging betrayal.

In short, Zaden's an asshole, but he's an asshole with a heart.

I sigh. All I know is that I want to spend more time with him to figure it out.

Boots stomp from somewhere nearby, and I realize guards are approaching.

A section of rock slides forward seamlessly, so perfectly integrated with the wall that I hadn't even noticed it. I curse myself for not using my Gaze the instant my eyes fluttered open. It should have been my first instinct to use my skills to assess my situation. I've only had Gaze a few days, so I suppose my instincts still haven't caught up with my abilities.

Hells below, I have to do better.

The slab of rock slides soundlessly to one side side with none of the crunch you'd expect from two massive slabs of stone, revealing an opening that shines with the light of a thousand suns compared to my cell's gloom.

A guard blocks the doorway, his features lit by the flickering flames from my wall sconce, a broad nose and prominent eyebrows. His uniform is dark gray with a slash of indigo running down each sleeve from shoulder to cuff.

Indigo is VanDyke's color—I recall seeing his footmen wearing livery in that hue. That means he is the fucker who kidnapped me.

So much light pours through the open door that my senses are overwhelmed. It seems as though the guard glows as brightly as an angel, but that can't be right—it must be my eyes adjusting from the gloom.

I rise to my full height, which is on par with his, and lift my chin. I may be a prisoner, but I won't allow myself to be cowed by anybody.

"Have you come to release me?" I ask imperiously, figuring I might as well try to stamp some authority onto this crapfight.

The guard just grunts and steps aside, disappearing into the darkness. He wasn't glowing—it was the angel behind him.

Count VanDyke.

I blink several times, trying to clear my vision. My nausea is ebbing, but a headache seems determined to take its place. I find the well of power within my chest, the one that controls my vestigial abilities, and I cast a gauze across it, turning down the intensity of Gaze so I can see the angel without going blind.

I am one of the rare few people alive with Gaze, which is why all these shitheads keep kidnapping me. They want to control it for themselves.

Too bad I can barely control it myself. Especially in my drug haze—another gift from the dickwad before me.

Still, I can wield it enough to dim the angel's shine while I assess him. He's beautiful. White blonde curls frame his pale, chiseled face, with fine features and a hard jaw. He towers over me, looking absolutely pristine in a cream linen suit. If a cherub mated with a God, they would produce Count VanDyke.

His perfection is marred by a bandage covering his right cheek, although the broken nose and shattered jaw Zaden gave him have already healed. I guess angels heal fast from flesh wounds, but his sliced flesh from the celestial blade is still bleeding. Good.

I want to ask how he keeps his suit so clean in such a disgusting dungeon. Instead, I tilt my chin higher and channel poise and grace. "How kind of you to have me as a guest, Count." I aim for insouciance. I don't want him to know how rattled I am by being taken prisoner—again—by a power-hungry male.

I'm getting really sick of this bullshit. But the last thing I want to do is expose any weakness to my enemy.

He shifts his weight, and the fabric of his shirt pulls tight against his chest, exposing the hard body underneath. I force my regard to remain on his face, knowing he is trying to distract me. I refuse to give him the satisfaction.

In any case, I wouldn't fuck him even if he was my ticket into heaven.

His fine lips curve into a slight smile, and his dark blue eyes twinkle in reflected torchlight. "I am glad you're taking this little... detour... so well. I know you hadn't planned to visit my castle so soon."

His smarmy grin makes me regret the tone I set for this conversation, but I suppose it's too late to go for pissed-off energy now.

I choose the middle line. "Look, Count," I say, refusing to acknowledge his status as an angel. "I don't know what game you're playing, but I want no part of it. Release me now, and I will spare your life. Again." I gesture toward the bandage on his cheek.

His blue eyes harden at being reminded that he owes me his life. The last time I saw him, Count VanDyke lay on the floor of the Undercity at Zaden's mercy, and if it wasn't for me, Zaden would have struck down his angel enemy then and there.

Clearly, VanDyke doesn't appreciate the reminder. His nose wrinkles, and I figure this cell must stink, and me along with it. "Don't forget your place, mortal. Whatever meager powers you have, you inherited from angels. They are the merest trickle of an angel's power. No matter what you do in your entire puny life, you will never have the same magic I have. You will be dead in the blink of an eye, forgotten to history. So never presume to hold sway over me."

Good. I'm pissing him off, and I couldn't be happier about it. The edge in his voice shows that I've gotten under his skin, and I know exactly how to burrow even deeper.

"Oh goodness." I smile broadly, proving that he hasn't affected my mood. "Somebody has a little inferiority complex. Now, remind me." I put a finger to my mouth as though deep in thought. "Who has the power of Gaze, which everybody seems to want so badly?" I tap my toes on the stone floor, pleased at the bunching in his shoulders which speaks to his growing anger. "Oh, that's right. It's me. And you can't kill me for it because it doesn't work that way. You have to wait until I die of natural causes. Which makes me, dickwad, immune to anything and everything you can do to me."

I put my hands on my hips in triumph, delighted at the effect I'm having. If I'm going to be his prisoner, I'll damn well irritate him for the duration.

The angel pulls himself together and smiles. "Oh, I'm so glad you mentioned that you'll have to give me Gaze on your deathbed. Because that's exactly how long I intend to keep you here."

The smile on my face falters, and I shove it back into place.

The angel steps closer, and cleanliness wafts off him like a bath of pure hot water. It makes me realize how dirty I am and how filthy my cell is. It also makes me want to run my hands along his cream suit and leave a nasty streak of grime.

VanDyke changes tack, smiling again, but this time with hooded eyes and a slight cock of the head.

"Perhaps I can make your stay more enjoyable," he purrs with a predatory smirk.

Gaze blesses me with the ability to see the power of angels, and I watch a bright orange tendril growing from the Count's open palm and snaking around my waist. It encircles my body, awakening every nerve ending. His finger of magic creeps upward and gently brushes against my breast, tugging on the nipple slightly.

I can't help it, my body tingles in response, and heat pools between my legs.

I may be able to see his power, but I'm not immune to it.

Rather than stepping away, which would only show my

discomfort, I smile sweetly and step closer until his wave of magic encircles both of us, and mere inches separate his chest from mine.

Skin tingling, I lean upward as though to kiss him, lowering my eyes to keep him unaware. But at the last moment, I drag my filthy hands down the lapels of his cream shirt, leaving a beautiful, satisfying trail of grime.

Count VanDyke snorts in disgust and steps away. "You might resist me today, mortal. But one day, you'll fall to my charms. He pauses in the doorway to look over his shoulder. "After all, you will be here for a long, long time."

Scarla

As soon as VanDyke leaves and the door slides seamlessly back into place, I kick my ass into gear and assess the space.

I remove the blanket from my internal well of power and allow my Gaze to flare. I scan my surroundings, and sure enough, the doorway shows up as bright lines outlining the rectangular shape in the rock. There are no other doorways or windows and nothing of note on the floor or ceiling.

I am too full of energy to sit, so I pace, thinking hard, pushing my headache down. I will not stay quietly under VanDyke's thumb for the rest of my days. Two plans quickly form in my mind.

The long-term plan is to play nice, eventually gain his trust, hopefully score a more comfortable bedchamber, then escape when he's least expecting it. That could take months or even years, depending on how gullible VanDyke is and how good my acting skills are.

The second plan is to fight like a mountain lion and escape using violence as soon as the chance arises.

I like Plan Two.

Minutes dwindle into hours, and the only marking of time's passing is the burning down of the frost wood in my wall sconce. It's called frost wood, but of course, in the extreme temperatures of our world, there are very few forests left, and wood is far too precious to use for fuel. Instead, we use compressed bundles of grogum stalk soaked in blubber. It burns slowly, but even so, the length of fuel is becoming shorter, filling my cell with the stench of smoky fat, and eventually, it sputters out.

The final spark traces through the air and disappears, leaving me in utter blackness.

Panic bubbles in my chest at being alone and at the mercy of an angel who is prepared to leave me to suffer in the dark. I reach deep inside myself and allow my Gaze to reach its fullest, hoping the trickle of light from the rocks will keep me company in the gloom and ease away my fears.

I don't consider myself afraid of the dark. Certain twists and turns in the tunnels of the Undercity are unlit; the farther you wander from the main cavern, the longer the distance between wall torches. But, call me crazy, being drugged, kidnapped, thrown into a cell, and having no light, has put me in a bad frame of mind.

"You're fine, Scarla," I tell myself, seeking company in the sound of my own voice. "You've seen worse."

I flick through my memories, searching for evidence that's true, but, in fact, I've never been in a shittier situation than this. At least when Zaden kidnapped me, he kept me in high luxury. Here, I seem doomed to spend the rest of my days in filth.

Powering my Gaze produces light from the doorway, a dull orange glow that delineates the opening from the surrounding rock. I experiment and try to turn the Gaze up even higher, wondering if that will make the gloomy light shine more brightly. As it is, I can't see my hand in front of my face.

Supercharging Gaze tires me. I never considered before that it must use energy. I only have a sense that it resides in the pit of my belly, and that's where I access it from. But clearly, using it at high levels fatigues me.

When I first inherited Gaze from Fra Perkins, Zaden showed up shortly afterward. I had no control over the power level back then, and he shone as bright as a star. I suspected he was a Sun God walking the earth. I've since learned that all angels shine brightly, each in their own color.

Zaden shines vibrant white and purple like he sleeps in starlight. It's stunning, with a distinct pattern and hue that is at once calming and exhilarating.

I wish Zaden was here now. His arms would wrap around me and hold me tight, and I would feel safe.

Perhaps he will scoop in and rescue me, then I won't need to rely on Plan One or Plan Two. Sadly, I can't be sure I have the patience to execute my long-term plan, and I lack the fighting skills to manage the other. Which makes Zaden my best bet.

Either way, I need to get out of here. My heart beats hard for a few seconds, and I get the sense it aligns with the drumming of Zaden's, wherever he is.

"Shit, Scarla," I tell myself. Zaden doesn't even know where I am. How will he rescue me?

Even worse, when I left his castle, he was on his sickbed, still recovering from his last fight with VanDyke. Hopefully, that means VanDyke is weak too, which gives me some chance to escape under my own steam. But, besides the bandage on his cheek, he looked freaking perfect.

Sick of pacing, I sit with my butt against the wall and pull my knees close to my chest for warmth. I hope the patch of rock beneath my ass isn't covered in that green slime. I wiggle and, thankfully, don't slide. I think I'm in the clear.

With my vestigial Gaze at full power, another light suddenly shines through the rock, far above me. It has the quality of an angel's glow but is much dimmer, and I wonder if I'm seeing VanDyke through layers and layers of rock.

But why am I just detecting him now? Does that mean my Gaze is growing stronger? Or has another angel entered the castle?

My breath hitches as the image of Zaden forms in my mind. It vanishes as the cell door slides inward. I leap to my feet, inwardly kicking myself—I didn't hear the footsteps approach. I have to do better.

This time, no blinding glow is exposed behind the door, so I can see instantly that VanDyke isn't present. It's just a pair of guards wearing their gray uniforms with the slash of indigo down each sleeve.

The same guard from before, the one with the prominent eyebrows and general Neanderthal look about him, pulls me to my feet. "You're coming with us," he says, more grunt than words.

I bite back a sarcastic comment. I'll save my backchat for VanDyke. Instead, I go willingly.

Wherever they're taking me can't be worse than this.

Can it?

Scarla

The guards lead me up a never-ending set of stone stairs that curls around a central pylon. At least the air is sweet because I'm sucking in lungfuls of it.

Seriously, if I don't emerge all the way up in heaven—or at least as high as the clouds—I want my money back.

"Is it much further?" My thighs ache with the unaccustomed exercise. I can walk horizontally as far as you want, but up and down? No, thanks.

The Neanderthal dude grunts, and the other makes no noise whatsoever.

"Where are we going?" I persist. These guys are more likely to give me honest answers than VanDyke, but they're not talking. Not even a grunt this time. Obviously they've been ordered not to speak to me. Or they're just pricks.

Finally, we emerge into a corridor in the castle proper, no grimy stone floors and poorly lit spaces here. A light gray rug bordered in indigo runs the length of the hallway, and my eyes widen as I pass statues of naked women carved from actual wood and carved busts of some old white dude who VanDyke must consider important.

The outrageous waste of wealth forms a ball of anger in my chest. This is even more lavish than Zaden's castle, and I gave him a real hard time.

It still bugs me. The amount of riches being thrown away here is disgusting when it could be used to make poor lives more bearable.

Intricately woven tapestries along the walls are interspersed with oil paintings depicting long-forgotten scenes of people picnicking outdoors in the midday heat.

Can you imagine? Actual people going outside while the sun is shining? Apart from angels and the odd freak like me, nobody can survive full sunlight. It will singe a person's eyebrows right off before boiling their brain in the cauldron of their skull.

I shake my head. Before long, I am deposited through a doorway, and the door slams shut behind me.

I throw an angry glance behind me, but it soon melts from my face at the glorious vision before me. This room is forged from stone but lovingly carved and cleaned. A stone bath sits in the center of the room, filled with steaming water, fragranced with petals and blooms.

A silver panel hanging from the wall is polished to such a high shine that I can see my reflection in it. I quickly glance away, not wanting to face how disgusting I look.

Two maids wearing cream skirts and indigo aprons stand on either side of the bath with their hands folded demurely.

Nobody else is present. This could be my chance to escape—although I'm sure those guards are right outside the door. But before I do anything rash, I need answers.

Seeing the maids has jogged the final missing memory from what happened yesterday. I wasn't alone at the market, I was accompanied by my maid, Molly.

Not just my maid, but maybe my best friend—my list of

buddies is rapidly shortening, and Molly is definitely up near the top.

"Where's Molly?" I demand.

One maid, the softer of the two, with slanting eyes and delicate bones, glances nervously at the other. I figure she's the weak link, so I aim my next question at her.

"Molly is the maid who was captured with me, and I need to know where she is. I need to know that she's all right. So tell me, please, where is she?"

The woman pales, her waxy skin turning almost translucent. Her black eyes dart toward her colleague again, but she doesn't answer my question.

I shrug. "Fair enough, I get it. You're intimidated by my beauty, my beautiful clothes, my general air of superiority. Don't worry about it." I'm wearing filthy rags, my hair sticks out in every direction, my breath is rotten, and I stink—I have never looked worse.

The pale maid's mouth twitches in the beginnings of a smile, and I can see I'm getting through to her.

"Please, just tell me that she's okay, and I promise I won't ask any more questions."

The maid stares at her shoes, resting her focus anywhere but on me.

I sigh. I'll have to think of another way to get the information I need. On the other hand, it's hard not to be enticed by the aromatic steam rising from this hot bath. "I assume this is for me?"

The servant nods. Opening up this trickle of communication feels like a small victory.

I untie my apron around my waist and let it drop to the floor. Instantly, both maids are at my side, helping me out of my clothes.

"I can do it myself." They ignore me, of course, and keep pawing at me until I relent and allow them to unbutton my dress and pull it over my head. They even unhook my bra and tug my panties down, which feels utterly ridiculous.

How do rich people enjoy this?

Honestly, I would so much rather do that myself. Now I'm standing naked, filthy, and as awkward as fuck in front of two women who barely acknowledge my existence.

Hurriedly, I step into the bath, eager to hide beneath the layered petals on the surface.

Space in the Undercity is limited, and groups of families sleep together, so I'm accustomed to changing near others. But we are all masters at turning our backs and averting our eyes, so the intense focus of these two women is disconcerting.

Heat from the bath scalds my toe when I step in, but I don't let that slow me down. I practically dive under the bath's surface and submerge my entire body for an instant before coming up for air.

The nervous maid glances at her colleague, and I can tell what she's thinking.

Why doesn't the heat burn her?

Perhaps they've heard of my heat resistance, another vestigial power I inherited over the years, in which case, they'd be thinking something different.

So, the rumors are true.

Yes, the rumors are true. My imperviousness to temperature is my most useful skill. Loitering outside as the sun comes up has gotten me out of many a fight in my time—it's my trump card. Also handy when the sun goes down, and the world turns to ice.

I smirk a little, pleased to have confounded these maids.

Soaking in the tub feels magnificent, as though my reserve of happiness is being restored. Every second beneath the hot, fragrant water brings me more contentment. Plus, it signifies that the Count intends to let me live aboveground in a proper bedchamber, possibly with my own personal maids. Plan One is progressing nicely.

Without a word, the nervous maid rubs shampoo into my wet hair and massages my scalp. Now, I hate power imbalance and the whole master-and-slave deal as much as the next girl, but having somebody massage my head is pure heaven and enough to make my ideals fly out the window. I could definitely live like this.

The taller, more self-assured maid brings me a towel and holds it out, expecting me to rise from the bath and into its folds. Well, I decide not to. If she doesn't have the decency to engage me in conversation, I'll happily play dumb.

I ignore her, close my eyes, and sink deeper into the blissful liquid.

The maid clears her throat, and I count that as another victory. Finally, she's made a damn noise. I peer at her through half-open lids, shake my head slightly and resume my repose.

I feel maybe ten percent bad for my behavior—after all, these maids are just following orders. But on the other hand, they have it much better than most poor bastards living outside the castle walls, and they choose willingly to work for a rich asshole like Angel VanDyke.

So, mostly, I feel good.

Until the maid begins tipping buckets of cold water into my bath. That erases my joy real fast.

With as much dignity as I can muster, I rise and step out of the bath into the waiting towel. The taller, crankier servant walks away to find a hairbrush, and I whisper to the other. "Why am I getting this wash? Is something special happening?"

She glances around to make sure her friend won't overhear, then whispers. "You're going to see the angels."

Scarla

If I hate wearing a servant's dress, then putting on an evening gown makes me want to scratch somebody's eyes out.

After the maids dried me, they puffed and preened me then stuffed me into this floor-length indigo dress that exactly matches the color of VanDyke's livery.

It is so low-cut at the back that if I sit down, my butt cheeks will probably flop out onto the chair, and so low in front that I need to walk smoothly and avoid sudden movements to keep my girls in place.

And no, I had no choice.

The guards meet me on the far side of the bathroom door, and the Neanderthal one appraises me openly, which I repay with a scowl. "Keep your eyes to yourself." I'm not above flirting with gents to get my way, but these guys aren't offering me any information, so I keep my hair flips to myself.

Besides, with so much skin showing, I feel vulnerable and exposed. Which is precisely the effect VanDyke wants, I'm certain.

He may be able to control my clothing, but he can't control my face. I settle into a filthy expression as the guards fling open a grand set of double doors into a dining hall.

Two men sit at a table, which heaves under the weight of

a banquet that could feed twenty. Roast chicken, hunks of unidentifiable red meat, plus platters and bowls of vegetables. All of it drips in rich-smelling fat.

"Here she is, my favorite prize." VanDyke beams at me. He has gone full cherub again, wearing a pristine suit in ivory that closely matches his tight blond curls and straight white teeth. He is immaculate, as always, and glows with his angel's shine. The only consolation is that bandage still covering his right cheek.

The other man shines just as brightly, in a vibrant green. He's clearly an angel too but not one I've seen before. At least, not as far as I can tell. He is stocky but wears a mask obscuring his face from hairline to chin, leaving no skin exposed.

The only parts of his body I can see are his short, stubby fingers, glistening from the fat of a dead animal.

The masked face turns toward me slowly, and my gut churns. A strong sense of power emanates from him, but I cannot detect any magic other than his green angelic glow.

Something about his stillness and intangible energy is disturbing, and his bone-white hand dripping in animal juices makes me shudder.

I am accustomed to sensing powers in others, but it usually comes with the visual—a stream of magic visible to my eyes through Gaze. But not with this man. He flings me right off my pedestal and back among the masses, who can only gape in awe at angels' abilities, unable to see their magic at work.

"What a pretty specimen she is," the angel says, looking me over and making my skin crawl. "Come here, pretty girl."

I don't move an inch, but all my muscles bunch, ready to flee. The way his eyes roll over my half-naked body makes my skin itch as though spiders are scuttling down my arms and chest.

His voice hardens. "You'll do as I say, mortal."

I summon my anger to keep my voice steady. "I'll do as I please, angel." I never gave in to Zaden, and I don't intend to start now.

I watch a line of grease drip down the angel's wrist and into his cuff before he answers. He chuckles darkly. "You will obey me."

Pain stabs through the palm of my left hand, and I double over in agony, holding it against my chest. I glance around for my assailant, expecting somebody with a dagger or a longbow, the fingers of my right hand seeking to staunch the flow of blood.

But there is none. The skin of my tormented hand is unbroken, pale and pink and not running with rivers of blood.

I look up at the masked man in horror. Frantically, I search for a sign of his magic, but no stream of particles lights the air, and I can't figure out what's happening. My breathing shallows and the pain in my hand is crippling. I can't think straight.

"Everybody bows to me, girl," the masked man says, and I suddenly understand.

He's using Inflict. A dark vestigial power that can only be inherited by murder. This male has killed a vestige, so he won't think twice about my life.

I glance at VanDyke, who regards me through lowered lids as though watching his favorite play. Clearly, he's enjoying the show.

I can't get past that word *murder*. But I'm sure VanDyke has killed too, and I know Zaden has. Famously, that's what angels do.

22

"You have Inflict," I gasp, and the agony in my hand subsides instantly.

The man adjusts his blue jacket, and the grease from his fingers transfers to the lapel. "Very good." I can hear the smile in his voice though I can't see his face. "I also have Gaze. Just like you. Always remember, mortal, that I am superior to you in every way."

The masked man has Inflict and Gaze, the dyad. He is the Cloaked King. His disguise makes sense—his identity is always protected to keep him safe from the vengeance of other angels.

I fold my arms across my chest and shake my head. "No, you'll always be a disgusting slug with filthy hands. At least I'm clean."

It's childish and superficial, but I can't help it, I need to get under his skin. That's been a lifelong problem—my need for conflict and the inability to put up with anybody's bullshit.

Pain lances up my arm, a bolt of lightning zapping from my fingers to my shoulder. I cry out in agony, unable to hold the torment in. My entire forearm must be in flames, but it isn't. Impossible. My limb twitches with electricity, and I know it will be damaged beyond use.

I sob and nurse my arm against my chest, but nothing eases the torture. I fall to my knees, weeping, and I don't even care. Right now, I don't give a fuck how weak my enemies think I am. I'll do anything to ease the fire in my limb.

The Cloaked King releases me from torment, and I sag in relief. My body is wracked with sobs, and it takes me several moments to calm them. I wriggle my fingers tentatively. Insanely, my hand is uninjured, my digits still work, and my arm is fine. But pain's memory lingers, and I doubt I'll ever forget it.

The King leers at me as I climb to my feet. "You'll learn, girl," he says, smiling like a benevolent teacher.

Count VanDyke leans forward, grinning as though this is the moment he's been waiting for his whole life. "Oh, she's a very slow learner. Aren't you, Scarla?"

A serving girl drops a steaming hot roll onto the Cloaked King's side plate, and he seizes her around the waist, making me jump at the sudden movement. The girl squeaks and struggles, but the arm around her middle is an iron band. The King grabs her pussy with a fat, greasy hand, and the serving girl stifles a scream and wriggles to escape, but then she collapses into his embrace with a soft smile and rubs herself against him.

He is inflicting her with pleasure. I throw myself at the King to knock him off her, but one of the Count's guards grabs me roughly, and I can't get to her. I just have to witness this fucking horror.

"Get off her," I scream, but the King grins like I'm adding to his enjoyment, so I shut the hell up.

Finally, he releases the poor woman. The disgust on her face mirrors that crawling down my spine, and I want to shake the Cloaked King's shoulders until his brain rattles.

But I can't. His ability to inflict pain is too potent, and I am utterly vulnerable before it. I watch the serving girl scuttle away then keep my eyes anywhere but on the Cloaked King.

At a nod from the Count, the guard releases me. My blood has settled enough that I refrain from attacking the Cloaked King, though I would dearly love him to experience a tenth of the pain he inflicted on me. The serving girl is safe enough now, and I'm sure she won't return.

I train my Gaze around the room, doing my best to block

out the glare from the two angels, looking for something, anything, that might help me escape.

It didn't take Gaze to find it. Four windows along the wall are open. Open! I've never seen an open window in my life. Over in Zaden's Castle in Malanox, the dining hall has windows overlooking Penngrove Forest, which I thought was fancy enough. Malanox Castle is insulated using sorcered stone and Maker-knows what else, but nothing potent enough to allow the windows to remain open outside dawn or dusk.

But here, the windows are flung wide despite the stars twinkling in the night sky. It must be freezing out there, yet servants line the walls without solidifying into human-shaped icicles.

I amble closer to the table, throwing in a saunter and a hip sway to distract the two angels. It seems to be working. They follow my progress but make no move to stop me. I walk behind VanDyke's chair, running a finger along his back, noticing the fineness of his suit material beneath my touch.

I lean down close to his ear, catching his soapy lavender scent. "No grime this time, I promise."

He smiles wickedly, and his lust magic kisses my skin for a moment, but I refuse to be distracted and quickly move away.

I've made it to the windows, but both males still stare at me. Peeking out, I see the grass three floors below. Cool air laced with the aroma of actual flowers in the garden brushes my face and tousles my hair, and I long to get outside. But three stories is a long way down.

Would that jump kill me?

Even a set of broken legs would be bad enough to halt my escape. I imagine throwing myself out the window, freedom tasting like rushing wind and cold air but ending in a painful thud against the solid ground.

No, that won't work. I might be about as patient as a toddler with a bladder problem, but I will have to wait.

The perfect opportunity for escape will come at some stage. It has to.

Scarla

I refuse to watch the cloaked king stuff oily food beneath his mask, and though my belly grumbles, I can't bring myself to eat a mouthful.

Thankfully, I only have to endure the lingering looks and spine-crawling stares for a little longer, and the evening finally ends.

A guard escorts me along the corridor, and I'm pleased to note we aren't returning to the long, winding staircase that descends to the dungeons. It would hardly feel fitting for somebody dressed as I am.

My indigo gown sweeps the floor, covering my ox-hide boots. "Where are you taking me?" The guard doesn't answer—no surprises there. "Look, I know how it is. You've got a wife and kids to feed, you're working for the man. So you think you have to do whatever he says. But if you talk to me, I promise I won't tell. Go on, spill the tea. Where are you taking me?"

The guard looks at me as though I'm a nuisance, which I suppose I am. This guy is more buttoned up than the Margrave on solstice.

"Strong silent type, hey? I can respect that. Maybe you could mime it instead? You could act out what the room's like, or just point. I'm not fussy."

I'm so relieved to be out from under the stare of those privileged, entitled twats that my mood is buoyant. And this poor quiet guard is taking the brunt of my happiness.

He remains stoically silent, but after I'm quiet for a few moments, he glances at me as if to check if I've disappeared. His regard soaks me in the scent of raw onions.

"Yep, I'm still here. Although if you could escort me to the exit, that would be fine. I can make my own way home from there."

The guard's eyes narrow, and no sign of amusement crosses his features, so I can't mark him down as a potential ally. Too bad, I'll have to keep working on that.

We tunnel through a maze of hallways and finally stop outside a plain wooden door. My lips curve at the thought of sleeping in a comfortable bed and having ready access to fresh water and clean clothes.

Wow, does that make me an entitled princess? No. Even in the Undercity, folks have plentiful water and mattresses. I'm perfectly justified not to want to sleep on a stone floor in a rat-infested dungeon.

Satisfied, I push open the door and step into an unadorned room with simple furnishings and three beds. First things first, I glance to the wall, looking for a window and potential escape route, but find none.

Then I'm ambushed. "Scarla!" Molly engulfs me in a hug, and I squeeze her back so tight that she protests.

She's slightly shorter than me, so my cheek rests against the top of her brown hair, and her thin body presses against mine. I breathe in her hay smell and smile. She's still wearing her Malanox castle serving clothes, the same coarsely-woven beige dress and cream apron as my not-a-disguise disguise.

"I'm so glad you're safe, babe," I say, pressing her tightly again before releasing her. The tight knot in my chest releases somewhat at seeing her, and I realize how worried I was for her safety. "I wasn't sure if you were taken too."

I smile. Molly's brown eyebrows knit together, and the large freckle above her lip wobbles. "The last thing I remember is being at the dawn market, then I woke up in this room. I... I thought maybe they...." Her intelligent eyes look up at me with such angst and concern that I can see she was more than a little worried for me.

"I'm fine," I assure her.

She puts her hands on her hips. "No thanks to you," she scolds. "I told you it was too dangerous to go to the market, but did you listen to me? No. Next time, listen."

"Okay."

"Promise?"

"Promise. Besides, we're together now."

She clasps my hands and squeezes. "Thank the Maker." Then she steps back and assesses me with a tilt of her head. "And what exactly are you wearing? I don't recall squeezing you into that dress."

I shrug, feeling the soft silk of my evening gown shift along the curve of my hip. "I figured I'd frock up for our big reunion," I joke, and Molly finally cracks a full grin.

She is definitely on my friends list. I rack my brain to think of somebody in my life that I'm closer to, but I draw a blank. Since my allegedly "best" friend Leo betrayed me, I've been searching for a replacement for the top spot.

And it seems like a maid hired to spend time with me is my best option.

Still, with that funky grin and the dancing freckle on her top lip that jiggles and wiggles with every sentence she utters, I can't feel disappointed with my selection.

"This is Bwadu," Molly says, flinging out an arm.

Frustration at letting my guard down again floods my body, and I whirl around to take in the room properly. The stinky onion breath guard has departed and closed the door behind him, but Molly and I are not alone.

Three beds are evenly spaced on the far wall, and lounging on one is a muscular, ebony-skinned woman who looks as though she could skin me alive with a flick of her wrist. Instant respect.

Molly's sudden, half-wild introduction to the woman gives me cause for pause, and I reel in my initial instinct to smile and introduce myself. I'm done being the sweet female.

Instead, I search inside for my well of power and control its release, so only a trickle fills my body, and the slightest hint of Gaze is unleashed. The last thing I want to do is blind myself if she turns out to be another angel.

I scan Bwadu from head to toe. She certainly isn't an angel, she lacks the bright shine those assholes have. Nor is she a vestige like me. Vestiges have a trickle of angels' power, created only when a mortal witnesses an angel's death and passed on from deathbed into suitable receptacles. Like me.

Vestiges have a subtle glow—much dimmer than angels—but Bwadu has none.

Inside her, the thin line of power runs from her head down her spine, as though I can see her very essence. The same as any other human.

Apart from those bunching muscles and that predatory expression. Her cheekbones are prominent, and a small tattoo of a curling orange leaf graces her left temple. The symbolism in the tatt is obvious, a reminder of the dying trees and a scornful comment on society's power structure. She must be from the Resistance.

Or I'm reading way too much into her ink.

I briefly cast my Gaze around the rest of the room to check for danger before sucking it back into the well within me. "Bwadu, my name is Scarla. I'm pleased to meet you."

The dark-skinned beauty reclines on her bed, but the pose is anything but relaxing. She looks like a coiled serpent, ready to pounce at the slightest provocation.

"You already know my name," she says without a smile.

I can't deny the eerie feeling of meeting a woman who doesn't flash a smile. It happens so rarely, and it is genuinely intimidating. I silently pat myself on the back for not offering her a grin either. Hopefully, that will make me seem fierce and capable, as she seems to me.

"Bwadu is from the outer city," Molly explains, although that doesn't help me understand anything.

"The outer city?"

Bwadu's voice is strong and clear, like a gong ringing in a library. "We are in Solren. The inner city is protected by a sorcered dome impervious to temperature changes. People can go outside at any time of day or night." That's right, I remember learning that on my last—and first—visit here. "The outer city is the ring around that. We have no protection from the elements and can only step outside at dawn or dusk."

I shrug. If she expects me to be impressed by that, she's got another thing coming. Back home in Malanox, even the rich folks don't have the protection of a dome and must stay within their own houses for twenty-three hours a day.

"So, you're from the poor part of town. That doesn't seem like a reason to detain you." I turn and jiggle the handle on the door, confirming that we're locked inside. "Are we captives here?"

Bwadu lifts one shoulder, looking as fierce as fuck. As soon as I'm alone, I'm going to practice that move in front of a reflective pool. "It could be that, it could be something else," she says.

Molly leans in and whispers. "She killed a guard."

I quirk an eyebrow, hiding how impressed I am. And scared. "A city guard?"

A lock of Molly's brown hair that has escaped her bun snags on her lips as she shakes her head. "No, a man from VanDyke's personal unit."

"Why?" I demand, whirling on Bwadu. If I'm going to be stuck playing sleepovers with a murderer, I'll damn well find out her mettle.

With fluid ease, she rises to her feet in one movement, and I'm surprised to see she is almost as tall as me. I'm so accustomed to being taller than other women, and most men, and I can see the same shock cross her features.

She takes a predatory step toward me, all feline grace. "I didn't like the way he looked at me."

I refuse to back away as she steps closer, but my heart picks up, thrumming a tune. "Well, that makes sense then," I quip, pleased I'm keeping my cool.

Bwadu stops stalking me, and her lips twitch in a smile. The curling leaf tattoo on her temple jumps. "Good. I'm glad we're on the same page."

I'm not at all sure that we are. She seems to be on the page where you kill guards for no good reason or not one you're keen to disclose.

But I'm reading from an entirely different book. I have been captured for my ability to use Gaze, nothing more or less. I'm not here because of my actions; nothing I said or did resulted in my abduction.

At least Bwadu is here because she stabbed a man. I eye her sideways, realizing I have no idea how she killed him. From the look of those muscles, she could have strangled him barehanded.

Not me. I'm here because of who I am, not what I did, and that thought rattles inside me like a ricocheting projectile.

It's not fair. But I plan to do something about it and get the hell out of here.

I meet Bwadu's eyes again, who still stands there, watching me with her hands on hips and muscles bulging, still waiting for a reply. I could learn a thing or two from her.

A thought occurs to me. Her strength and attitude might be just what I need to help me escape.

I smile. "Perhaps you're right. Maybe we are on the same page."

Zaden

I wake up with memories of Scarla's lips chasing me from my dreams. It takes more than a few deep breaths to shake those thoughts away.

I pull myself to sitting and lean against the bed head, rolling my shoulders to assess how quickly my injuries are healing.

Damage from a celestial blade heals slowly, but I'm pleased to feel less pain and know the jagged wound running between my shoulder blades must be almost invisible.

I'll regain my full strength in a few more days, although the scar will never heal completely.

Then I can take Scarla up on her suggestive smile when I last saw her exiting my chamber. Her burning kiss still sears my lips, and the sway of her hips is imprinted into my mind.

She won't know what hit her when I regain my strength. I won't let her get away with a saucy suggestion without staying longer by my side.

I frown. She hasn't visited me in over a day. I hope she's not angry with me. Again. She tried to kill me a few days ago, but our relationship has changed a lot since then. I hope.

So why hasn't she come to see me?

Bright sunshine streams through my bedroom windows, lighting the tapestries and rich furnishings with a golden glow.

For the first time since I was injured, I pull myself to my feet unassisted. Gingerly, I take a step, gaining confidence when my knees don't buckle and the pain in my back is just a dull throb.

I intend to find answers. Even if that Maker-be-damned mortal hates me, I want to hear it from her lips. Then I can set about removing it, either with kisses or with the lash of my tongue.

For the first time since I was injured, I leave the safety of my bedchamber and step into the hallway. The carpet is soft beneath my bare feet, and I stride quickly through the twists and turns toward Scarla's room, knowing the castle as well as I know my own heartbeat.

I barge into her bedchamber without knocking, not caring if she's in a state of undress. She should have thought of that before ignoring me for almost forty-eight hours.

Her bed is beautifully made, and on the nightstand rests a full jug of fresh water. Her room is pristine, and if she slept here last night, the servants were quick to put things to rights.

Snarling, I step into her adjoining bathing chamber, half hoping to find her submerged in a hot bath. But it is empty.

I return to the bedchamber, my eye lingering for a moment on the place where she sleeps, imagining her face is soft repose upon that very pillow when my superior hearing picks up a faint scuttle in the doorway.

A serving girl, probably attracted by my stomping and growling, glances at me for a moment with alarm, her eyes wide, then ducks her head and dips into a small curtsy.

"Forgive me, Margrave."

She darts away but stops in her track when I snarl, "Stop!"

She is one of many serving girls; I don't know her name or

want to. I just want to know where Scarla is.

"She... I don't know, Margrave," the girl stutters when I demand to know Scarla's whereabouts.

I step toward the girl so that no more than six feet separate us, and she cowers but doesn't dare move backward. "Tell me everything you know. When was she last seen?"

"She... She went to the dawn market."

"Today?" I roar. I explicitly forbade her from going there. The dangers are too numerous. Scarla may be capable and fierce, but she is no match for an avenging angel, and one of the most powerful angels in all of Aubia is on her enemy list.

The maid shakes her head. The contrast between her and Scarla couldn't be more stark. Whenever I try to inflict my fury on that damnable mortal, she tilts her chin at me and snaps right back.

But this woman is all meek terror. "No... No, sir. Yesterday."

"Yesterday?" I step closer and struggle to keep my rage contained. If my celestial blade Ashmodu was in its rightful place at my hip, it would sing for blood and slice through this woman before I gave it a moment's thought.

As it is, an image of Scarla's frown flits through my mind, and I make do with balling my hands into fists.

"Why did nobody tell me about this?" I spit through gritted teeth. She cowers more, too frightened to talk, so I school my voice into calmness. "You may speak and fear no repercussions for your words."

She bobs another quick curtsy. "She asked us not to tell you, milord."

"And does the household answer to her now instead of me?" My voice is quietly contained fury.

"N-no, Margrave."

Clearly this woman has no more to tell me, so I shoo her away like the nuisance she is. "Leave."

She scuttles out the door, and I cross to the window, trying to figure out where Scarla could be.

She hated me once and vowed to kill me. She even obtained a celestial blade capable of causing mortal harm to an angel to accomplish that task. But, in the few short weeks since then, I like to think she has changed her mind and grown at least a little fond of me.

Her window overlooks the curving river that springs beneath my castle and curls around as a protective moat before heading south toward Solren. Across the river, the tall buildings of Hightown cluster around the river's curve for ready access to freshwater. Beyond it lie the hovels of Lowtown and, in the distance, the mountain that protects the poorest of the poor from the elements.

The mountain where Scarla was born and raised, where she spent so many years tending to the sick. If she hadn't witnessed so many deaths in the infirmary of the Undercity, she wouldn't have inherited so many vestigial powers. Her ability to withstand temperatures, for one.

And Gaze. Gaze is the one I need to return to heaven, from which I was so unfairly cast.

I am a Fallen Angel, the greatest shame that can be born by a celestial being. Heaven calls to me, singing with longing, and my soul will never be complete until I return. And return I will. But to find the gates of heaven, I need Gaze.

A long sigh escapes me. Can I really forgive Scarla for having conflicting emotions? I myself can barely reconcile my need to control her with my desire to worship her.

I run a finger along the window sill and find a clumped lock of copper hair. Upon closer inspection, I can see where a blade sliced through one end, and I realize she must have cut off her hair as a disguise.

Damn foolish mortal.

Anguish rises within my body, an unwelcome visitor with which I am unfamiliar. Usually, I am in command of everything I see and at the mercy of nobody and nothing.

But the prospect that Scarla may have fallen into her enemies' hands makes me feel powerless, and I detest the sensation. Worse, it brings back memories I've spent years trying to forget. Memories of Elanora and my absolute fucking failure to save her. If Scarla becomes another Elanora, I will lose my damn mind.

I fling open the window and climb onto the ledge, barely able to fit my shoulders between the stone sides. Bright sunshine warms my face, and I turn it upward, straining to remember what heaven feels like. Then I throw myself out into the bright day and fall toward the red earth, letting that feeling swoop in my belly for a moment before I snap open my wings and soar.

For the first time since I was injured, I am flying.

I have spent decades ensuring that rumors of my existence remain precisely that. Rumors.

No, it's probably been centuries by now. Nothing instills fear and panic as quickly as something that people don't understand, so it's easiest to keep my celestial nature hidden.

But here I am, in broad daylight, soaring over the stone manors of Hightown, and the ramshackle huts of Lowtown, beating my wings occasionally to keep my altitude.

Wind rushes through my hair, and the hot sun beats down on my back and feathers, but I don't care. I am intent on reaching my destination as fast as possible, and wings are faster than horses' hooves.

I soar to a landing right outside the entrance to the Undercity and snap my wings back into place, then cover them with a glamor. The motion ignites a river of pain across my back from my recent injuries, but I pay no heed.

I stride into the cavern entrance, sparing a glance for the guard on duty. His soapy smell reminds me of Scarla.

"You do not need to remember this," I tell him, lacing the words with a sprinkle of magical intent to help them take root in his mind.

I push aside the heavy ox-hide hangings, and the temperature immediately plummets. Past the second set of hide hangings, the heat falls again to a comfortable human level, and the main cavern, which could just about fit my castle, buzzes with people. The scent of the kitchen and the chickens and goats housed beyond it assaults me.

Many faces turn to look at me, and I glance down at my clothing. I've come straight from my bed without even bothering to don a cloak, so it's no wonder I'm attracting attention. My black shift is so short it barely covers my junk, and the bunching muscles of my thighs are on full display.

Even with this realization, I don't pause a beat. It doesn't matter what Undercitysiders make of me, especially since most of them will forget they saw anything. Their gazes tend to slide off me as though my years of hiding my true identity have made me invisible to mortals.

Without breaking stride, I climb the stairs at the far end of the main cavern, the steps cold and dusty underfoot, and emerge at the mezzanine level reserved for councilors.

A group of gray-haired men in various shades, but very few women, greets me, and I turn my scowl to maximum.

"Where's Leo?" I demand. If anybody knows what happened to Scarla, it is her weaselly fucking has-been of a friend.

Scarla

"I assume you want to get out of here as much as I do," I say to the ceiling, lying on my bed with my hands behind my head.

"Obviously," Bwadu answers from her own bed.

She is sitting up facing me. I sense her staring at me and force myself not to look back. It feels as though she's assessing my strength, and if we're going to work together, I need to impress her.

"How much do you know about the castle's layout?" I ask.

She snorts a laugh. "Enough to know we can't just find a window and leap out." I glance at her sharply, wondering if she has some vestigial ability to read minds because that's the very plan I considered over dinner last night.

I'm reassured by her lack of glow and return my focus to the ceiling. Stiff stalks poke through the mattress into my back. "Why not?"

From my peripheral vision, I see her shrug. "Two concentric rings of castle walls, the outer one with manned watchtowers and guards patrolling the ground. Some kind of sorcered tripwire alerts them to unauthorized movements on top of the walls. The shifts rotate daily and randomly switch between different duties, so they can't be bribed."

I turn to my side, staring at her, forgetting about trying to

appear cool. "Hells below! You know a shitload about that."
I've heard rumors of guerilla groups forming a resistance to
the Lords and Counts and Margraves who have so much when
the poor have so little.

Am I having a conversation with a guerilla?

A shiver runs down my spine and a thousand questions birth
on my tongue. How many resistance fighters are there? Are
they ready to strike? What are their plans? Do they know that
most of the world's rulers are actually angels?

And how do they plan to deal with those celestials?

I've only ventured out of Malanox twice, both times coming
here to Solren, both times in the last couple of weeks, and both
times under duress. But I can't honestly say it's been all bad.
Spending time in a bigger city has made me appreciate how
vast our country, Aubia, is.

Bwadu herself is evidence of this. Back home, the resistance
fighters are nothing but murmur and conjecture, but here she
is, living and breathing and smirking, a rumor personified.

"We've done our research," she answers cryptically, making
it clear she really is part of a group.

I swing my legs over the bed's edge and sit facing her, hands
on my knees, our faces mere inches apart. "Are you a guerilla?"
I whisper.

Okay, so I've definitely lost any cool points I might have
earned with her, but I can't help it. I'm like a kid on solstice,
staring up at the fireworks and having my first taste of mulled
honey. I need to know everything.

Her mouth twists, and I can't tell if it's a smile or a frown.
The tattoo of the curling orange leaf on her temple shimmers
in the reflected torchlight. She parts her lips to answer, and
I hold out my hand. "Stop. You can't tell me. Not yet." I

remember that I live in Malanox Castle with the Margrave of Malanox as my lover—sort of—so maybe she shouldn't tell me her plans. I would've jumped at the chance to take the rich bastards down a month ago, but now I feel compromised.

She leans in close to whisper, and my pulse thumps. "I'm pretty sure resistance fighters don't spill their plans to everyone they meet," she says, then reclines back on her bed, smirking.

Riiight. Sure. That makes sense. She doesn't know me from a bar of soap, so why would she confide her deepest secrets?

Come to think of it, the only thing I know about her is that she's in this room with me. She *said* she killed a guard, but we don't know if that's true. Maybe she's a spy, trying to get information from me about the Margrave or aiming to butter me up so I'm happy to spend my life in this hell hole.

I turn my back on her and face Molly, whose bed is on the other side of mine. Somehow I ended up with the crappest bed in the center.

She rests with her eyes closed, hands folded neatly on her belly. Her chest rises and falls shallowly, so I can tell she isn't asleep. "Are you okay, Moll?"

At being addressed by her mistress, she sits bolt upright. "Yes, thank you."

I sigh. "Cut the crap, Moll. We're equals, all right." She's had a lifetime of serving, so it goes against her instincts to treat me as a normal human being.

"Sure," she says, lying down slowly. "So why do I always fetch the water?"

A laugh bubbles up within me, and I let it free. Molly's face creases in a grin, her freckle dancing on her lip, and she brushes a stray strand of brown hair from her face.

"Fair point," I say, still grinning. But a little worm inside my chest wriggles at her words, and I wonder why I didn't notice before that she does all the work.

Perhaps I'm not as enlightened as I like to think.

* * *

I lie on my bed, staring at the ceiling and listening to Molly's gentle exhales, when a thump on the door sends adrenaline through my veins.

Molly and I spring to standing like soldiers being inspected, and Molly is so erect I think she's going for an award. Bwadu couldn't give a shit—she leans against the wall languidly, inspecting her fingernails.

The door swings open, revealing Leo. I search for the cheeky grin and easygoing charm of my childhood friend, but his dull glow is distracting—it's the muddy, murky hue of a vestige who got his powers through an act of evil. Even his bright red hair seems muted and dull.

His eyes find mine, and his lips quirk. "Scarla. Are you okay?" The concern in his voice sounds genuine, but I can't trust anything about him anymore.

A sarcastic response comes to my tongue, but I don't want to give him the satisfaction of engaging in conversation, so I stay quiet.

"She's not okay," Molly says, taking half a step forward to protect me. With each panting breath, her shoulders rise and fall, and a wave of gratitude washes over me.

"Will you join me for a walk outside?" Leo asks me, ignoring Molly.

I glance at Bwadu, who shakes her head slowly, *no*. "Is that a request or a demand?" I ask.

Leo lifts one shoulder in a half-shrug. "I have guards out here who will do as I say... but I'd rather you came willingly."

The idea of taking a walk with Leo disgusts me—he betrayed me so deeply that I can still feel the twist of his knife in my gut. But this is an excellent chance to survey the castle and plan my escape, so I might as well take advantage of that.

It's not like I have a choice anyway.

I swan past him into the corridor, irritated at the trace of a grin on his face. I used to love that grin—now it makes me shudder.

Leo leads me along a maze of twisting corridors, and I try to memorize them. Having lived most of my life underneath a mountain, I'm excellent at navigating blind, and the patterns of the interconnecting hallways burn into my memory.

We pass a window, and I see the sun blazing outside. I'm confused when he leads me to a grand door, which obviously opens to the garden. Leo nods to a guard who swings open the wooden door without hesitation, then Leo—the guy who starts sweating before the burn even starts—steps out into full daylight.

I follow him, hoping he'll burst into flames or melt into the flagstones, but he doesn't. I forgot about the sorcered dome covering the inner city of Solren.

It is perfectly comfortable out here. Which neutralizes my key skill. Bloody Hells below.

I immediately see the benefit of a mild climate. Gardens surround the castle, lush and green, with actual flowers blooming for no reason I can see other than because they look pretty. None of the species have medical applications, as far as I can tell.

"It's beautiful," I breathe, forgetting to be angry. Even the gentle floral fragrance is delicious, and I'm surprised I can't taste the flowers in the air.

"I thought you'd like it. That's why I brought you here." Leo grins as though he did me a favor by abducting me.

Nine-foot trees form a green tunnel that leads toward a wooden bridge crossing a stream, enticing me. I forget to be mad and dash along it. "Let's go this way."

Leo follows with a chuckle. "This is the first pathway I went down too," he says, as though we're still old friends.

His tone annoys me. "Don't pretend we have similar tastes."

"But we do. We've always b—"

"I've never kidnapped anyone, so there's that."

He pauses a beat. "Look, Scarla, you will never understand how difficult that was for me. I—"

"You're right about that. I'll never understand."

He sighs. "I'm doing what is right for the Undercity. Even if it feels wrong to me." I stomp across the little wooden bridge, too pissed to reply. His voice chases me. "What would you sacrifice to make the world better, Scarla?"

The question judders through me, crashing into my bones and making whirlpools in my blood. I don't know the answer. And I hate that he's asking. It's tough to be impartial when the person he's sacrificing is me.

But I'm saved from having to respond by him blundering on. "You're the one who taught me to fight for my beliefs, Scar."

"Don't call me that," I snap. "You've lost the right to be familiar with me." I'm still thrashing along, crunching over pebblestones and shoving aside the small branches that get in my way.

Leo grabs my wrist and forces me to stop. "Scarla, listen to me. I need to control Gaze so I can run the Undercity. Then I can make it a fairer place to live."

Concern pulses in Leo's deep brown eyes, and I hate that our friendship is so lost. I believe he is trying to make the world a better place, I really do... but he's going about it the wrong way. Everything about him is wrong. "You haven't thought this through. Do you really think VanDyke will let you take Gaze? He wants it for himself."

Leo's fingers dig into my wrists, but they loosen slightly at my question. "I figured that you and I could work together. Together we can do anything. We're stronger than anyone."

I laugh. Leo's talking like he's a kid straight out of creche. Like he hasn't realized the world is run by angels who don't give a fuck about mortals. Like the words "you" and "I" might still mean something.

"So your plan is to keep me prisoner until I die of natural causes, then take Gaze and rule the Undercity? You'll be eighty years old, idiot. Good luck with that."

He releases my wrist entirely, but I don't walk away for some reason. I need to hear his answer so I can understand his plan. Because what I know so far makes zero sense.

"I don't want Gaze for myself. I just want... I want you by my side. Like I said, together we're stronger."

Leo and I have been friends since forever. A couple of months ago, his emotions changed into something deeper. I used to feel guilty that Leo caught romantic feelings for me like it was somehow my fault.

But now, I just chuckle darkly. I don't think he understands the difference between romance and coercion. "You and I will never work together again. You lost that chance when—"

"I fucked up."

47

I pause at his admission. A leaf blows through the small space between our bellies, reminding me of everything else that's come between us. Even if he admits that kidnapping me was a mistake, I still can't forgive him. "Big time. Anyway, your plan sucks. Even if I wanted to work with you—which I never, ever will—controlling the Undercity isn't the problem. The issue is all of Malanox. Actually, it's all of Aubia. You're an idiot if you don't understand that."

He flinches at my tone, and that makes me happy. It's not the highest moment of my moral life, taking pleasure from his pain, but he's hurt me so thoroughly that I enjoy seeing the misery in his face.

He reaches out a hand toward me but drops it in mid-air. "I'm sorry."

I push on, relishing my small victory. "The last time you attacked me, you were beaten by the Angel of Malanox, my lover." Leo recoils when I spit the word *lover*. "And when he comes for me this time, he will be pissed as Hades."

Zaden

The gray-haired men crowd around their table looking startled.

It seems I've appeared during an Undercity Council meeting, although all conversation died when I turned up.

"Where's Leo," I repeat, and I don't have to inject anger into my tone, it's seething with it.

These Undercity mortals have their own power structure; apparently they even believe in it. But it's laughable. As if I couldn't bring down rocks and cover the cave mouth with a flick of my wrist.

As if they don't owe their lives to me entirely.

As if the real power in the Undercity isn't mine.

A grizzled lump of a man with more gumption than the rest dares ask me a question. "Leo who?"

"Leo Billson Farmer," I clarify, remembering their custom of identifying workers based on their parent's name and their occupation. It doesn't extend to retirement, and I never bothered to grasp the complicated naming system they use after that.

"H-he's been gone almost two days. I assume he's in Solren. H-he has some high-ranking acquaintances."

I growl at the reminder of Angel VanDyke assisting Leo, and

my fingers curl into fists.

"Where is Scarla's father?" I snarl, and if they ask *Scarla who?* I will circle the nearest man's neck with my iron grip and squeeze.

The sad old men mutter quickly among themselves, then their spokesperson clears his throat. "Luca Bradson Farmer is working in the mines today. Mary will lead you there."

A girl emerges from the shadow. I almost ask "Mary who," noting that her last name wasn't provided. Are women treated differently in the Undercity? That might explain the fire in Scarla's belly that I can never quench.

Mary appears strong enough and doesn't talk, which is fine by me. We go down the stairs and dive into the tunnel leading north from the far end of the main cavern. It slopes down quickly and has various offshoots, but the path isn't difficult to follow. It clearly leads deeper into the mountain, and Mary's chilly discomfort radiates from her.

"Hurry up, girl," I snarl, and she breaks into a trot, sucking the stale air in lungfuls. I lengthen my stride, but it does nothing to ease the tension in my body.

If Scarla isn't in the Undercity, I can only assume she's with Leo.

And last time I looked, she wasn't going anywhere near him willingly.

The ring of pickaxes striking rock reaches me well before the sight of dark figures wielding heavy tools in the dim tunnel ahead.

Mary's voice is strong. "Pa Luca, you have a visitor."

Scarla's father is weary and lined, but the resemblance to his daughter is clear. Although his face is half-submerged beneath a bushy beard, they share the same copper locks and big brown eyes, and I instantly warm to him.

I make it my business to know what's happening in the Undercity, and I paid particular attention to Scarla's father these past few months. Her love for him is her biggest weakness, and I wasn't foolish enough to let that go unnoticed. I'm not above threatening an innocent man to get myself back into heaven.

So I know enough about him. He does odd jobs for the Undercity Council and picks up the slack when folks are sick. He lives in the night hub, so he is usually asleep during the day, so he must be making up for a shortfall of mine workers today.

He looks at me fearfully, and I'm disappointed not to see any of Scarla's fire in his eyes. "Hello, sir."

He appears like a grizzled wolf from a distance, and I want to test his mettle. "My name is Zaden." I don't usually tell people that, but I want to see his reaction. He knows that a man called Zaden killed his oldest daughter Leesa, so I expect him to lunge at me; perhaps he'll swing that sharp metal pickax at my middle.

Instead, he ducks his head. "Hello, Zaden."

Disappointment filters through me. "Scarla must get her fire from her dead mother," I say sharply. I watch keenly to see how he'll respond to my overt lie, whether he'll rise to the challenge. We both know exactly the events surrounding Scarla's mother's departure from the Undercity and precisely how dead she is.

But he disappoints me. He nods his head. "Yes, sir." The tension in his neck shows me he didn't mean to say that—it just slipped out. I have that effect on people. It's one of the perks of being a terrifying angel.

"Where is Scarla?"

Finally, I've provoked an emotion in this rodent of a man other than submissive fear. He stands taller, and his face turns up to mine, his jaw tense. "I thought she was with you."

Good. Now we're getting somewhere. He's admitting that he knows who I am, which means he knows that I killed Leesa. Yet still, he does nothing but cower before me.

"When did you last see her?"

His shoulders droop. "Not for days."

My heart sinks. He is telling the truth, I am certain. If he hasn't seen her in days, then she is missing. How did I not notice her departure? A detestable sense of vulnerability flutters through my chest like an errant butterfly, but I squash it with an iron fist. She's gone, so it's time for action.

And if Leo is gone too, then he took her.

I just need to find out where that imbecile is holding her, then I'll tear his fucking throat out.

* * *

I return to the castle on foot. I want to launch into the sky and pound out my anger in the clouds, bringing thunder and lightning in my wake.

But first, I need to obtain the facts. I hold my rage close against my chest and walk.

I must have followed this path a thousand times. A million. Malanox has been my home for centuries, a small isolated town on the desert's edge, overlooked by most of the Cloaked Court.

Its solitude was a drawcard when I first moved here, looking to escape all the politics and bullshit of the other Fallen. I have no desire for power on earth—my only goal is to return to Heaven.

Hence my other reason for choosing Malanox. This is a dense conclave of vestiges, and I figured I would find Gaze one day, so I might return to Heaven.

I just never expected it to come in a package of fire and spit and a lovely fucking mouth. A mouth I can't stop thinking about, even here, walking through the hot damn town in the middle of the day.

She brings a new perspective to the life I've lived so long. These streets, which I've walked a million times, look different since I met her. I hear her voice telling me it's unfair that the poor have so little, and looking at these clapped-out shitboxes in Lowtown, it's hard to disagree.

But it never occurred to me before I met her.

The dirt road shifts to cobblestones and the low buildings grow taller and stronger as I walk from Lowtown to Hightown.

There's a weed with a faint astringent aroma poking through the stones, and I wonder if Scarla could brew it into a healing tea.

I've seen weeds before. I've drunk tea. But the color of this plant is more vibrant than any other I've seen, as though she brushes aside the cobwebs of longevity and makes life new again.

The last time I felt this way was when I first came to earth before I fell. That time, I messed up, and the joy was snatched from me by Elanora.

My wonder turns cold, and a shiver tickles my skin despite the burning sun. I won't let Scarla repeat Elanora's mistakes. Nor will I repeat mine.

Scarla

Leo's question tumbles through my mind.

What would you sacrifice to make the world better, Scarla?

I'm lying on my stupid bed, staring at the stupid ceiling, and his stupid freaking question keeps circulating through my head like a crow stuck in a cave banging its stupid tiny head against the walls.

What would you sacrifice to make the world better, Scarla?

The thing is, I don't have an answer. He and I share ideals—a world where food, resources, and materials are shared equally among everybody. It sounds so simple, yet it's so far from our reality.

But maybe for me it, they are empty ideals. Like a shiny new crate of blyberries, but when you remove the hessian sacking, you find the box is empty.

I feel more and more like a barren blyberry box the longer I stare at this stupid freaking ceiling.

What would you sacrifice to make the world better, Scarla?

Maybe I wouldn't sacrifice anything. Perhaps I'm just full of pretty words and no substance.

Leo, of course, had an answer.

I'm working to make our dream come true, Scarla. And I sacrificed the most important thing in the world to me...my friendship with you.

It was hard to be angry with him when he phrased it like that. Not only was he paying me a massive compliment by saying I was so important to him, but he was taking action.

His blyberry crate is full of fresh, ripe berries, while mine is empty.

"Maker be damned," I mumble under my breath.

Bwadu and Molly are each on their own beds and glance up when I speak.

"Are you going insane already?" Molly inquires politely.

I shake my head, and a grogum stalk tickles my ear. "Not yet, babe." I'm so sick of this plain white room with its windowless walls and flat ceiling. "I'm beginning to miss my dungeon," I tell Molly.

She quirks an eyebrow. "I'm sure you could arrange to go back there. Just attack a guard or something. Maybe throw a fistful of grogum mash in his eye."

A man brings us meals three times a day, bringing some of the worst crap I've ever tasted. Squished, doughy grains that have been boiled to death and then served to us in their afterlife.

I have a new appreciation for the culinary skills of our cooks back in the Undercity. It's almost like the chefs here are trying to make the stuff taste bad.

Bwadu joins the conversation, speaking over her shoulder without turning. Her back is to us, and she's leaned over like she's whittling wood. "Their armor has a weak spot under the shoulder," she informs us.

Does she think we're serious? "Good to know. I'll squish some mash into the next guard's armpit."

I earn a grin from Molly, but not Bwadu. She holds out an

object that is sharpened into a point at one end, about the length of her hand. "This would be more effective."

"Where'd you get that?" Molly gasps, standing to walk nearer.

"From the bed. It's not much better than an oversized splinter, but it's better than nothing."

Okay, that's impressive. Bwadu arrived the same day as me, and she's already fashioned herself a damn shiv.

The door clicks open, and the splinter disappears into Bwadu's waistband so smoothly that I almost miss the movement.

One guard enters while the other stays in the corridor. They don't say a word. The closer guard marches right up to Molly and grabs her arm roughly.

She squeals. "Hey, get off me."

The man drags Molly toward the door, but I'm faster. I dart to the doorway and block it with my body. "Where are you taking her?"

The guard grunts and shoves me aside, but I plant my feet on the stone floor like I'm growing roots, and I don't budge.

He snarls, "Get out of the way, girl."

With my natural height advantage, I'm looking directly at the man. Gray eyes stare back at me, unblinking, but two can play that game. "Tell me where you're taking her first."

The second guard is right behind me—I've left myself open to him. He grabs his forearm around my neck and yanks me so my back presses against his body. He breathes into my ear, his rank breath burning the tiny hairs inside. "You ain't a princess in your castle anymore. Now siddown and shut up like a good little girl."

His arm squeezes so tightly against my throat that I struggle to breathe. My lungs burn for air, searing hot. I twist my head to the side, seeking the release of the extra space where his elbow pokes out, and suck in a tiny sip of oxygen.

He shoves me aside, and I land on the floor on all fours, panting, gulping in air, feeling weak and vulnerable.

The second guard smirks at me while Molly's captor drags her roughly from the room.

I hate feeling weak. I hate feeling vulnerable. I remind myself that I am the most valuable player in this game because I have the one thing that everybody wants.

I climb to my feet, and my voice pours from me like thunder. "Stop," I command, but Molly has already disappeared from view, and that second guard just stands there with that irritating smirk on his ugly face.

Lightning erupts from the well of power within me, my fury directed at the man to wipe that vicious scowl from his features.

In a burst of color that I know only I can see, the column of light inside the guard's body flashes brightly, then he falls to the ground.

I'm struck numb. What the fuck just happened?

The guard lies motionless, and Bwadu is already kneeling by his side with two fingers on his neck. The orange leaf tattoo at her temple pulses with every beat of her heart. After I've watched it pound a hundred times, or maybe a thousand, she glances up at me. "He's alive."

I sigh with relief. I didn't want to kill him. He's a dickwad, but he's as much a victim as me, forced to labor for an angel who values his life below a skitter beetle's.

The door is ajar, and Bwadu watches it but doesn't move.

Why doesn't she run out and try to escape? Why don't I?

Shock roots me to the spot because I still don't know what I freaking did.

Bwadu's focus lands on me. "Do you want to tell me what the fuck just happened?"

I do. I want to tell her exactly what happened, but the words don't come. "I have this ability...."

She spends another three seconds staring at me before she moves to the door. "Come on, this could be our only chance to escape."

I blink stupidly. "You want me to come with you?"

"Yeah." She looks me up and down, and her lips twist into a half-grin. "Turns out you're more useful than you look."

Zaden

Wind whips across my cheeks, turning them red. It stings my eyes and burns my face as I soar above VanDyke's castle.

It is gaudy and opulent, festooned with marble columns. Every balustrade is lined with gold leaf reflecting moonlight, making the whole thing sparkle like a fucking firework.

But I know that beneath the ostentatious façade lies the skeleton of a fortress. This Fallen Angel's castle won't be easy to penetrate.

Dozens of tiny rectangles twinkle with candlelight, and I wonder which one is the chamber where Scarla is being kept.

It had better be one of them. If VanDyke is keeping her in an underground dungeon, I'll slice him from neck to pelvis and eat his fucking spine. Ashmodu tingles at my hip, thirsting for blood.

I spot my landing, right outside the palace's outer gates. If he didn't have a sorcered protective dome over his castle, I'd land on his roof. As it is, I'm forced to ask for permission.

My wings snap into place, hidden and invisible, when my right foot touches the flagstones, and I walk without breaking stride.

My entrance was about as dramatic as possible because these guards need to know who I am. They need to fear me. The nearest guard looks at me, dread living in his eyes.

"Do you know who I am?" I demand.

He shrinks into his jacket. "Ye-yes, milord."

"Then open the fucking gate."

My eyes must be burning black with rage, and the man scuttles to obey.

The castle gates creak open slowly, and impatience burns through me. As soon as they are shoulder-width apart, I stride through. My rough boots echo loudly on the cobblestones, and my black cloak flows out behind me.

At the inner wall, the guard on duty dares to question whether Count VanDyke is expecting me.

Every moment's delay might be causing Scarla pain. She may be moments away from permanent injury. VanDyke might be torturing her to the point where her mind breaks. Gaze doesn't require a sound mind, so he has no need to keep her intact, only alive.

And here is this minion asking whether I've been invited like I'm here to attend a dinner party.

My hand slides across my body in a practiced gesture, and Ashmodu slides free with a ringing of metal.

"Sorry, Lord," the guard says, pressing the lever to release the mechanism to open the gate.

With supreme self-control, I let the man live, but I don't return Ashmodu to its scabbard.

My celestial blade will do more good in my hand, and I flex my grip on the gleaming silver hilt, watching the black veins pulse along its edge. Here in the inner sanctum of VanDyke's castle, I expect he will be alerted to my presence sooner rather than later.

Fury inhabits me like a living beast, begging for a fight. I want to curve my fingers behind the Count's Adam's apple and pull it from his throat, then drop the bloody pit to the filthy floor and grind it beneath my boot.

But the smarter move is to find Scarla and get her safely away before the Count finds me.

I need to be smart.

Count VanDyke wastes his time and his money on earthly pleasures. His taste for luxury is his greatest weakness, and I intend to exploit it.

Three tall turrets adorn the castle's center at staggered heights. I figure the tallest one contains his bedchamber, so the second tallest is probably for guests. If he's trying to show off his wealth and superiority to Scarla, that's where she'll be.

My wings snap out, and I pound hard, driving down the wind and soaring into the sky. Now that I'm inside his inner wall, there is no restriction on flight. I circle the second tallest tower, climbing higher with every beat of my wings, glancing in the few open windows I pass but learning nothing.

Of course, the tower has majestic windows on the top floor, so VanDyke's guests can see the beautiful view. I land on the white stone sill, which is broad enough to stand easily and tall enough even for me to land without stooping.

I snap my wings closed and then drop into the room, scanning for Scarla or danger in that order.

The opulence of this room is disgraceful. A massive bed is against the far wall, covered in gold and deepest red silk cushions. Calling it a bed is an understatement—it takes up a third of the room and could sleep twenty close friends.

A dozen women lounge on the bed wearing just bras and panties. Strong perfume layers the air, and febrile flesh is everywhere. I search the upturned faces methodically for

Scarla's.

Bile rises in my throat that she might be here, and I suddenly hope she isn't. Not here, not in this room; this is clearly the Count's personal harem. In the instant before the women notice me, in that moment before they slap sexy smiles on their faces as a façade, I see expressions of boredom and despair.

Are they willing participants? Or is this just the best out of their limited shitty options?

I shake my head. Scarla's incessant talk about the rights of the poor is getting under my skin.

I've seen enough orgies in my lifetime, and participated in enough, that they don't tempt me. They, like everything else in this mundane world, bore me.

I've done everything and seen everything, and none of it holds any appeal to me.

Except Scarla. She is a spark of interest in a gray universe, and that's why I'm so desperate to find her.

But she isn't here. A quick glance is enough to tell me that.

The nearest woman is already running a hand down my bicep and crooning. "Would you like me to help you off with that long, thick cloak?"

I put a hand under her jaw and squeeze until her lips pout ludicrously. "Where is Scarla?"

The woman doesn't blink—I guess she's used to rough treatment. "I don't know anyone by that name. But you can call me whatever you like.... I'll be your Scarla."

I fling her aside, face first, and turn to the next woman. "You! Has anyone named Scarla ever come here? Long, tousled, copper hair." No, I remember the lock of cut hair I found in her bedchamber and amend my description. "Short copper hair. And a bad attitude. Do you know anybody like that?"

The second woman shakes her head.

"Where would they keep a prisoner?" I demand, and every eye in the room stares at me.

"I-in the dungeon?" one suggests.

"Where else?" I stride toward the door, thinking hard. "Are there any bedchambers without external windows?"

I push my way past a woman who clearly has the wrong idea about why I'm here. She presses her breasts against my back while I'm standing at the door, and I take a deep breath to keep my calm.

Scarla would not be impressed if I killed these women while I was here to rescue her.

"You could try the servants' quarters, honey."

I whirl on the woman. "Where are they?"

She simpers under my gaze. "First floor in the western wing," she purrs, and I leave, slamming the door in her face.

I take the stairs three at a time, glancing out the windows as they fly by so I can keep my sense of direction intact. I hit the bottom step running and follow the hallways to the west.

It's obvious when I reach the servants' quarters because the glamorous façade disappears. Here, the floors are plain wood, and the white walls are unadorned. It's just a long corridor with closed wooden doors.

Screams from behind one door stop me in my tracks, my pulse thrumming. I cock my head, listening intently. One of the bonuses of being celestial is having enhanced hearing, and I can identify the tone of this woman's voice.

It sounds familiar, but it isn't Scarla. The screams have the tonal quality of one of my servants but not one whose name I know. I guess Scarla was kidnapped with a Malanox servant.

That means I'm on the right path. Dismissing the bloodcurdling yells, I keep running.

The corridor is plain and white, with wooden doors at even intervals on either side. At every door I pass, I plant my foot, then kick with my heel right where the lock enters the doorframe. It's quicker than trying the handles each time, and I can check for Scarla at a glance.

I get into a rhythm. Run, kick, scan. Run, kick, scan.

It's agonizingly slow, but I can't see another way to make sure I find her.

Eventually, when my unknown servant's screams are already far behind me and inaudible to the human ear, I reach a slightly ajar door.

I duck inside and see three beds, the middle one of which has a trace of Scarla's blyberry scent. She slept here.

A guard lies unconscious on the floor, and I can't help but grin.

Well played, mortal.

She's escaped from her room, so I figure she's in these corridors or already outside.

She'd better still be inside. If she's made it to the grounds, she has zero chance of making it out alive through the sorcered dome or past those armed guards. She is as good as dead.

I stop kicking doors and just sprint, pounding my arms to drive myself forward with every running step.

Zaden

My feet skim across the wooden floor so fast I'm almost flying. But the walls are too close to permit that.

I have to find that mortal before VanDyke does.

My heart pounds in my chest, and I feel alive—more alive than I've felt in centuries. But I don't like it. I don't fucking like it one bit. If anything has happened to that woman, I'll have VanDyke begging for mercy that I'll never give him.

Blood pumping, my feet batter the floorboards, and the doors whip past. Around the next corner, a streak of copper hair flashes in the distance.

"Scarla!" I call.

At the sound of my voice, she stops in her tracks and turns.

Even at this distance, I can make out her features perfectly. Her copper hair has been cut short, but it is still wild and tousled, framing her pale face dotted with light freckles. She is the only human who spends enough time in the sunshine to earn sun kisses, and they mark her as special. Her wide brown eyes stare into my soul, and she looks at me unblinking.

I stare back. It really is her.

We are two beings at opposite ends of a hallway, and opposite ends of the world, in more ways than one. Mortal versus angel. Undercitysider versus Margrave. Cave-dweller versus ruler. But in this moment, I know that no matter how many differences we have, we share a single soul. She and I belong together.

She hesitantly takes a few steps toward me, checking that it's really me. Her mortal eyes are almost blind in this light. I could cross the distance between us in a few moments, but I don't want to scare her away. Besides, my feet have grown roots in the wood.

After a few more strides, she breaks into a run, her face creasing in joy.

A newborn star never gave off as much light as Scarla's smile.

She leaps into my arms, and I wrap them around her, holding her tight, inhaling her, and I can't wait a moment longer to taste her. I smash my lips against hers, sucking on her, drinking her, never wanting to let go.

But I need to make sure she's okay. "Scarla, are you hurt?"

"No." Her mouth moves against my neck when she talks, and the heat of her breath on my skin makes my cock jump. This woman has brought back to life all the parts of me I thought were dead.

"I want you," I murmur, and she waits a moment before answering as though that's not the complete sentence. As though she's expecting a command.

I want you to follow me.

I want you to stay silent.

I want you to fall to your knees and take my cock between those full fucking lips.

She smiles softly when I put her down, then she stands on one leg, thrusting out a hip. The motion of her body beneath my hands is intoxicating.

"Actually," she says with a sassy grin. "You've interrupted

me. I was just in the middle of escaping...."

I quirk a brow, my lips curving upward. This mortal can always surprise me—and surprise is worth a thousand years to somebody as old as I am. "Yes, I can see that."

She bites her lip; now they are all I can think about. "So, can this wait? I'd love to stop and chat, but...." She hooks a thumb over her shoulder

"I reach an arm around her and pull her to me, splaying my palm across her lower back. "You're not going anywhere without me," I growl. I've spent centuries searching for this woman, and if she thinks she's leaving alone again, she's wrong.

She runs her fingers lightly across my chest, placing a flurry of fireflies lighting my skin. She pretends to think for a few moments, chewing that damn lip again. "Okay. You can come too."

She turns to run, but as she does, I catch sight of her throat. A dark red welt mars the side and back of her neck in a clear marking of strangulation.

I grab hold of her thin wrist in an iron grip.

She looks back at me uncertainly. "What? We have to go."

My fingers encircle her wrist easily, and I'm not letting go. Not until I find out what happened. I trace the fingers of my other hand along her injured neck, and she winces.

I strain to keep my voice low. Somebody has hurt my mortal, and I need to know who. "Who did this to you?" The mark is an angry red against her lily throat, and the sight turns my blood volcanic. "Tell me who did this so I can rip his skull from his spine and send his rotting flesh to his family. Nobody hurts you, Scarla. Nobody."

Scarla watches me, her eyes filled with an emotion I can't

catch. She glances down at her wrist, and I realize I'm holding her too tight, so I loosen my grip—but I don't let go.

Pure energy drives me; I thirst for revenge. "Was it VanDyke?" She shakes her head, no. I school my voice to be calm but even to my ears, it sounds quiet and dangerous."Tell me who it was."

She parts her lips. "Just one of his guards."

I picture the man unconscious in her bedchamber and commit his face to memory. I will repay his wounds a hundredfold as soon as I have Scarla to safety. "Was it the man lying on your floor?"

Before she can answer, a muscular woman with long legs and the speed of a panther sprints along the hallway from behind Scarla. "She's not telling you anything," the ebony-skinned woman says on a snarl.

In an instant, I shove Scarla behind me, putting my body between her and this new assailant, assessing her stance and approach. A curling leaf tattoo marks the woman's temple, a clear sign that she is a troublemaker, a terrorist. She undoubtedly possesses the skill of a warrior, but it is nothing; she will be like raindrops falling into a volcano if she tests my rage.

"Stop!" Scarla tugs on my shirt. "She's a friend." I swear, nothing but Scarla's voice could free me from my fury.

I assess the woman for a moment longer, then make up my mind. If Scarla says she's reliable, then I trust her. For now.

"The closest exit is back this way," I tell Scarla, turning back the way I came.

Count VanDyke must know I'm here by now, so I expect his not-so-welcoming committee to turn up any time.

Scarla pulls on my hand, snagging my full attention. "We

have to find Molly first. She was taken with me, and they removed her from our room this morning. We need to find her before we can escape."

I sigh. Damn this fucking mortal and her fucking moral code. We don't have time for this.

"Molly, your maid?" I say, thinking quickly. I recall Scarla being pissed at me a couple of days ago for not knowing who Molly was, so I remember she's the servant. She must be the woman I heard screaming behind a closed door near the tower entrance.

"Yes," Scarla nods, pleading with her eyes. "I'm not leaving until we find her."

"Molly's fine," I lie. "I saw her being set free as I was arriving. They said they didn't need her, only you, so they let her go."

"Really?" Scarla hangs onto my lapels like she's holding a lifeline. Molly's life doesn't matter at all—only Scarla's is of any value. I don't feel bad for lying to her—it is the right course of action.

I need Scarla to be safe.

For Gaze, obviously, but it's more than that.

I can tell myself as much as I want to that I only need her for Gaze, but I'm lying. She is the only interesting thing to cross my path in over a hundred years, and I'm never letting go. I don't just need Scarla for Gaze.

I need Scarla for Scarla.

Scarla

Zaden is so huge he almost takes up every atom of space in the corridor. I sniff the air between us and am disappointed not to detect his usual forest-of-the-lilies scent, just the leather of his pants.

He looks like some kick-ass guerilla ninja, dressed head to toe in black with muscles upon muscles.

His grip around my wrist is like iron, and the danger in his voice makes me hesitate.

But I need to find Molly, then we need to get the hells out of here.

"Come on," I urge, tugging my arm but making no headway in loosening his grasp.

Even his eyes are raging black. I've dreamed of his piercing green irises these past few days, how I'd feel when I finally saw them again.

But they're entirely absent, replaced by these murderous black pits of rage.

Indecision flashed across his face when I mentioned Molly's name, but he seems to make up his mind and reassures me that she's fine. "They let her go," he repeats.

That makes sense. VanDyke and Leo have no reason to keep Molly here—she's useless to them. I'm glad they freed her...

but spending the rest of my life in an enemy's castle without her would be the worst punishment.

Zaden cocks his head and listens for a moment, and I wonder what he can hear. Running boots of approaching enemies? Or just the overexcited pounding of my heart?

His fingers curl around the palm of my hand, and he pulls me in, then presses his lips to mine roughly. A flame coils inside me in response, but the moment is over in an instant.

"Let's go," he barks, then runs along the corridor in the opposite direction than he indicated earlier.

"That's exactly what I was saying," I mutter before following him.

He isn't heading back toward the castle proper, so I assume he heard guards approaching.

Bwadu and I sprint along the corridors, doing our best to keep up with his long muscular legs, but I sense he is going slowly for our benefit. Still, my lungs are burning. Just how big is this freaking castle?

Finally, Zaden pushes through a door, with Bwadu hot on his heels and me bringing up the rear. We spill out into broad daylight, which is completely disorienting. I was sure it was the middle of the night. That windowless room really messed up my sense of time.

I'm still blinking under the bright sun when Bwadu picks up a long sturdy stick and jams it against the door so any guards chasing us won't be able to get out.

But it won't stop the guards who round the corner and run at us along the gravel path.

I barely have a moment to take in my surroundings. We're in a beautiful garden with lush green grass and abundant flowers. Honestly, it's like something out of a fairytale, like the stories the old folks in the Undercity tell about their great-great-grandparents' lives. Nothing like this exists anymore, or so I thought.

The colors are overwhelming. I've spent a lifetime looking at brown and gray, the hues of drought and dirty snow, the only two seasons I know, and they both come every day.

I've always done my best to make up for the lack of color in my life, trying to dye my clothes blue with macerated blyberries, for example. My copper hair doesn't hurt either.

But I never imagined anything as spectacular as this. The flowers beside me are such a vibrant orange that I want to fall to my knees and pray to them. I could spend a thousand years exploring this garden and never get bored. And the sweet, rich aroma is so thick I feel like I could hide inside it.

But I have less than twenty seconds before those guards will be upon us.

"Let's fly." I throw myself at Zaden, but he pushes me away.

"I can't carry both of you."

"Shit."

"And I can't fly through the castle's dome. We have to leave via the gates." He runs to the east, where the castle gates lie, and Bwadu and I follow as fast as we can.

The approaching guards change direction, peeling away from their original course in an arc aimed to intercept our path. It's going to be a close thing whether we make it to the gates before the guards make it to us.

Zaden is pulling away, so I put my head down and force my Maker-be-damned legs to pound harder and faster than they ever have.

It becomes clear why Zaden streaked ahead when he reaches the gates and fells the two guards on duty with two flicks of his wrist. His long sharp sword flings drops of red blood onto the lush green grass.

Black veins line his blade, ringed with purple smoke, the exact color of purple that tints Zaden's otherwise pure white angelic glow. I suppose that means that Zaden and his sword are bonded on some deep level. He certainly wields it as though it is an extension of his being, and a pang of jealousy at his physical prowess rings through me as he yanks down on the rope to open the gate.

He is so freaking good in a fight. Even Bwadu is better than me. She has beaten me to the gate and faces back toward the approaching guards in a fighter's stance, though she's armed with nothing but that wooden stick she sharpened into a point.

With a heaving chest and burning legs, I finally reach the gate and slide under it. In the same instant, Zaden slices through the rope that operates the mechanism, and the metal jaws smash into the ground, kicking up dirt.

We're through, and the guards are stuck on the other side.

Panting and grinning, I climb to my feet. But my grin washes away. This bloody castle must have two sets of walls and two sets of gates. Which means two sets of guards.

There is no out-running the menacing men before us. They already surround us, at least a dozen of them in dark leather armor punctuated with VanDyke's indigo stripe running from shoulder to wrist. Obviously these guys were forewarned.

Every one of the bastards holds a sword at the ready.

"Shit," I breathe.

Do we have a chance against a dozen armed and trained soldiers? I could maybe take down one, and I reckon Bwadu would be good for two. But that leaves ten men for Zaden and, angel or not, he can't be in ten places at once.

But we have to try. I won't go back into VanDyke's castle. And I doubt the Count will be as merciful toward Zaden as I forced Zaden to be to the Count at their last meeting.

The image of Zaden with a celestial sword sticking out of his chest sends a pulse of adrenaline through my body that makes me move.

Already, Zaden is dancing with the first man who approaches, swirling his deadly blade in a whirl of flashing silver and purple smoke.

I revise my assessment. Zaden can take all of these men. He's already leaving a wreckage of bodies. But I don't know if he can take them in time.

The guard nearest to me approaches slowly like he doesn't want to kill a girl.

Well, this girl has no qualms about killing him. I used to be hopeless in a fight, but then again, I used to be many things.

I've grown up a lot.

The man approaches with his sword to one side. "Put these on, and you live." He unclasps something from his belt and throws it at me; by instinct, I catch it before I even realize what it is.

It is cold and hard. Handcuffs. "How about I cuff you to the gate while I kick your ass," I counter.

The man is still approaching steadily, and I resist the urge to back up. "Fine," he snarls. "We'll do it the hard way."

I throw the cuffs to the ground. "Yeah," I agree. "That sounds like more fun."

The man's eyes narrow, but I force myself to stay calm. He is still hesitant to hurt me, and I use his hesitation to my advantage. I channel Gaze and see the line of light that runs through the man's body from his head to his toes, seeking the narrowing of the light beam behind his throat.

I concentrate on that slight thinning of light and pinch it, but nothing happens.

Dammit. Why isn't this working?

My blood pumps faster, thundering in my ears.

Glancing to the side, Zaden's graceful, lethal dance distracts me for a moment. The spice of blood fills my nostrils, and the clanging of swords is almost as loud as the pounding of my pulse.

The last time I felled a man by squeezing the glowing inside his neck, I wasn't under direct threat. That time, Zaden had been in danger, not me.

Perhaps my growing panic is interfering with my abilities. But how am I supposed to be calm in the middle of a battle?

Bwadu is wrestling with a man up close like she's giving him a hug, getting inside the arc of his sword, but I don't have time to watch her.

My attention is back on the man approaching me. He raises his sword, and it looks like he will kill me.

He's going to fucking kill me. What happened to me being safe because these power-hungry bastards all need to inherit Gaze when I die of natural causes? I'm pretty sure violent slaughter during a battle doesn't count as a natural death.

Maybe this dude didn't get the message.

He swings his sword, and I finally give in to panic. A rush of energy pours from me, and the guard freezes for an instant, looking as though he's been struck by lightning, although I'm the only one who can see the flash of brilliant light that charges from my body.

But I guess he can feel it. He topples to the ground like a discarded doll, inert and boneless.

A moment later, it's all over. Bwadu looks me up and down, then nods as though she's satisfied with my performance. "Good," is all she says before she begins running.

Zaden comes back and trails a hand along my cheek. His touch startles me from my coma, and I allow him to pull me into a run.

I knocked that man unconscious, that's all. I'm glad I didn't kill him. Really. But the surge of power I emitted felt so damn good, and I know that I could've killed him if I wanted to.

Two guards are on duty at the second gate but offer no resistance. They stand aside and watch as Bwadu heaves on the rope that opens the gate, then they stand mute as we run through.

"You have to tell me how you do that," Bwadu says, eyeing me sideways. But I can't tell her. The more people who know about Gaze, the more danger I'm in.

"Meet us in the forest," Zaden says to Bwadu, then he wraps one arm around my waist and snaps out his wings, beating hard and pulling us into the air.

My belly swoops as we soar upward, banking away from VanDyke's castle, leaving all that danger and imprisonment behind.

Scarla

We soar higher and higher, but I'm pretty sure my stomach is still on the ground far below us.

Zaden's arm is wrapped firmly around my waist, and my back is pressed hard against him. After being cooped up in a windowless room for days, flying feels freaking amazing.

But as soon as we hit the clouds, Zaden dives back toward Earth like he's forgotten something important.

Did he leave Ashmodu behind? I can't think of anything else he'd go back for.

But we don't return to the castle. A sweep of dark green beneath us resolves into a forest canopy, and when we get closer, I can pick out individual trees.

When we are near enough that the branches could tickle my toes, Zaden neatly snaps in his wings while we drop through the canopy, then flicks them open again to flutter us gently to the leafy ground.

Amazingly, we land right beside Bwadu, who is leaning against a tree sharpening another piece of wood.

She glances up at our arrival, a grim expression on her face. "So angels really do have excellent hearing," she says in a non-sequitur.

I frown, but Zaden follows her line of thought. "Good

enough to hear you panting like an injured desert fox," he retorts.

I scan Bwadu for injuries because she is dripping in blood, but none of it seems to be her own. Or maybe it is—I can't tell. Next, I sweep my gaze over Zaden, again finding the information pointless.

Blood? Yes. Injuries? No damn idea.

Bwadu and Zaden seem to be in some kind of pissing contest. She's staring at him with her arms folded across her chest, and he's looking at her without blinking.

Bwadu scrapes a sharp stone along her newest piece of wood, flaking off a curl of timber. "Who do you think you are?" she asks Zaden.

He pulls himself up to his full height, an impressive shitload taller than either Bwadu or me, and we're not exactly dwarves. "I am the Margrave of Malanox." Authority and power drip from his words and stance, and a tendril of purple haze accompanies his tone, wrapping around her, trying to influence Bwadu.

Still, she isn't impressed. She hocks a gob of spit onto the ground. "And I'm the Queen of the Gypsies. Bite me."

This lady just gets better and better. I can't hold in my snort of laughter. "Did I mention how much I like this chick?" I ask Zaden.

"A little respect wouldn't go astray," Zaden snarls.

Bwadu stiffens and stands at her full height—which is pitifully unimpressive next to the angel.

It seems like the real pissing contest is about to begin, so I lean against a tree trunk to wait it out.

"I don't respect people who hide in castles and steal resources from the poor," Bwadu says, and I've got to award her points for attitude. She looks badass.

Zaden relaxes slightly, though I doubt his opponent could tell. But I detect a subtle softening of his shoulders and loosening of his muscles. "I meant because I rescued you from your jail cell."

Ha! I've got to give kudos for that. I wish I had a scoreboard or some of those oversized numbers that the councilors hold up to judge the singing competition on solstice. I'd give Zaden an eight.

"Except," I interject, "we were kind of already escaping when you turned up."

Bwadu points at me. "That. Exactly that."

The angel regards me, and finally I see those piercing green eyes that haunt my dreams. "And do you think you would've made it here on your own?"

Not a chance in Hades. But I won't be telling him that. "We would've given it a damn hot go," I say instead.

I hate that he's right. I used to be absolutely helpless in a fight. Sure, if I could escape outdoors, nobody could chase me, as long as it was day or night. And if I happened to get in a scuffle during dusk or dawn, then the only tactic I had was to prolong the chat until the sun arrived or left.

Now, I'm a lot more accomplished. I've knocked out two men today using my twist on Gaze, and, frankly, it felt freaking fantastic. But I'm still vulnerable. I can handle one man on my own, as long as he moves slowly, but any more than that and I'm in trouble. I'll have to do something about that.

Now that Zaden's focus has snagged on me, he doesn't tear it away. "With a little training, you'd be... formidable."

Bwadu turns on me too, and I regret interjecting in their little argument. Now all the attention is on me. "What the hell are you doing exactly?" she demands. "Who are you? Are you one of them?" She hooks a thumb toward Zaden and narrows her eyes.

An unrefined, uncool giggle floats from my mouth. "An angel? Hardly. I hate those assholes."

Bwadu twists her lips. "Really?" She looks slowly between Zaden and me. "That's not the impression I get."

I refuse to blush. I drop my head, trying to hide my face behind a curtain of hair, forgetting that I chopped most of it off. What an idiot.

The truth is, I don't hate all angels-not even a bit. My feelings for Zaden swing far from hate. There is a shitload of lust in there, at the very least.

But that's hardly surprising, given that he is the hottest freaking male on the planet. In the dappled light of the forest, his shirt pulls across his shoulders and biceps whenever he shifts his weight, revealing his hard form underneath.

I need to change the course of this conversation. "Bwadu here is a member of the Re-"

"I have to get going," she interrupts, throwing me a loaded look like she's asking what the fuck I'm doing sharing her secrets with a ruling angel.

She has a point.

Not caring if I look uncool, I cross to my new friend and pull her into an embrace. We're both tall, but she is way stronger than I am, so hugging her is like cuddling up with a tree trunk.

"Where can I find you if I need you, babe?" I ask.

She looks at me stonily, and I sense her weighing me up. The risks and benefits of telling me. Probably weighing my heart against my head, weighing up my values to see if they match hers.

Given that we're in the presence of an angel, who I suspect is her sworn enemy as a Resistance member, it's remarkable that she shares as much as she does. "Ask for me in the Rim," she murmurs.

Everybody in the Undercity has heard of the Rim. I don't know exactly where it is, but I associate it with unsanitary filth, crime, and murder. I'll have no trouble remembering she lives there.

She nods a farewell at the angel, then turns and jogs deeper into the forest at an even pace, looking as though she could keep it up for hours.

"You keep interesting company," Zaden remarks dryly.

I watch Bwadu recede into the forest for a moment longer before turning away. "She... she's impressive, isn't she?"

Zaden laughs, and the sound lightens my soul somehow. "That's not the word I would use, but I suppose you're right."

"What word would you use?"

Zaden is toying with the top button on his bloodied shirt. "Ungrateful. Rude. Skilled."

I nod, happily agreeing to all three of those adjectives. "Exactly," I say, triumphant. "Impressive."

The top button of his shirt pops undone, then he moves on to the next. I tilt my head. "Er... What are you doing?"

"Blood."

I give him a moment to explain properly, then harrumph. "If that's your highly articulate way of saying that you are covered in blood, then yes, I can see that. But I'm pretty sure the laundry can wait until we are farther away from VanDyke's guards, who are almost certainly pursuing us and will be here at any second."

Zaden shakes his head and undoes another button. "Nope."

"Really? It can't wait? You're overcome by a fit of housework and need to bust out some soap ASAP?"

Another button pops open, and my eyes are transfixed on Zaden's hand, moving steadily down his body and exposing more of his hard chest. "Nope," he says again.

"So you can't form an entire sentence, but suddenly you can do laundry? Don't you have a house full of slaves to do that for you?"

He glances up, grinning. "I do."

"Good. Then fly me home, angel, before those guys with big pointy swords arrive."

Zaden's shirt is completely undone now, and he shrugs out of it. I swear those shoulders could knock me flat out. It's extremely difficult not to be distracted by the display of firm flesh and corded muscle.

"The guards saw me fly into the clouds with you, so they know full well that we are far from here."

I furrow my brow, watching how his nipples jump when he's trying to make a point. "But then we landed again. And we aren't far from here. We're exactly here."

"True."

"And here is very close to VanDyke's castle. So let's flappy-flap the old wings and get farther away. You've already acknowledged that the guards had eyeballs, so they would have seen us diving into this forest."

A few flecks of blood have made it through Zaden's shirt, marring his golden skin. "Nope," he says with another little leap of his nipple.

This is too much. I march up to him and put my arms around his neck. "Fly," I demand. "You are so fucking irritating, you know. Just fly."

His arms snake around my body, pulling me close to his chest. "I've told you before that people only see what I allow them to see. The guards saw me take off with you but never saw me emerge from the clouds and land. We are perfectly safe here for a few minutes."

I slide my hands along his back, over the curve of his shoulders, and rest them on his biceps. "A few minutes?" I ask. Something about his voice is so calming that a few minutes seems like plenty of time.

What am I even worried about? If one indigo-slashed fucker shows his face between the tree trunks, Zaden will have us airborne in an instant.

"Exactly," he murmurs.

Scarla

"That's plenty of time," I say, not exactly sure what I mean. His biceps are so large beneath my hands and pulsing with heat.

Warmth coils in my belly and seeps lower, pooling between my legs. I'm breathing faster, and my breasts push against his chest with every intake.

Zaden catches sight of them, and his breath hitches. I run my fingers down his chest and pinch those nipples that kept snagging my attention.

Running the palms of my hand down the forms of his muscle, lower toward his belly, I trace the ridges and planes of his belly.

I push back a little to make room between our hips, and Zaden reluctantly loosens his grip around my waist.

"You have a little blood... here," I say, tugging at his belt.

His hands run up my back, over my neck ever so delicately, and into my hair, which he grabs fistfuls of while I unbutton his pants and lower them.

He moans in a loud growl when his cock springs free.

I take a sharp intake of breath at its size. I haven't seen it this close before, and it is truly an impressive work of art. I reach out one finger and touch the base, then trace a path upward slowly, slowly, enjoying the velvet texture and my control over this male's breathing, higher and higher up to the rim.

I circle the rim once with my finger, then follow the curve up to the tip.

That single caress feels amazing, and from the pained expression on Zaden's face, he feels it too.

I go back for more, unable to resist another stroke of that silky steel, but he grabs my wrist. "Fuck, Scarla. Stop."

We are stuck in a tableau that reminds me of when he saw my injured neck and stared at me like he was about to burst into flames. Like then, his fingers circle my wrist like iron manacles, and his gaze is black and intense. "You're wearing too much, mortal."

I smile darkly. I'm enjoying the power I have over him, the way his nipples dance when I frustrate him, and the way his cock reaches for me, yearning for my touch.

But it's true. I am still fully outfitted in a maid's dress, complete with a frilly white apron and my ox-hide boots. Zaden reaches down under my skirts and runs his hand up my leg, leaving a trail of blazing fire. It takes him an eternity to reach the apex of my thighs, and by the time he finally gets there, I am begging for his touch.

His fingers meet my soaking wet panties, and it is his turn to smile. "I can see you're ready for me, Scarla," he purrs, and I can't deny it. He rips my panties off, and I'm sure he's left a red mark at the top of my thigh where the bamboo threads broke.

But I don't care. I just need the friction of his touch against my aching core. But as soon as he casts my panties aside, he removes his hand from my skirts.

"Don't you dare fucking stop, angel."

He chuckles. "I like seeing you beg for me."

I stiffen. "I'm not begging. I could walk away if I wanted to."

Liar. I'm not going anywhere until this male pummels me to oblivion.

"Are you sure?" Zaden bends down and kisses me passionately on the mouth, tasting and teasing and sucking, and I want nothing more than to spend eternity kissing him back.

No, I'm not sure. I don't know if I can ever walk away from this male.

But I push away. I can't let him get the upper hand, so I trail a line of kisses down his neck, over the swell of his chest, pausing to lick and nibble at his nipple before kissing my way down to his belly.

His enormous cock reaches all the way to his belly button, so I don't have to bend over far to kiss the top of it.

Before I do, I hover over it and address Zaden, making sure the heat of my breath brushes his hard length. "Would you like me to stop now, angel?" I ask archly.

In an instant, Zaden pulls me off the ground and into his arms, fishing under my skirts with one hand while he holds me tight against him. "I need to be inside you," he growls. "Now."

He has me high against him, and I wrap my legs around his waist so my core presses hard against his chest. He slowly lowers me until his tip rests against my clit.

I moan as he rotates my hips with his hands in tiny circles, allowing his cock to pleasure me. My back arches and I wish he had a spare hand to clamp over my aching breasts.

With supreme control and his biceps and shoulders bulging, he raises me ever so slightly and tilts me so his tip rests against my pussy. Our faces are level, and I can't help but fall forward, claiming him in a kiss.

He begins to lower me gently onto him, but I whisper, "Stop."

He growls loudly, frustrated, but does as I say.

I hook my ankles together behind his back so he doesn't put me down, misunderstanding my intention. I lean forward and find his ear. "Fly," I murmur.

With another growl-that-could-be-a-moan, Zaden snaps his wings into existence, seemingly out of nowhere. The sight of his silken black feathers, as dark as night, pushes me to the edge of a cliff I want to dive right off.

A soft moan escapes me, high and light, and Zaden clutches me tighter to his chest. Then he lowers me slowly over his hard length, every millimeter deliberate and divine, and I close around him, slick and ready.

I think he is entirely inside me, and I whisper into his ear again. "Fly."

I was wrong; he wasn't fully inside me. But, in an instant, he is.

Zaden shudders, his warm muscles vibrating right through me, then launches himself up into my body, filling me with his cock in the moment before he carries us both up, through the canopy of trees, and into the sky.

With every powerful beat of his wings, he drives himself a little deeper in, and lifts us higher into the bright sunny sky.

This swooping isn't just in my belly. Every part of my body is singing, alive with sensation, as though I've dived into a giant pool of freezing water. My nerve endings are ringing, and my brain is overwhelmed.

The monster between my legs is a little painful, and as he drives deeper up into me, the pain is tweaked. But when we reach our cruising altitude, the sensation changes completely. I relax around him, and the sense of being filled entirely becomes plain amazing.

The clouds are low above us, like a soft white mattress that looks fluffy and snuggly. But when we fly through them, I come away cold and sprinkled with dew.

Zaden's arms grip me tightly, one behind my back and one supporting my ass. I am hanging from him, barely able to wiggle my hips and definitely unable to keep my lips from his.

"Have you done this before?" I ask, but the wind whips my words away, and I don't think he heard.

He slows down, and I get into the rhythm. His chest is firm and pressed against me hard as if we were in love, not just lovers. His arms feel so sure and secure that I know he will never let me go. He is completely in control. He has, literally, my life in his hands. And my pleasure too. He controls every thrust, every grind, every moment of slippery friction between us.

His hand squeezes my ass, and I clench around him, earning a masculine moan that makes me even hotter and wetter.

He thrusts into me with increasing speed as clouds drift past us and cold wind rushes over my spine.

I dig my fingers into his back, underneath his feathers, which brush against my hands. The touch of a single angel's feather is enough to make me climax, and now I have a whole bladeful of them brushing against the backs of my hands.

Heat rises within me, and my breasts grind against his hard chest, my nipples seeking the relief of pressure. His hand grinds my ass against him as he thrusts deeper and deeper.

I clamp my mouth around his and suck greedily, digging my fingernails into his back.

I have no idea how he's managing to fly through all this. He doesn't seem to be paying any attention to the mechanics of the flight other than occasionally glancing up. But his focus is entirely on me, as mine is on him.

If I was piloting this thing, we'd have crashed by now.

Stupid emotional words linger at the tip of my tongue, wanting to leap from my mouth into his, but luckily, I am able to hold them back.

But I can't hold back the growing ache within me, the feel of his feathers on the back of my hand, his strong arm behind my back, the grinding and rubbing of my breasts against his chest, and his hand on my ass. Even the rush of wind along my face and legs.

Most of all, I can't ignore the pounding of his enormous cock inside me, pulsing, jumping, thrusting, and how it feels where every inch of my body meets his.

My muscles clench tighter and tighter until I feel as though I might collapse into a ball of pure twitching energy, and with one last thrust, I shatter. Every muscle in my body contracts, and those deepest in my core squeeze tightest of all, breaking me apart into a million pieces that scatter all over the distant land beneath us.

The angel senses my release and follows me, shattering with a look of pure agony on his perfect features and an incoherent growl that somehow contains my name.

I stare up at the firm lines of his lightly stubbled jaw, full lips, broad forehead, and those startling green eyes. I could watch that face all day.

Already, he seems distracted, looking out ahead to see which way we're going. But then he leans forward and kisses the lobe of my ear. "You're fucking amazing, mortal."

Scarla

Returning to Malanox castle feels like coming home.

I alight from the Margrave's horse-drawn carriage, pleased to have solid stone beneath my feet. Rich people may have enough money to afford horses and carriages, but they don't have enough brains to invent a more comfortable form of transport.

Rich dudes are dumb. My sister's voice filters through my mind, and I smile. She died fourteen months ago, and I'm finally at peace with her passing. I spent so many pointless hours wrestling with her death because I knew there was something more to it than what everybody said.

And I was right. The Margrave, my angel, killed her. But only to ease her suffering. That knowledge nestles inside me like a warm light, and I relax into it whenever I need comfort. Leesa's final moments were peaceful and at a time of her own choosing—Zaden was just the weapon she wielded.

Leesa would never have believed I might end up calling the castle home. It rises above me, gray and forbidding, with a tall tower at each of the four corners.

I used to think this place was a fortress, but it's nothing compared to VanDyke's castle. Here, the river acts as a moat, and the only bridge across is guarded by Zaden's men, but it is otherwise unprotected.

No looming walls surrounding the castle, no impenetrable sorcered dome, no phalanx of guards.

I revise my assessment of the place. It isn't menacing, it's beautiful. Honey flows along my veins as I step inside, feeling safe again, finally.

The entrance hall appears less ornate now that I have something grander to compare it to. Sure, the ceiling is double height and soars far above us, intricate red and gold carpets cover the floor, tapestries and paintings adorn the walls, and that grand marble staircase curves and splits. But it is somehow simpler and more honest than the gold and white marble trinkets that littered every spare surface of VanDyke's palace.

"Home, sweet home," I say with a sigh.

Zaden, who traveled home with me in the carriage from Solren, instantly picks up on those words. "Did you say home?" he asks, raising an eyebrow.

We haven't discussed our living arrangements recently. In our last conversation about them, he was prepared to keep me a prisoner here until I die.

Things have changed. I assume.

"I'll stay here on one condition," I tell him, stepping onto the lush rug and feeling it give way deliciously underfoot.

He comes up beside me, his hands clasped behind his back like a perfect gentleman. "Oh yes? Do tell me your condition, milady," he mocks. "I'm certain I can accommodate it."

I purse my lips. "I may come and go as I please. And if I choose to give Gaze to somebody else on my deathbed, then that's my choice, and you can't stop me. Thirdly, I may invite anybody from the Undercity to visit me as my guest, whenever

I like. Finally, I will always have access to my own bedchamber and not be forced to share with you."

Zaden paces away, nodding thoughtfully. "I'm not sure I can agree to all of them," he says.

My hands fly to my hips. "Oh really? And which one of these perfectly reasonable conditions are you struggling with?"

He strokes his chin. "The last one."

I managed to contain my splutter. "That one is non-negotiable." Honestly, all I want to do is to hop into bed with this male and never get up, but it's way too soon to be backing down on any of my points.

When I speak, Zaden pauses pacing to look at me, then resumes. "I see. I thought you said you'd attended classes in the Undercity."

I can see he is leading me into a trap here, but I can't figure it out. "Yes," I say warily.

"Then you will be aware that one does not equal four," he says, still pacing as though trying to solve a complex problem.

"Yes, I am. Would you like a gold star for pointing out the obvious?" I ask.

"Not at all," he says, scuttling back and forth in front of me like a lost skitter beetle. "I just want you to acknowledge that you have four conditions, not one."

I huff, really whooshing out a big puff of air. "Fine, you want it in one condition? The condition is this. I do what I want, not what I'm told. Period."

I can feel my whole posture stiffen as I wait for his reply. If our living arrangement is going to work—and I really want it to—then he has to agree to this. I will not be here as his servant or slave or prisoner. I will only be here because I choose it.

The angel stops wearing a groove in the carpet and stays put in one place. I hope he's finally taking this seriously, but his smirk worries me. "You do what you want and not as you're told?" he asks.

I fold my arms across my chest and nod. "That's right."

His smirk deepens. "That's not so much a condition as simply your personality. If I thought I could get away with telling you what to do, no amount of begging on your part would change that."

"I..." It feels like he's disagreeing with my condition, but he isn't. Not really. "Good," I finish with confidence.

Zaden steps closer and twists a lock of my hair around his finger, then cups my cheek. "It doesn't mean I won't try," he promises with a twinkle in his eye. "Watching you get pissed with me is as sexy as fuck."

My legs turn to jelly, and I have to lock my knees to keep from falling. "Then prepare to be constantly aroused," I retort.

"Oh, mortal," he says, leaning in and whispering the words against my lips. "You're in so much trouble."

* * *

Zaden agreed to me having my own bedchamber because I didn't give him a choice. But he suggested I bathe in his room, and I couldn't find a single reason to disagree.

His room is in the northwest tower. I've never been permitted entry before—it is always guarded by an armored dude with no personality, who I've never been able to charm my way past.

I'm dying to know what it's like inside.

Zaden pushes open the door, and my breath hitches. How does an immortal being choose to decorate his personal space?

Will there be mummified bodies of ex-lovers? Works of great art gifted to him by famous painters from the past, like Mordeus or Hasbern? Or will he have a collection of extinct animals roaming one corner like an out-of-time zoo?

Nope. He has a bed, a table, and a bookshelf.

Fascinating.

"How... impressive," I say dryly. "I can see you spent centuries honing your style. This place really reflects your personality."

"Thanks," he deadpans. "It took me lifetimes to get just right."

Even the bookshelf is paltry compared to what he could have. It is no taller than his extended arm and only as broad as his outstretched arm span. There can't be more than a couple of hundred books on there.

"These are your favorites?" I ask. Perhaps I'll be able to glean something about him from his choice of books.

Zaden shrugs. "I haven't read them all."

I walk closer to examine the cracking spines. The bindings are old cracked leather, and the gold lettering is mostly faded. "Are you waiting for some time to open up in your schedule before you start?" I joke.

Zaden comes to stand beside me, his presence almost tangible, although we aren't touching. "You know, most things get pretty old when you've lived as long as I have. Even reading."

I clutch the book in my grasp to my chest protectively, as though he's insulting the damn thing. "But there are always new stories. How could you get bored of that?"

"If you stick around long enough, you can get bored of anything." His green eyes tunnel into mine. "Almost anything," he amends.

I open my mouth to protest, but I suppose he's right. Sadness winds through his words, and suddenly a life as long as his seems like a curse.

"I'm sorry to hear that," I falter.

He reaches out toward me but falls short of touching my face. "Not everything is boring," he murmurs, and the muscles deep inside me clench. "But how about we wash some of the blood off first."

I raise an eyebrow. "First? And what comes second?"

His lips curve into a grin, and my skin tingles alive with sensation. "We'll just have to see where our bodies lead us."

Steam rises from the giant stone tub in the bathing room that adjoins Zaden's bedchamber. The idea of immersing myself in that hot water is heavenly. I am filthy and disgusting and covered in splatters of dead men's blood, so I readily agreed to take a bath.

I pull off my dirty maid's dress and let it drop to the floor, wishing Zaden would turn his back., But he doesn't. His eyes watch every movement I make like he's studying for a test. I feel awkward and exposed, standing here naked before him, a flawed version of the marble women that adorned VanDyke's castle.

It's nothing he hasn't seen before, I remind myself. And from the hungry look in his eyes, he doesn't mind seeing it again. His jaw twitches as his gaze sweeps over the 'X' carved on my hip, but at least it is healing nicely.

I slide into the bath, and little waves lap and burble against my body while bubbles of lavender burst above the surface. The hot water soaks through my muscles and erases the blood of battle from my skin. I immerse myself completely, taking a moment to anchor myself in the here and now. I am no longer a prisoner in a dirty dungeon, worried for my life and Molly's. I am back home, in the safety of Malanox Castle, and this is where I will stay—for as long as I want to, and not a second longer.

I surface and breathe in a gulp of air. I clean my body with scented lotion and scrub my skin with soap until I have washed away every trace of my imprisonment.

I emerge from the bath feeling human again and dry myself in a huge white towel that is softer than a mother's love. I could sleep for days. I slide in between the crisp covers of Zaden's bed and close my eyes for a moment, listening to the sounds of the angel having his own bath, splashing and humming a tune. My lips twitch in amusement—I wouldn't have picked him for a hummer.

A minute later, he comes out of the bathroom totally butt naked, with an enormous freaking erection. "Hi, mortal," he purrs with hooded eyes and irises swirling with black.

The sight of his perfectly sculpted body and that huge, eager cock, has me squirming under the covers and melting into a pool of honey. For an instant, his wings flare out behind him, sending a pulse of desire through me.

"Holy hell," I murmur. "That's an impressive wingspan." He smiles wickedly and stalks closer.

Zaden

Scarla is hidden under the sheets in my bed, her hair damp and rumpled from the bath. I rushed my own washing and never got the image of Scarla's naked ass swishing to the bed out of my head.

Not just any bed. My bed.

Her mouth is slightly open, and she's staring at my cock, making it harder. When I flew her home from Solren, I felt the inside of her, but that was frantic and animalistic and rushed.

Now I want to feel her long and slow and soft.

I cross to her bedside and stand proud. She surprises me by leaning forward, half-sitting, and placing a delicate kiss on the end of my cock. I make a little startled grunt, and she leans back against the pillow with a self-satisfied smirk.

I fence my hands on either side of the pillow and soak up her slight blyberry scent. It's tinged with musky arousal, and if I drew back the sheets to reveal her skin, the whole room would be filled with her flavor.

"You kissed my cock," I growl.

"Yes."

"How very presumptuous."

Her fingers run up my jawline. "Thank you."

"It wasn't a compliment," I tell her, but really, most of my

97

attention is on how her finger runs down the shell of my ear.

She smiles softly. "You're welcome."

Honestly, this damn woman is a witch. I lean closer, the heat from her face warming me. "Are you trying to bewitch me?" I growl, then claim her mouth with mine, savoring her taste, lingering on her lips, letting her tongue slide over mine.

She nips my lip. "I thought it was the other way around," she says with a sexy fucking smile that I want to lose myself in.

I peel back her sheet to reveal one breast, which I claim with my lips, my tongue, my mouth. Her back arches into me, pressing her harder into my mouth, and I back away, not relinquishing control. She presses a hand against the back of my head, and I give in, letting the pressure build between my tongue and her tit.

Her soft moans are intoxicating. I could come from those alone, thrilling and aroused and all kinds of pleasurable.

But I need more. I plant kisses across to her other breast and softly bite her nipple, earning another sexy groan that almost tips me over the edge. I run a hand down her soft belly, over the gentle curve of her mound, and along her slick folds.

She is so fucking wet that my cock gets even harder, and I press it into the side of the bed. I'm kneeling on the floor, my mouth clamped over her breast and my hand on her clit. I experiment with different movements and firmness until I find the pressure that has her bucking under my hand.

"Please, Zaden," she whimpers, and some of my control returns. She is the sexiest thing I've ever laid eyes on, but I need to keep myself in power. "Please, fuck me, Zaden."

Her breathy voice is irresistible, and I can't wait any longer. I throw her sheet aside and the sight of her whole body, lily white and as sinful as hell itself, has my cock jumping.

I growl and lower myself on top of her, careful not to let my full weight crush her. She's strong and tall for a human, but she's still a mortal.

I rest the tip of my cock at her entrance while I place my lips on hers, then I plunge my way into both, our mouths and bodies enmeshed. Her center is warm, soft, dripping with desire, and I've never felt anything better.

Even heaven can't have been this good.

I push against her, and my hips meet hers completely. She gasps, and her muscles contract around my cock, pulling me in, inviting me, wanting me.

Struggling to maintain control, I ride in and out, and she's writhing, her breasts pressed against my chest. We find a slow rhythm that builds, a push and pull, a sensual dance, and finally, she begins to release.

Her eyes are closed like she's visiting a personal paradise where I can't follow her, and the soft curve of her jaw tightens. Her muscles ripple powerfully along my shaft, and I finally let myself go.

I plunge into her, so my balls press against her folds, and she arches up, her moaning high-pitched and lavish. When she finally shudders against me, I let myself release into her with my final thrusts.

Entirely spent, I slump onto the mattress beside her and prise her fragile arm out from under me. I leave a leg slung across hers, too sated to care how she interprets that small piece of intimacy.

Staring at her face, I will her to look at me. She does, and her eyes look soft for once. My chest constricts.

My eyes roam over her vulnerable form, and I remind myself

why I brought her here and seduced her.

But keeping an emotional distance is getting harder and harder.

"You know, for an angel, you're awfully good with human bodies," Scarla murmurs.

I chuckle. "Well, your body is awfully good." I run a finger down the curve of her waist, the swell of her hip, and she nuzzles against me.

"You've obviously been around females before," she says. She rests her head on her hands, using my chest as a table, and grins mischievously. "Or do you get some kind of sex training up in heaven?"

Reminders of heaven and everything I've lost usually piss me off, but her tone is so light and teasing that I can't help but smile. "No sex training. I've just put in a lot of hard practice."

She stares up at me through that halo of short copper hair, which always manages to reflect every beam of candlelight in any room. "That I believe. Anyone in particular?"

Lying in the warm, sex-scented sheets, limbs entwined with this fascinating woman, the words flow from me like mother's milk, though I've spent decades keeping them locked inside me. "I loved somebody once. Her name was Elanora." I think back to that woman and describe everything I see. "She had hair like moonbeams over water, silvery and ever-changing, and slanted eyes that could turn a man to liquid. She was better than heaven, and I would have given my life for her. I would have given her the whole world."

Too late, I realize Scarla has stiffened beside me. I've clearly upset her, and I cannot help but feel a warm glow of satisfaction that she's jealous. It's not a gentlemanly response, but fuck it, I'm not a gentleman.

But Scarla's tone is smooth and teasing, and I take mental note of her ability to deceive. "What happened? Did she grow tired of your massive cock?"

"No. She was a mortal, and she died." I've never spoken those words aloud, and I'm surprised at how easy they are to say. The wound of Elanora's death is no longer fresh—it is healed and only evident in the scar on my soul it left behind.

"A mortal?" Scarla whispers. "But you hate us."

Well, fuck, if she hasn't figured out by now that's a lie, she's not as smart as I thought. The only thing I hate about humans is the brevity of their lives. There's no point getting to know one because I blink my eyes, and they're gone, replaced by the next version. Like Xerxes. I'm losing count of how many damn Xerxes I've been through.

"Yes," I say, running my hand in a circle around her warm hip. "I hate you." Then I lean in and plant a soft kiss on her cheek, wondering what the hells I'm getting myself into.

Scarla

"Where are you going?" a low voice demands from the dark.

I pause with my hand on Zaden's bedchamber door. I can hardly deny that I'm sneaking out, but it isn't to get away from him. "I'm going to see if Molly has returned yet," I tell him.

"I already told you she's not back."

"I know." That's why I was trying to sneak while Zaden was asleep, but I'm beginning to think that angels don't even need sleep. I've certainly never seen the Margrave close his eyes for longer than a blink. "I just want to check for myself," I say.

"Of course you do," he murmurs, and I can hear the amusement in his voice. "You never believe anything unless you see it for yourself."

I peer toward the sound of his voice, trying to make out his features in the dark. I let my Gaze trickle on, and he lights up like a lantern on solstice. His smirk is on full wattage.

My hand still rests on the doorknob. "I've learned to rely on myself."

Growing up, I was under the care and protection of my mother, with whom I spent so many long hours in the Underwing, watching while she tended to the sick. After she died, Dad was stricken with grief and couldn't look after us properly.

Nobody in the Undercity goes hungry, of course. The whole

community makes sure of that. We have coal to trade and food enough for all, although it's mostly grogum porridge, with chicken and berries once a week.

But that isn't the same as feeling nurtured and loved. The closest I've ever come to that was with Leesa, but now she's dead. And then Leo, until he betrayed me.

Zaden is beside me in an instant, and his arms wrap around me. "You have me now," he murmurs, and his words ring with honesty.

"I know." I relax into his embrace. "But I want to go down and ask around in the servants' wing. It's not that I don't believe you, I just—"

"Let me come with you," he offers kindly.

I chuckle. "Yeah, because the servants are all so comfortable around you. You have a real reputation as a big old cuddly teddy bear. The maids are bound to relax and open up if you're with me."

His brows pinch together. He knows as well as I do that most people in Malanox are terrified of him, including the servants in his castle. "Fine. If it'll make you feel better, go do it."

He squeezes my shoulders and lets me go, and I step out into the cold hallway, regretting the lack of his warmth, folding my arms across my chest. I know this castle's corridors as well as the twists and turns of the Undercity, and I pad along the hallways and down the stairs swiftly and quietly.

The name Elanora dances through my thoughts. It's hard to come to grips with the fact that the mighty Margrave of Malanox was in love with a mere mortal. I hate the bitch, obviously. Jealousy curls my fingers into fists and heats my blood. But I'm glad he shared his history with me.

And I feel like I've learned a lot about him. Like why he

hates mortals so much—it's a distortion of his love lost. The strength of his emotions must have twisted into hatred when Elanora died. I only wish he'd told me more about her, but he clammed up when I pressed him.

Which is probably just as well because I already have the image of her freaking moonlight hair, I don't need any more details of her perfection, or I might scream.

This is my favorite time of day. The sun isn't up yet, so most people are still asleep, and I have the whole world to myself. If I go outside, the world will be covered in white; if I watch the sunrise, the snow will sparkle like the heavens before it melts.

But I'm not going outside, not this time. I pad down to the first floor and into the narrower corridors where the servants live. A young man, Rory I think, nods his head at me in a slight bow. What must the footmen think of me? I arrived a prisoner, and now I share the Margrave's bed willingly. They probably don't know whether to pat me on the back or curtsy.

"Hi, Rory," I say, wanting him to treat me as an equal. "Is Molly back from Solren yet?"

"No, milady," he says in an even voice, and I can see I'll have to work on that whole equality thing. I'm not sure if I got his name right, and judging by his demeanor, he wouldn't correct me if I didn't.

I knock quietly on Molly's door and then let myself in. It's a small simple room, but she has it all to herself. "I don't have to share with anyone," she once told me. "And that's exactly how I like it."

Molly is naturally tidy—either that, or she's had it beaten into her—so I can't tell at first glance if she's slept here recently. The bed is perfectly made, and nothing is out of place, not even an errant stocking. She certainly isn't sleeping now.

With a huff, I back out into the hallways and roam, stopping every person I see and asking after Molly. After my fourth "No, milady," I have to admit she really isn't here.

Not that I thought Zaden was lying. He's always been truthful with me. Even when I asked him if he murdered my sister, he didn't lie; he didn't even hesitate. He told me the truth. Yes, he killed her, but only because she begged him to.

My belly rumbles with hunger, so I climb the central staircase to the second floor and cross to the dining hall, wondering if the Margrave will be eating there this morning.

He isn't, but my arrival causes a flurry of activity. Footmen nod and servants scurry, and moments later, a plate of eggs and fruit is placed before me at the massive wooden table.

I take a seat on the long edge so I can see out the windows toward Penngrove Forest. The gardens here aren't much to talk of, just red dust with the occasional hardy weed poking up between the flagstones. But I like the view anyway. The trees of the forest cling together in the distance seeking refuge en masse and reminding me that there is a bigger world out there and that I can go visit it anytime I please.

I must keep remembering of that. I don't want to fall into the habit of believing that I can't leave the castle or that I shouldn't. Even worse, I don't want to get to the point where I don't want to leave.

All these power-hungry men who fawn over my Gaze—and are prepared to kidnap me to control it—have me valuing my freedom more than ever. So I eat my steaming eggs and sweet fruit while staring over the forest and reminding myself that I can go there anytime I like.

The dining hall is beautiful. Vaulted ceilings covered in

ornate paintings soar far above me—this is another double-height room. The walls are lined with wood panels and tapestries. Even the sunlight streaming through the windows is dancing on the stone floor.

After breakfast, I go in search of Zaden. I need somebody to train me in hand-to-hand combat because I never want to feel as vulnerable as I did at VanDyke's palace. If anybody lays a hand on me uninvited, I want to be able to remove it, no questions asked.

I reach the foot of the grand central staircase, wide and curved with intricately carved banisters of expensive hardwood and marble treads. This is where the Margrave brings his important guests to impress them, I suppose. Up these stairs and into the ornate dining room.

But the man who blocks my path isn't a guest. His long oily hair and narrow face with pinched lips raise an instinctive shudder in me when he sneers at me from beneath those dark eyes. I am looking at a ghost. A dead man. I back away, fear pricking my spine, until my brain kicks in.

This isn't Lord Xerxes the Fuckwit. The man before me is younger, gangly and immature, with just the dusting of a beard on his chin. He couldn't be older than eighteen or nineteen. But he's definitely related to the Fuckwit—he's the spitting image. Maybe a younger brother? Certainly not the same man. For all I know, Mini Xerxes is a cute little puppy with a joyful personality.

Even from three feet away, the rancid stench of his breath carries to me when he speaks. "Well, well, well. If it isn't Scarla Rosedarter Healer from sleeping hub S2A7 of South Undercity."

Mini Xerxes recites my old address as a threat, and I know

that's what he wants me to think. He knows precisely where I sleep—or used to sleep—and where my father still does. So if he wants to inflict terror on my family or me, he can do it easily.

Guess he's not a puppy. Dammit.

"Who are you?" I demand. This oily teenager doesn't scare me. He's just a man, one solitary human. Even if he's related to Lord Xerxes, the man at the top of my enemies list. That list used to just contain Sadie, the thug from North Undercity, but it's grown out of control lately. Lord Xerxes, Count VanDyke... even Leo.

Mini Xerxes' sneer contorts his face. "I am Sir Reginald Xerxes, second son of the Lord of Pravu. My older brother told me everything about you and your schemes, and you'll get nothing past me. If you try anything, you can say goodbye to your dear old father." He slices a finger across his throat. Asswipe. Anybody who threatens my father deserves to die; this guy just signed his own death warrant.

I am not frightened of him though. Either he's less scary than Fuckwit Senior, or I'm more confident than I used to be. Mini Fuckwit seems all posturing and bravado and no substance. I focus on the ribbon of light running inside his spine and the point where it narrows behind his neck. I could squeeze that narrow light using Gaze until he passed out. I've done it before, although with mixed success. I just need a little more training.

But I know he can't hurt me. His doublecrossing older brother has been exposed—and killed—so Zaden is unlikely to trust this oily man. But why the Margrave let him into his castle in the first place is a damn mystery. That bloodbond to his family has a lot to answer for.

I adopt a light tone. "I'm a bit surprised to see you here, Mini Xerxes," I say, refusing to use his title. "I thought the Margrave had cleared out all the trash."

To climb the stairs, I have to pass right by this disgusting man, and my fingers clench, and my breath stops as I approach him, alert for an attack. My entire body is tense as I walk past, but I keep a light smile fixed on my face.

His beady eyes watch me as I saunter past, assessing and calculating and throwing a beam of pure hatred at me.

I don't breathe again until I'm beyond him and several stairs above, climbing to the third floor, keeping my pace sedate though it almost kills me.

Once I'm out of sight of Mini Xerxes, I let myself break into a jog that carries me to the northwest tower. The guard on duty looks at me, but he steps aside rather than challenging me.

I strut past, pleased at my access to the Margrave's private tower. The stairs here hug the tower's outer walls, so I climb them in an upward spiral and burst back into Zaden's bedroom at a run, clawing for breath.

"You have to teach me to fight," I tell him.

He stands by the window that overlooks the town, leaning against the sill, wearing nothing but a pair of low-slung black pants that sits low on his hips. "But put on a shirt first," I say, not wanting to be distracted by the acres of muscles.

His lips twitch as he turns to face me. "You want to learn how to fight?"

I throw my shoulders back. "Yes."

He assesses me, studying my face and reading my serious intent. He nods. "Good."

Scarla

We're training in the yard where the guards work out and practice how to kill.

I don't come here often. A red dirt floor provides a softer landing than stone, and a sorcered roof offers protection from the sun and snow so the men can train any time of the day or night. It's a simple wooden structure on the northern side of the castle, detached from the main building. It's large enough that a hundred men could gather for a meeting, and a small regiment of sweaty men is clanging swords in one corner of the yard.

As we approach, the men stop their training and stare.

"Do you always train here?" I ask. From the looks of amazement on the men's faces, their Margrave coming to fight with them is a rare sight indeed.

Zaden's strides are long and don't falter as we enter the arena, heading straight for its heart like an arrow. "I have a private training room," he says curtly.

I hate that I have to scurry a little to keep up with him, but his legs are so damn long that I do. "So why don't we train there?" I don't want to fall flat on my ass in front of a dozen gawking men, and I'm sure I'll do exactly that.

I've trained my Gaze somewhat, but my hand-to-hand skills

are woeful. I imagine I'll spend most of the morning with my legs in the air and my butt in the dirt, flailing like an overturned frost beetle.

"Nobody goes into my training room except me," the Margrave snarls.

Immediately, I want to go there. I want to see for myself what's so special about the place that his High-and-Mightiness won't permit me to enter. I open my mouth to say so, but he cuts me off.

"You're not going there, Scarla. Just drop it."

Fine. I'll save that battle for later. Maybe having a gaggle of giggling men watching me fail will drive me to succeed.

The Maker knows I need to. I want to eliminate every ounce of vulnerability within myself. Gaze helps, but I need basic fighting skills too.

"Are we starting with swords?" I ask, looking around for a weapons rack.

Zaden smirks. "Fists." He drops into a fighter stance and shows me how to do the same. He runs through the basics of posture, weight, balance, and agility.

I can't wait until I've mastered this. I picture Mini Xerxes sneering at me from the high ground of the stairs, his image morphing into that of his older brother, and my blood boils. One day, I will slap that sneer off his face and watch him flail about in the dirt trying to find it.

"Why do you let Mini Xerxes stay here?" I demand, steel ringing through my voice. "His brother tried to fucking kidnap me. He betrayed me to VanDyke if you recall. He betrayed *you*." My voice rises on the last word.

The Margrave dances around my defensive stance and darts in fast, slapping me on the cheek with an open hand. "Raise your fists, stay alert," he instructs.

I try to do is he says, but he sneaks in another slap on my cheek, seeming to come out of nowhere. "You killed all the other servants who were involved," I persist. "And you killed your precious Lord Xerxes. So tell me, why is his brother still breathing?"

Zaden slaps me again, lightly but enough to sting. Anger rises in me, and I hold my fists higher and move my feet, dancing on the spot, trying to keep my eyes on him.

"I told you once before," he says on a breath. "I owe his family a bloodbond."

This time when the angel strikes, I see it coming and manage to swat him away at the last moment, so only the tips of his fingers brush my face. I smile triumphantly. "But why? Something about his great-great-grand-somebody, right?" I can't think of anything that Xerxes' old relative could've done that would justify bringing his great-great-grandson under Zaden's roof, under his protection, after his brother betrayed the Margrave he was sworn to serve.

"Good," the Margrave says, approving of me batting away his palm. "You're paying attention. Don't lose focus." Out of nowhere, his fingers tap my cheek—that Maker-be-damned angel moves faster than sunlight.

"Tell me the truth about Xerxes, and I promise I'll focus," I offer.

Zaden's arms fall loose by his side. "I thought we were doing this because you want to learn how to protect yourself?"

"I do."

"So, no deal." He darts in and lays another finger on my cheek, and my pulse rises.

I narrow my eyes and keep my feet as light as possible,

raising my hands to protect my face completely. There's no way he's getting past me again. "Why won't you just tell me the truth?"

I watch his face intensely, looking for any sign of movement. His eye twitches. "I've never told anybody."

That doesn't surprise me. This angel ain't exactly an open book. He holds his secrets closer than Fra Lennox holds her cards during a game of Aces over Nox. "Then it's about time you did," I say, dancing to my left to keep a distance between us.

He nods approvingly. "Good, you figured out you're allowed to move."

I scowl at him. "And have you figured out you're allowed to share with people?"

I expect him to glance around furtively to ensure nobody can overhear us, but I suppose his angel hearing would pick up if anybody was close. "Years ago, when the old Cloaked King died, before the current one took the throne, there was a power vacuum and a struggle among the Fallen of Aubia. There were great battles throughout the lands, as each angel pitted themselves against the others."

That doesn't make sense. Surely I would have heard if there was some giant celestial battle on earth. Most people don't even know that angels exist, they're just rumors that sensible people don't believe.

"Blood ran through the streets of Solren, Desert's Maw, Bilgon, everywhere."

My mouth falls open. "You're talking about the seven-year war."

Zaden's jaw twitches. "Yes. I believe that's what mortals called it."

"But that was about control over the hardwood forests of Leyva," I blurt out. Every creche child knows the story of that war. It happened five hundred years ago, and thousands of fighters, farmers, and miners died battling for their own cities and townships. It was all for control over the precious hardwood forests of the North, which contained Rosen trees, the hardiest and sweetest smelling wood.

"No, it was never about the forests," Zaden tells me, and I know he's telling the truth. He always tells me the truth. "That war was about succession of the Cloaked Kingship. It was a bitter battle between angels over who would rule the Cloaked Court because none of us had the dyad of Gaze and Inflict. They used their townsfolk as fodder, but it was always a war among angels."

History rewrites itself inside my mind, like pieces of a jigsaw puzzle coming together in a new way to form a completely different picture. "So it was always about the angels?"

Zaden isn't attacking me anymore with his damned quick fists, now he's just pummeling me with information. "That's right. They made a bloody mess of it all."

That pricks my attention. "They?"

He shrugs. "The other angels. I wasn't involved. Like I keep telling you, I'm not interested in power. I just want to return to heaven."

I can see it now. He is a Fallen Angel who's just looking for his way back home and, meanwhile, getting caught up in the blood feuds of others. I misjudged him so badly, and my heart melts at how I treated him. "So what happened with Xerxes's grandfather, or whoever it was?"

Zaden's jaw twitches. "There was a complication. A personal issue he helped me solve."

I stand flat-footed and scowl. "That's it? That's all you're telling me?"

Zaden's regard shutters and the brief glimpse of openness is gone. "That's all you need to know."

Zaden no longer dances around me; his arms are limp by his sides, so I let mine drop too. "I see."

But I don't really. I've seen Zaden kill a man for looking at me wrong, yet he brings the brother of the man who betrayed him under his protection. I'm frustrated that Zaden only half-shared with me but pleased that he didn't cover his silence with a lie. Trust is the most important thing in the world; we can work on intimacy.

My cheek stings with another slap, this one harder, and I look up through narrowed eyes to see a cheeky grin on the damn angel's face. "Don't let your defenses down, mortal. Ever."

"I'll bear that in mind," I say, raising my fists. There is no way he's getting through my barrier again.

He slaps me on the belly this time, grinning. "And don't overcommit your defenses to one area."

"Is this a training session or battle strategy lecture?" I grumble.

He quirks his brow charmingly. "Both. What's with the sudden bloodthirsty streak anyway? Usually, you're the one begging me to spare people's lives because humans are apparently so important."

"We are!" I say indignantly.

He dances around me fast, and I spin to keep him in sight. "So why do you want me to kill Sir Reginald Xerxes?" he asks.

That's an excellent question. It takes me a few moments to admit the truth to myself—I really do want that asshole dead.

Out of the castle, out of Malanox, and hanging with his brother in hell. No point denying it. Even though I've only just met him, his charms are already clear to me. He's the first person I've ever truly wanted dead. Unless you count Zaden, who I used to dream of murdering.

Mini Xerxes is as rude as his brother and clearly shares all the same traits. I have no problem smearing his character with the faults of his brother, who terrified me by sending men after me in Penngrove Forest and betraying Zaden by attempting to kidnap me. Mini Xerxes has been just as much a creep as his bro.

"He's a fuckwit," I summarize.

Zaden comes in slowly for a jab at my belly, but I see it coming and block him. "And do you think everybody who's mean to you ought to die?"

Studying the male's face, I don't think he's teasing. He is genuinely interested in my answer. "No, of course not."

Zaden cocks his head like he's trying to figure me out. "Just him then?"

I nod. We keep dancing and fighting—well, I keep bouncing on my toes and being slapped—but Zaden's question keeps running through my mind.

Why do I want Mini Xerxes dead? It's true that I forced Zaden to spare the lives of both Leo and VanDyke and that my revenge on the Xerxes family has already been paid in blood. So what's so awful about Mini Xerxes?

I think it's because the first words from his lips were a veiled threat against my father's life. I won't allow anybody to take my father away from me—he's the last real, solid part of me I have left. Everything else has been torn away. Mom, Leesa, Leo. Dad is the only thing that remains.

And I would kill somebody to protect him.

That thought lights me from the inside, burning through me like a forest fire, filling me with adrenaline. I remember Leo telling me why he did what he did. It was to protect the people—the Undercitysiders—that he loves.

The fire inside me sputters out and leaves an ashen residue. Leo is prepared to kill to save the people he loves.

Maybe I'm not so different after all.

Scarla

Weeks bleed into months, and my workout schedule only gets fuller. My body is changing too, becoming stronger and tighter, more like the warrior I want to be. We usually work in the guards' training yard but sometimes in the castle forecourt or, on one memorable occasion, inside the inner maze, the network of crisscrossing passageways inside the castle's very walls. The walls were so close and the space so narrow that I had an advantage over Zaden, who could barely pull back an arm and certainly couldn't draw a blade.

"You have to be able to fight anywhere," Zaden keeps reminding me.

Molly still hasn't turned up. I look out for her every dusk, staring down at the road toward town, and I ask after her every morning down in the servants' halls.

I've fallen into the habit of playing nursemaid to the castle, tending the sick or injured in a makeshift infirmary in the servants' rooms. I guess those skills I spent a lifetime developing are paying off. I can lay my hands on a feverish patient and ease the chills, reduce the heat. If that doesn't work, I try my hand at herbal medicine, but I'm far from expert at that.

Still, I reduce some suffering, and that makes me happy and the servants grateful.

And a grateful person is a handy person to have in your debt. I store up all the debts I'm accruing for later when they might come in handy.

Lunch is usually a quick bread roll and a hunk of cheese that I pilfer from the kitchens. Xerxes the Mini Fuckwit avoids me most days, so I don't have to worry about him smacking the food from my hands like he tried one day. Still, his continued existence annoys the living fuck out of me. I guess I'll deal with him when my training is complete. A bloodthirsty beast deep inside me stirs at that thought, and I wonder how long I'll have to keep it chained.

"I have a new training idea," I tell Zaden one morning over breakfast.

He puts down his croissant and pays me his full attention. I love it when he does that—his focus is like a blazing spotlight, making me feel like the only person on the planet. "You're not in charge of training. I am."

I cradle a mug of warm tea. "Don't be an asshole. Okay, I'll do you a deal." He doesn't say a word, just narrows his eyes, so I barge on. "Tell me about your bloodbond with Xerxes, and I'll stop coming up with brilliant suggestions to improve our training."

He crosses his cutlery neatly and lays them on his plate. "What do you want to know?"

"How do you make a bloodbond?" I take a slow sip of tea, pretending I'm not staring at his face and cataloging his reaction to my question.

He snags another bite of his pastry before answering. "All angels have the ability to cast a bloodbond, which they can perform on others or themselves. We access our deepest power, the link to the primordial, and forge a promise to forever link the bloodlines of two individuals. As long as the underlying promise between the two beings is kept, the bloodbond is secure."

Holy crap. That seems like a big deal. I can't suppress a shiver at how intense that sounds, and Zaden's deep rumbling voice only makes it more impressive. "So, what happens when you break the underlying promise?"

Zaden's jaw tightens, and he chews on his croissant harder than strictly necessary. He and I both know he killed the Fuckwit and thereby destroyed their bloodbond.

Obviously I've hit a nerve. But he's not in a sharing mood and throws his pastry to his plate. I wait out the silence, hoping he'll answer my question, but he doesn't. It's hard to beat an immortal being at a game of patience.

I place my mug carefully on the table. "If you're not going to answer about the bloodbond, you need to listen to my training idea."

He lifts his head. "Yes?"

I keep my voice light, steering us back into safer territory. "We should train in Hightown. Those streets and alleys are more like a real fight than our arena. Or maybe Lowtown. There's plenty of makeshift weapons down there, like sticks and rotted poles. It would keep things interesting."

Zaden picks up his croissant again. "No. Too many people. Somebody could get hurt."

I chew my lip and tilt my head. "I'm pretty sure that's the idea of fighting."

"No, I mean somebody innocent. A townsperson."

I put my hand to my chest in mock horror. "Are you saying I'm not innocent?"

Zaden shoots me a look laden with sensuality. "Oh, you are

119

far from innocent, mortal."

I shiver, and not from the cold. His loaded look has my panties instantly wet. But I have a point to make and don't intend to back down. "Since when do you care about hurting mere humans?" I ask.

"I care about not being seen by a bunch of nosy insects," he counters. "Especially insects who get all riled up when one or two lose a head and come knocking on my door annoying me. It isn't worth the hassle."

Okay, perhaps he's less of a sensitive gentleman than I thought. His description of humans as insects doesn't annoy me anymore because I know about Elanora and that his disinterest is just a distortion of his love. My lips curve into a smile. "We're not going during dawn or dusk, so no precious humans will come to any harm," I tease.

He growls. "I told you, I don't care abou—"

"In fact, let's go right now." I scrape out my chair and stand, refusing to accept anything other than total obedience from my tame angel. "On your feet, lover boy. Let's go."

He throws me an annoyed look but climbs to his feet with a resigned expression on his beautiful face.

Scarla

The overnight snow has melted and flowed into the snowmelt catches, which the townsfolk use for drinking water, and into the river, where it flows south. As we cross the only bridge over Malanox River, we walk through a fog of steam as the top layers of the water evaporate under the blistering sun.

"I hate crossing at this time," Zaden grumbles. "My cloak gets all sodden."

An image of a scowling angel dripping wet fills my mind, and I suppress a chuckle. "Poor baby," I comment mildly, earning that scowl I imagined.

"This is a stupid bloody idea," he says.

We step out of the hot rising mist into full sunshine, and our clothes immediately begin steaming under the dry heat. "I never knew you were such a whinger. Shouldn't you be all about hell and brimstone and fiery eyes and avenging missions? And less about the grumpy pants?"

Zaden glances at me. "I can be both."

"Sure, sure. I guess you can complain in your downtime."

His lips twitch as he stares at me, his boots ringing out on the cobblestones of Hightown. "Exactly. And I can smite people in between. I can't be smiting all the time, you know."

I throw back my head and laugh. This angel continues to

surprise me. "You're not like I expected," I tell him.

He turns right and ducks into a small laneway that leads away from the river. "Well, given that you expected me to be a murderous prick, I'm glad to hear that. Now how is this for a training spot?" He gestures to the narrow alley, and I nod. Light and shadows plays along the narrow lane, which I'll use to my advantage. Or try to. I'll try to angle him so sunlight blinds him.

"Here is fine. And, for the record, I still think you're a murderous prick. You're just funnier than I anticipated."

He hooks his thumbs into his pockets. "So, I'm a murderous clown."

I chew my lips, thoroughly enjoying his discomfort. "That sounds about right." I dart in and peck his cheek, brushing my mouth against his cheek at the point where his stubble meets his skin, amazed that I am comfortable enough with an angel to kiss him whenever I feel like it.

Before I can move away, he clamps an iron arm around my waist and whispers into my ear. "Just don't tell anyone the truth. I have a reputation to uphold."

He winks, and I giggle. "My lips are sealed."

"Not too sealed, I hope," he purrs, leaning in and claiming me in a kiss. I melt against him for a moment, then take full advantage of his vulnerability and punch him in the kidney. We are combat training, after all.

He releases his grip around my waist, and I dance away with an enormous grin. "Don't let your defenses down, angel," I tease. "Ever." That's his favorite training phrase, and it's wonderful to throw it back at him.

Zaden's eyes narrow and darken, and he watches as I back against the tall building. Hard, bumpy stone pokes into me.

The richest folks live here in Hightown, inside high stone buildings terraced side-by-side like animals huddling for warmth.

The sun isn't yet high in the sky, so the tall houses cast long shadows, and our little alleyway is mostly shaded. But it's still hot enough to boil an eyeball—unless you're an angel or a vestige like me.

Zaden pretends to spot something off to one side, but I don't fall for it—I keep my focus squarely on him, watching his weight shift. When he darts at me, I'm ready for it. I duck under his attack and whirl behind him, landing a forearm on his knee as I pass.

He nods approvingly. "Well done. You're improving."

"I'm sick of your guards laughing when I tank."

"Funny," he smirks. "I quite enjoy that part."

A scowl creases my face but doesn't reach my eyes. "Hilarious. Did anybody ever tell you how funny you are?"

He ducks in low this time, aiming for my middle, but I leap to the right and evade him, splitting my face in a grin. "You're getting slow, Margrave."

I know he's going easy on me, but I still get a thrill from how much I've improved. Just in these past few months, I've become faster and stronger—my aching muscles from hours of daily exercise are proof of that.

His eyes darken, and a devilish grin lights on his face. "Is this fast enough for you, Scarla?" In an instant, faster than I've ever seen him move, he is in my face, his arms caging me against the stone wall behind me.

"You've been holding out on me. I didn't know you could move like lightning!"

"I can't let you know all my tricks," he says.

"What else can you do?"

He leans forward until his sweet breath brushes my cheek. "I can fly," he whispers, bringing to mind the last time he did, with me in his arms.

Thank the Maker he's kissing my neck and can't see me deepening into red. It's hard to pull off being stylish and sophisticated, as though I always expected to become an angel's lover when I'm flushing with embarrassment every second minute.

I'm standing with my back flush against the wall, so I don't have a lot of room for a backswing, but I aim a weak punch in his ribs. Unfortunately he's expecting it and catches my fist in his. "You don't get to fool me again, little human."

"Dammit. Leo used to fall for it every time."

"He did?" The angel stiffens in my arms. "I wasn't aware you used to kiss him." His voice deepens. "Or fight him." Zaden's jaw is so hard I could cut coal with it, and I wonder which option bothers him the most.

"Which would be worst? Kissing him or fighting him."

Zaden's voice is thick. "I don't care if you stick a chicken bone in his eye, but if he lays one soft finger on your precious skin, I'll flay him alive."

Okay, that seems like an overreaction, but I suppose for an avenging angel, it's pretty tame. It's almost a standard greeting in the circles Zaden moves in.

"Well, I did neither. These fists have never punched him." I hold up my hands to show him. "And these lips have never kissed him." I pout a little, teasing.

"What other parts have never been kissed?" Zaden asks, nuzzling my neck and laying a soft row of smooches across it.

His tongue is warm and slick, and the sensation of it sliding along my sun-heated skin is blissful. "This bit." I point to my clavicle, and he unbuttons my shirt to trace the area with his lips, his tongue, his hot breath.

"Where else?" he purrs against my chest, his light stubble gently scraping my skin and sending a ripple of vibrations straight to my core.

"A little lower," I say, straining my breast as though I can make the thin material covering it disappear with willpower alone.

He unbuttons my shirt some more, focusing intently on the soft flesh he's revealing. My skin is alive with sensation.

This is my last chance before I fall under his spell completely. I bring down the side of my hand on the back of his neck and watch triumphantly as he staggers for a moment—this could be the first time I've ever truly taken him by surprise on the battlefield, and it feels almost as good as his touch.

I dance away, but he ensnares me with a single tendril of purple magic that wraps around my middle and stops me in his tracks.

Whirling around, my mouth falls open. "Cheat!" I accuse.

He's recovered from my little love tap, and he leans an elbow against the wall so his shirt pulls across his chest, showing his perfect form. "How am I cheating?"

The ribbon of his magic coils around my body, and every part of me it touches sings with fire. It tightens around my waist, then loosens, teasing me and creeping higher, encircling my back, and then brushing the tip of my hard nipple so lightly I want to scream.

"You never use your sex magic on me!"

Ever since he realized I could see his seduction powers, he's stopped using them on me. But now, all bets are off, and he is

125

attacking me with pleasure.

Still leaning against the wall, his hips rotate ever so slightly, drawing my attention down to his massive erection. Those damn pants of his are low on his hips, hugging his ass, and way too small to contain his straining cock. "It isn't cheating, mortal. It's just another weapon in my arsenal."

I chew my lip. "Is this Inflict?"

"No," he growls. "Every angel can do this, it's in our blood. We're born to it. Inflict is a hundred times more potent. Every angel can attack briefly, but we can't cause prolonged pain. Only pleasure." He draws out the word, tasting it with his tongue.

I'm desperate to leave—I can't let him win another freaking training round. But there's no way in Hades I'm walking away from that snaking tendril that is bringing my damn veins to life with fire. It curls around my breasts and tweaks my nipples harder, but not hard enough. I need his hands clamped around them, his mouth sucking, the friction of his body pressed against mine.

Without noticing, I've taken the few steps toward him and am leaning against him, rubbing myself like a damn kitten against his chest.

He moans, a deep guttural noise, when my belly smooshes against his hard length, and the sound is so sexy that I almost come right there.

"Can we agree I won the training?" he purrs.

No. There's no damn way I'll agree to that. But my slutty mouth has other ideas. "Yes," I moan. "Yes. You win."

"Good." He slams me against the wall but cushions my head. He keeps one hand wrapped behind my head and presses his lips against mine, tasting and exploring and licking and sending me fucking insane.

His other hand snakes lower and unbuttons my pants with unseemly skill.

"What if somebody sees us?" I gasp.

"They won't."

"But... but what if they do?"

"I don't give a fuck," he growls, burrowing his hand inside my pants, tracing down over the thin fabric of my panties.

I don't give a fuck either. I widen my stance, and he snarls in approval and caresses me through the fabric before pushing it aside and pressing his finger against my clit. He circles and teases, and I squeeze his hand forcefully against me, needing more friction, more pressure, more of him.

"Wait," I breathe, and he pauses for a moment but doesn't remove his hand. "What about you? If we keep going, I won't last much longer."

He smiles deliciously and claims my mouth again, speaking into my lips. "I've gone decades without sharing my bed with any woman but you. I'm used to waiting."

I can't help it. I feel special. This incredible, skilled, handsome warrior hasn't slept with a woman in ages, and he finally has. With me. I want to climb into the clouds and shout to the world that I'm an angel's chosen.

But right now, I can't string two words together. Zaden slides two fingers inside me, and I groan his name.

"Scarla," he says into my mouth, and I pull on his lips as though that will fuse us together. Anything less will never be enough. With his fingers still inside me, he rubs my sensitive core with his thumb, and the heavens dance before my eyes.

I want to tell him he's amazing, to compliment his coordination in working all that magic down there, to whisper sweet words of approval. I'm one of those loser women who falls in love with every man she sleeps with, and I want to pour all those emotions out right now.

But I only manage to say one thing. "Fuck me, Zaden."

He presses his thumb harder and takes my aching breast in his mouth, which is too much for me. I crack and then splinter, falling into shards, utterly coming apart. The waves of pleasure reside, ebbing away deliciously, like a dozen tiny fractures of my body, until I'm left with a sense of absolute bliss.

I'm leaning against him, grinning like an idiot, barely able to support my weight. "You are spectacularly skilled at that, milord."

"What, fighting?" he asks, running a hand down my cheek.

"No. You're a terrible warrior," I lie. "Forget about it." I almost close my eyes and take a nap against his abs.

"Oh, I don't think I'll ever forget it," he rumbles.

Scarla

With every passing week, I become stronger, more skilled, and more confident.

Zaden has me training against his guards now as well as himself, and they are under orders not to go easy. Although I equal many of them in height, and my muscles are growing thicker and firmer, I still can't match most of the men in strength. Or speed—I'm quicker than one or two, but not all of them.

Even so, I have managed to best every damn one of them. Gaze brings me an advantage that nobody predicted. With it flicked on, the ribbon of light that dances down each man's spine becomes my focus and helps me to predict which way my opponent will move.

A slight blurring of the light to the left comes before the man's body moves that way, and I can duck out of the way and land a blow of my own.

It's almost as though I can read my opponent's intent. The more I train with Gaze, the better I can interpret that ribbon of light. A blurring to one side or the other indicates movement, and the longer the streak of blur, the faster the man will leap. A little twinkling down the side of the light stream means he'll just move his arm or leg, not his entire body.

Honestly, the guards are easy to defeat now that I've trained my Gaze and honed my battle nous.

They hate it. Especially old Nicholson, who practically spits in my face whenever I approach him in the training yard. I don't mind. It spurs me on, lights a fire under my feet, and has me dispatching him even faster.

I still can't beat Zaden, of course. Although I can sometimes see a thick ribbon of light down his spine, mostly he's entirely made of light, a luminescent glow that I still can't read. No matter how many times I squint at him, whether on the training field or off, I still can't interpret the flurries and sparkles that are constantly twinkling all over his damn body. They don't seem to correlate with movement, intent, or conversation. They are just as mysterious as he is.

As I leave the castle, I start humming, racking my brain to remember where the tune is from. It might be an old campfire classic or a childhood ditty I learned in creche; I can't quite place it.

It's early dawn, so the castle forecourt is teeming with guards. I nod and smile at the nearest ones and make my way around the side of the castle and set out across the red plain in the direction of Penngrove Forest.

The infirmary's supplies of herbs are short, so I'm heading to the forest to top them up. The ground is sludgy beneath my feet with the last traces of melting snow, but the temperature is comfortable, and the hum on my lips keeps me happy.

The first time I came to Penngrove Forest in search of Wilton's Dale, I'd been seeking it to help Molly, who was suffering from the sighing sickness.

She still hasn't returned to the castle, and I continue asking after her every day; part of me even worries for her. But by now, I figure she's starting a new life for herself in Solren. Perhaps my constant questioning of why she would live a life in servitude finally got through to her, and she's run away to start over.

I picture her by Bwadu's side, living in the Rim of Solren. I have no clue what that place looks like, but I imagine massive struts from a long-decayed bridge, with a slum town sprouting up among the hulking pillars. I trust Bwadu will take care of Molly because the Rim has a terrible reputation, and my sweet friend will need all the help she can get.

Could be way off, but it doesn't really matter. I just hope Molly is with Bwadu. And I wish she'd send me word that she's all right so I can stop worrying, although I doubt she can read or write.

When I reach the tree line, the sun is showing over the horizon, and I unbutton my cloak before plunging in. It's still dark in here, and patches of snow cling in the deepest shade around the broad trunks.

The relative darkness doesn't bother me. I know my route. Several clumps of Wilton's Dale grow at the base of yen trees a couple of hundred feet into the forest, so I head there now, keeping an eye out for probleroot to top up the tea supplies while I'm here.

Mulchy bark and damp leaf matter assault my senses, making me relax. I inhale deeply, breathing in nature's aroma, marveling at how rarely I am truly immersed in the natural world and vowing to take more frequent walks in the forest.

I wish Molly were with me. I'm pleased she's started a new life for herself, but I miss her. There aren't many I count among my friends; although I'm trying to work my charms on a few maids, servitude is so ingrained in them that they can't stand the idea of treating me as an equal.

It's exhausting. If Molly was here, she'd tell me to snap out of it, and then I'd say something stupid, and we'd have a good laugh.

I bend to gather the roots, pushing aside a covering of fallen leaves with a crackle and crunch, when a twig snaps behind me.

My body spikes with adrenaline, and I turn to find Xerxes the Mini Fuckwit sneering down at me. The forest canopy covers the sky completely, but there's no missing his wispy beard and narrow face.

I stuff the woody stems into my pockets, then stand to my full height. The first time I met Mini's brother, he slapped me and called me names, making me feel small, afraid, and vulnerable though I tried to put on a brave face.

When I returned from VanDyke's palace, my position in Zaden's Castle was much more assured, and I knew I had no reason to be scared of this man—but still, I was, and I had to plaster on a brave mask to hide my fear.

But now, feeling strong and skilled, there's nothing forced about my bravery. My adrenaline disperses into my blood, and I relax into a smirk of my own. "Are you following me again, Mini Xerxes?"

He hesitates at the surety of my tone, then a creepy smile lifts his cheeks. "I want to keep an eye on you, girl. You never know what danger you could get into out here, all alone in the forest."

I lean against the tree, showing him how unconcerned I am. "Are you trying to threaten me?" I ask idly. "Only, it's hard to tell because I don't feel at all scared."

He wipes a strand of black oily hair from his face with his

long fingers and narrows his beady eyes. "Watch how you talk to me, girl." He takes a step closer. "I don't like your tone."

I look down and check my fingernails. "And I don't like being called girl. Don't use that name again."

His thin lips quiver in delight as though I'm walking into a trap. "Or else what, girl? Your precious Margrave isn't here to protect you now."

Now I'm inspecting my fingernails; I see what a state they're in. I really must take better care of them. The nail on my fourth finger is too long, and the others are all chipped. "I said don't call me girl."

He steps closer, and his rank onion breath makes me recoil. "Or what, girl?"

"Or this." I brace my shoulders against the tree's rough bark and kick Mini Xerxes in the gut with my heel. He doubles over, and I keep a close eye on the glowing ribbon of light that travels the length of his spine, watching for movement. It shimmers, and he produces a dagger from his boot and thrusts it up toward my ribs.

I've already moved aside before he finishes his action, and I thump an elbow down on the back of his head, knocking him to the ground.

I dance away a few steps, grinning. This is the most fun I've had in days.

"You fucking bitch," he spits, and I'm delighted at the flecks of blood flying from his mouth.

I shrug. "I've been called worse. Like girl, for example. Do you promise not to call me that again?"

The Mini Fuckwit unfolds his gangly frame and stares at me with murder in his eyes. He stalks closer, clearly still not understanding the position he's in. "I will call you whatever I like, whore."

The light in his spine is vibrating in anger, which only exaggerates its movements, making it easier for me to predict his next move.

And easier for me to manipulate.

I focus on the narrowing of light at the base of his neck and squeeze ever so gently. Not enough to make him pass out, just enough so he topples to the forest floor like his bones have turned to snow.

He stares up at me, helpless. I saunter closer and slam my thick ox-hide boot on his chest. "I could kill you," I say calmly. "With my fist, with your dagger, or with my vestigial power. So many options to choose from."

His dark oily hair is splayed over the leaves, and a smudge of red mars his pallid face. He can't move, but his beady eyes are fixed on mine, and I know he can hear me.

"The only reason I'm sparing your life is because Zaden, for some reason, wants you alive. Not because he respects you, obviously, but because he respects your forebears. And I respect him, so your heart will stay pumping for now. But if you ever again call me whore or bitch or girl, I will cut out your fucking tongue. Do you understand?"

There's another reason I can't kill him. I don't want to taint my soul with murder because I will never get into heaven, where Zaden is desperate to return. And although I've barely admitted it to myself, the truth is I would follow that male anywhere, and if he's going to heaven, I'm following.

But Mini Man doesn't need to know that. He blinks rapidly, and the little finger of his right hand twitches, so I take that as a yes.

"Good. Now, you better get your act together and figure

out how to move your muscles before dawn's end, otherwise I guess the sun will do my dirty work for me."

I stride away, feeling very pleased with myself. That was awesome. I am a freaking sir-slaying super soldier. Invincible.

Unless you count Zaden or any other angel. Those celestial bastards are so freaking fast, and they can only be killed by a divine blade.

So, angels aside, I feel pretty freaking fantastic. I can defeat anybody in a fight. I haven't even worked up a sweat.

Gone is the vulnerable little girl caught up in men's games. And here am I. Scarla Rosedarter Healer, a woman for the world to reckon with.

Scarla

I want to run right back to the castle and into's Zaden's arms to tell him about my glorious defeat over Reginald Xerxes the Mini Fuckwit.

But my angel is away on business so I can't. Actually, I'm not sure how he'd react to me knocking out his right-hand man. I'm not clear exactly how far his protection over the Fuckwit extends, so it's probably best that I keep my victory to myself.

Zaden isn't often away, and I'm surprised how much I miss him. He's the person I wake up to most mornings and fall asleep with most nights, and the glowing ball of happiness inside me is all his doing.

I can't wait to nuzzle against his warm neck when he gets back, soak up his forest lily scent, and feel safe in his arms.

But since he isn't here, there's no point sleeping in his bedchamber. I make my way to my own, over in the guest wing on the eastern side of the second floor. My room isn't as grand as Zaden's, though it's still more luxurious than most places I've laid my head. At first glance it seems small, and I have to remind myself that five or six families would sleep here if this were a cavern in the Undercity.

At moments like these, I miss the Undercity community. Sleeping in a vast room by myself feels lonely. I grew up with dozens of warm bodies nearby at any time, often a quiet chat in one corner, or a mother taking care of a child, or the soft snuffles of gentle sleep.

I was never lonely in the Undercity, but this room is so vast, empty, and barren that a coldness seeps through my bones that has nothing to do with the temperature.

Zaden's absence makes me lonely. He has become my primary supply of comfort and love, and I wish he were here right now.

I settle between the cold sheets when a gentle knock sounds on my door. The servants don't usually knock—they scurry about like skitter beetles, ignoring eye contact, ignoring my attempts at conversation, and sticking to the edges of the room.

I sigh. "Come in."

Zaden appears in the doorway, looking tired after a long day. He's wearing finely spun navy pants and a cream shirt, a clear sign that he's been away on business. At home, he sticks to practical clothes with enough pockets for all his secrets.

The sight of him brings warmth to my flesh as though the sun has newly risen. "Zaden!"

He pads across the room and sits on my bed, dipping the mattress. "You weren't in my chamber, so I came looking for you."

"I'm glad you did."

"Really? Good." He bends to kiss me, his lips soft and his chin scratchy, and I run my fingers up his biceps, feeling the swell of his muscle beneath the fine silk fiber. He plants one hand on the mattress across my body, keeping me in a protective cage. "I heard that Reginald limped into the castle at late dawn. Barely made it back in time."

"Oh, really?" I ask innocently.

Zaden nods with a teasing twinkle in his eye. "Apparently he took a beating. Chipped tooth and a bloody face."

"What a shame."

He lifts a brow. "You wouldn't happen to know anybody who has a grudge against him and the skill to carry it out?"

I fold my arms beneath my breasts. "I can think of a hundred people. I guess the better question is, can we think of anybody he might attack when he thought they were vulnerable?" I scratch my face in deep thought. "I can't think of anyone."

Zaden's mouth tugs up, and I want to kiss the corner, right where his lips meet his cheek, but I resist. "Me neither," he says. "I can't think of anybody who'd be skillful enough to take him on."

At that, I sit upright and cross my legs. "Did you say somebody extremely masterful at combat took him out?"

Zaden shakes his head. "Oh, I wouldn't exactly say *masterful*."

"Yes, you would. In fact, I'm pretty sure you did. It must have been an amazing warrior."

Zaden backpedals. "Well, Reginald isn't exactly a soldier."

I chuckle. "You got that right."

My angel smiles. He stares at me, those vibrant green orbs penetrating into my soul. "I'm proud of you," he says softly.

My heart swells, and a mother's sweet lullaby fills my veins. I can't get enough of this man; he touches me in all the right places, and not just physically.

I can't hold back my caress. I run a hand down the side of his chiseled jaw. I wasn't sure how he'd react to me beating down his precious lordling. "You're not mad?"

He snorts. "Would you care if I was?"

I lift one shoulder. "Maybe," I tease.

He lays a kiss by my temple, then one on my cheek, then one on my lips. "I'm just glad you can defend yourself."

"Me too." I remember how triumphant I felt in the forest, as though I could take on an entire army. But I'm still vulnerable to monsters like Count VanDyke because I'm no match for an angel. And I never will be.

"Come with me." Zaden tugs back the bedcovers, and I shrug into a cloak, then pad after him through the castle's corridors to the northwest tower. "Are we going to your bedchamber? You know, we could've just stayed in mine."

"We're not going there." He leads me up the winding staircase but climbs past his bedroom door to the top floor.

"I've never been up here before," I whisper.

With one hand resting on the knob, he stops and watches me. "This is my private training room."

A thrill runs through my muscles. "The one you've never shown to anybody?" He nods. "And you're going to show me?" He nods again, and my heart swells, growing to fill my entire chest, so big it squeezes my lungs.

He opens the door, and I follow him through, intrigued at what I'll find.

This is more like what I expected to find in his bedroom. A sweeping curve of cabinets along one section of the round room contains curiosities and trinkets that I'm dying to explore. An array of swords and daggers adorn one expanse of a wall like decorations, but I know they're not just for show. In the center is a large open space for training, although several obstacles have been laid out.

"It's wonderful," I breathe.

Zaden smiles. He seems very relaxed for somebody showing

his deepest self to another. "There's something I want you to have."

He crosses to an opaque cabinet that looks as though it's forged from a single metal plate, folded and twisted into shape. A key appears in his hand, and he unlocks the cabinet and retrieves a long narrow object about the length of my forearm.

"What is it?" My voice is barely audible, although I'm sure his ears have no trouble picking it up.

Zaden crosses to one of the narrow windows, and I follow, leaning my elbows beside his on the sill and looking out over the desert and forest.

"Gaze is a precious gift, and there will always be those who seek it. It is one of the rarest vestigial skills, and angels and mortals alike would kill to possess it."

White moonlight bathes the forest in a cold hard light, and I shiver. It isn't yet snowfall, but the temperature has plummeted, and Zaden's words penetrate me like icicles.

"I promise to always do my best to keep you safe, Scarla. Always. But there may be a time when I fail. I've already failed you once."

"If you're talking about me being captured by Count VanDyke, you didn't fail me. I sneaked away and got caught and—"

"I vowed to protect you, Scarla, and I did not. That is a failure. You are now skilled enough to defend yourself against any mortal."

Zaden's tongue is usually overflowing with teasing words, telling me how terrible I am at fighting or how I'll never best him—often followed by his tongue teasing me in a more physical way. So his gravity is unnerving. His face is stony and severe, and I shudder.

"But your biggest threat comes from other angels. I am proof of what lengths an angel will go to to win Gaze, and I am not the cruelest or most ambitious of my kind. Despite what you might think."

I twist my hands before me, and the cold stone of the sill soaks up my elbows. "I don't think you're—"

"Let me finish, Scarla. I want you to have a measure of protection against angels. So I am giving you this celestial-tipped dagger."

He unsheathes a dagger that glints viciously in the moon-light, a dead straight blade with a fatal point and an intricate hilt encrusted with a single glowing emerald.

"I..." The polite part of me wants to refuse this gift, knowing that I could never in a million years repay him for this, for the enormity of what he's giving me. Celestial blades are almost as rare as Gaze itself, and I can never erase this debt. But the practical part of me knows he speaks the truth. With no way to protect myself from angels, I will never be safe.

"Thank you," I say, instead of the refusal that rose on my tongue.

It isn't enough. No words could ever be enough to show my gratitude for this gift. He isn't just giving me the gift of trust, handing me a weapon that I could use against him, but he's also giving me the gift of strength, of fortitude, of never again having to feel vulnerable.

"You're welcome, mortal. Just promise me you'll be strong enough to use it if the need arises."

He's telling me I need to be prepared to kill, to take the life of an otherwise immortal being. This feels like a moment of reckoning, where I assess my true worth.

Do I value my own life above an angel's? Am I the kind of

person who could kill?

Zaden's eyes bore into me like twin emeralds, reflecting the moon's cold light.

I nod. "I promise."

Scarla

I wake in Zaden's bed, coiled in his limbs.

I can't believe he gave me a celestial-tipped dagger. It is beyond doubt the most valuable gift anybody has ever given me, and the enormity of it continues to amaze me. I can just see the top of it from where I lie in bed, a rare prize with that emerald jewel and beautifully ornate hilt—although its true worth lies in the blade, not the jewels.

That blade could kill an angel.

It's hard to remember how I could have once hated Zaden enough to kill him. A shudder wracks me at how close I came to doing so. Lying here, bathed in his musky scent, it seems like that must have been a different woman. I've changed so much.

Zaden's face is serene beside me, his eyes closed and his body in repose, those muscular limbs draped along the silken sheets, with one leg hooked over mine.

I can't tell if he is sleeping, but he is undoubtedly resting, like a lion in repose—cute and adorable, but you just know those coiled muscles could go hard in a second.

I trace a finger down his arm, over the swell of his bicep, around the valley of his elbow, and along his forearm. Up close, his skin isn't as smooth and free from imperfections as it looks from a distance. Or perhaps that's just Gaze. Tiny nicks and old scars from previous battles crisscross his arm, barely visible.

My heart squeezes at the thought of all the wars he's been in, the fights he's endured, the blood he's shed. I want to protect him from that, protect him from his own impulses, protect him from future harm.

It isn't lost on me. The perversion of a vulnerable mortal like me wanting to protect an angel is ludicrous, and I smile at the thought. But that's not quite right. I'm not a vulnerable mortal anymore; I'm a weapon.

I plant a kiss on the top knuckle of Zaden's index finger, then extricate myself from his lazy limbs.

"Where are you sneaking off to, Scarla?"

I smile. Morning sun bathes his skin in gold, and every imperfection has disappeared again.

"Not sneaking. I'm just going."

"Where to?"

"Out." I can't give him all my secrets—I need to keep an air of mystery. Besides, the frown on his face is adorable and will keep me warm all day.

I shimmy into some pants and a long-sleeved shirt to protect me from the sun, then head outside for my morning walk. This has become a new tradition. In fact, I've stopped running downstairs to check if Molly has returned because I'm now certain she's started a new life in Solren. As soon as I get confirmation of that, I will be able to relax completely into my new life.

It's a glorious day. Folks in Malanox don't talk about the weather, although I hear that used to be a topic of conversation. It's hard to imagine how that might go.

"It's daytime. The sun is out."

"Yes."

"Just like yesterday."

"Yes."

Seems like a dead-end conversational topic to me, but people used to be strange.

Today is the first day that ever looked different from any other. I've missed dawn, and the sun is already up, but the shapes of the steam rising from the evaporating river seem ghostly and beautiful, like a galaxy of water nymphs returning to heaven.

I stop in my tracks when the realization hits me. I am perfectly happy.

Zaden is the perfect companion for me. Intelligent, with a ready wit and, deep down, a large heart. Every day I uncover a little more of his soft side, and him gifting me with that precious dagger feels like the final proof that he is kindhearted.

Did I say companion? I mean lover. He does things to my body that I never thought possible, taking me to the highest peaks of ecstasy and letting me tumble off them, shattering into a million pieces on the tundra below.

Honestly, that man never stops giving.

Although he certainly seeks his own pleasure too.

A goofy grin is plastered across my face, and I realize I am more than just happy.

I am in love.

I walk a full lap of the castle until my mind is made up. I will talk to my father.

Apart from Molly's continued absence, the only thing I feel compelled to do to complete my happiness is to tell my father about it. As far as he knows, I was kidnapped by Zaden and forced to stay here, living for fear of my life. Of course, I've told him that's no longer the case, but I haven't fully explained my relationship with the angel. It's time that I did.

Well, there's no time like the present. Instead of returning to the castle, I head toward the bridge, a narrow break in the wall of steam rising from the evaporating river.

I plunge through and emerge hot and wet, but that does nothing to wipe the grin from my face. I am in love with Zaden, and I'm going to tell my dad.

I set a fast pace through Hightown, following the main road toward the mountain, letting my boots echo dully on the cobblestones and not even minding the sweat dripping from my brow. As the paved stones make way for the gravel and dirt of Lowtown, I slow down, keeping an eye out for skitter beetles and ice gangs.

I used to fear the ice gangs, but that's definitely changed. It's the disgusting roaches that bother me now. With their hard carapaces and lack of flesh, they are ideally suited to the heat, and when the humans disappear indoors for the day, they take over. A beetle as large as my foot scuttles toward me, and I shriek and jump over it.

Hang on, I need to take stock. I am no longer the little girl scared of roaches, I'm a grown-ass woman with vestigial power. I wonder if Gaze works on the bugs.

I reach for my well of Gaze and channel a steady stream, focusing my attention on a skitter beetle that is climbing the outside of a mud hut. No ribbon of light runs through it like humans have, but its entire shell glows super dimly. I need to ratchet up the power of Gaze before I can even see it.

With humans, I can squeeze the ribbon behind the neck and render them unconscious. Can I do something similar with skitter beetles? I can't see any natural narrowing, any apparent weak point, but the entire covering is so thin that I feel I could pierce it anywhere.

Focusing, I pick a random spot on the round back of the bug, which is now clambering upside down under the hovel's eaves. Flexing Gaze, I imagine piercing the light shell at one point, like I am driving an awl through a thin piece of ox-hide leather. With a little more pressure, it pops, and the skitter beetle falls from the roof and lands on its back.

Excellent. My grin returns, along with a sense of satisfaction.

That's another skill I've gained and one less fear for me to hold.

Hell, I'm running out of fears. I never thought I'd say that.

I pass the water catchments, shuddering at the steady thunk of skitter beetles landing on the well cover far below and make my way through the outskirts of Lowtown.

A voice calls behind me. "Hey, you! You're runnin' a bit late, aren't ya? Why don't ya come over here, and I'll get you some water."

I recognize this man. He's in one of the ice gangs, who strap large chunks of packed snow around their bodies and terrorize stragglers who are late returning indoors after dawn.

"Not today, thanks," I yell. Humming a tune, I kick out at the man's companion, who lunges at me from behind a wooden hut.

Honestly, defeating these boys is no harder than eating a delicious bowl of pufferbuns and berries. I don't even have to use Gaze, although I could. But that would almost feel like cheating.

Instead, I take this as an opportunity to practice my new hand-to-hand combat skills.

I must remember to thank the boys back at the training yard for their excellent teaching.

I decide to leave the poor ice gang members with just a couple of scrapes and bruises, nothing more. It's like a little lesson for them.

At the Undercity, I breeze past the guards, winking and tossing a greeting. The temperature plummets once I'm beyond the first set of ox-hide hangings, and I cross to the second set in the blink of an eye, breathing in the familiar dank air. Beyond them, it's a perfect temperature for mortals.

Mortals. I roll the syllables over my tongue, tasting them slowly. It's funny how much that word has become part of my vocabulary, and I think of them as separate, different, human. Not different from me, really, although I am a vestige, but different from Zaden. And now he's the one I'm closer to. The castle's my home now.

The main cavern is quite busy, and I keep my eyes peeled for Dad. He still sleeps in our old night hub, good old S2A7, so he should be settling in to sleep. I plow into South Undercity, nodding and grinning at the guard on duty, and then plunge into the familiar warren of tunnels that make up my city.

Some passageways lead up, others down, and the farther you go along, the more they branch into an ever-widening maze. But I know it like the back of my hand, so being here feels like slipping between soft sheets. My sleeping hub is one of the closest, and I'm there within minutes.

Sure enough, the nighttime routine has begun—well, the daytime routine since all the families in this hub sleep while the sun is up and work with the moon. Parents are telling stories to their kids, people are changing into their nightgowns, and Fra Hutchins Miner is already passed out with her mouth agog, sharing her snores generously.

My heart lurches when I see my sleeping pallet. It used to be the four of us sleeping there, and now it's just Dad. Maybe he feels lonely having that huge pallet all to himself, or perhaps he shares with some of the larger families now. The edge washes off my happiness, as though my fingers and toes have been dipped in a shallow pool of sadness at the thought of not knowing how Dad spends his time.

I used to know intimately what he did with every waking hour—and every sleeping one—but I haven't been around as much lately.

"Scarla, dear. We haven't seen you in a while."

It's Fra Stollen who works in the kitchens. She's always chatting with somebody, but I usually don't get much of her attention. I don't give her much of mine either, but I need her assistance now.

"Hi, Fra. I'm just visiting. Do you know where Dad is?"

The older woman's nose wrinkles, and I can tell she is disappointed at my lack of social skills. I never was one for a chat. Surly Scarla, that's me.

But the name doesn't mirror my feelings right now. I am living a life beyond dreaming, with a sensual, giving man with the mind of a devil and the body of a God.

Perhaps she sees my inner glow, or maybe it's my ridiculous grin, but her face softens. "He's helping out in the mines tonight, dear. You'll have to wait until he gets back at dusk."

"Thanks," I sing behind me, already heading out of the hub.

No way am I waiting until dusk. I've decided to talk to Dad, and I can't put it off any longer. I'll just find him wherever he's working.

I've never ventured into the mines before—only miners are

allowed there. Every parent tells their children the tale of the brother and sister who played cat and mouse in the mines and got hopelessly lost. Their little bodies were found weeks later, several miles into the dark maze.

But honestly, that's probably just a story to scare little kids. How dangerous can a mine really be?

Scarla

Okay, so this cave is creepier than I thought.

The only reason I haven't freaked out completely is because of Gaze. With that, a trickle of light seeps through the walls, like blood-red veins running through the pitch. The veins taper the further I go from the main cavern, so I know I could turn around at any point and follow them back.

I switched on my limited charm out in the main cavern and discovered from a small bloke with a wiry frame and an oversized nose that the miners are in the quadrant N4P today. I've learned enough over the years to understand that code, even if I've never been in the mines. N is for North, four means I take the fourth major turning off the north tunnel, and after that, the sites are labeled alphabetically, so I guess P is a shitload of footsteps away.

I hum to myself to stay sane and drive away the heebie-jeebies. The darkness seems to eat the echo of my footsteps, and even with the glowing veins running through the walls, I'm sure if I spent any time here, I'd go insane.

Finally, a regular light glows in the distance, and I guess site P is approaching. It's further than I thought, and each stride barely impacts the space I have yet to travel.

In a six-hour shift, these guys must spend at least two of it walking. No wonder they come home looking so damn tired.

A high-pitched whine stops me in my tracks, trying to figure out what I can hear. It takes me several moments to realize that the intermittent sound is metal clanging against stone. The darkness behind me seems all-encompassing, so I break into a jog.

"I'm not scared," I lie, like I'm a fucking idiot who can fool myself.

Soon, the clanging is deafening, and the torchlight is enough to see my hands and feet.

I burst into a large cave with torches lining the walls and bunches of men and women singing.

Why are they singing? Are they mistaking this gloomy cave for a field of flowers at dawn?

With every song beat, another sickle falls, and I realize the tune keeps them working. Probably keeping them sane too.

In the flickering light, I pick out my dad's wild, shoulder-length copper hair and bushy beard, both of which are darker and grayer than ever.

I call his name, and he looks at me like I'm a ghost. "Hi, Dad," I say conversationally while he opens and closes his mouth like a puppet.

"Scarla. How did...? What are...? You don't even have a torch. How did you get here?"

I throw my arms around him, and he stands rigid for a moment before hugging me back. "I have to tell you something."

"Can't it wait until dusk? It's a miracle you found your way here. You could have easily gotten lost and starved to death. Plenty have."

I swallow my shudder. I guess those tales of people dying here aren't just to frighten kids.

The man working beside Dad is a young guy I haven't seen before, probably from North Undercity. He's almost as tall as I am, and his cheekbones cut the air, his lips a slash. He eyes me up and down, admiring.

Dad scowls at him, but before he can say something, I butt in. I don't need Dad to stand up for me anymore.

"If you have a compliment to pay me, mate, use your words like a big boy. Otherwise keep your eyes to yourself."

Dad's lips quirk upward, then he pulls me aside to an empty section where the coal has already been worked out, and nobody is near to overhear.

Worry creases his forehead. "What's wrong, Scar? Is everything okay up at the castle? We can leave together if you want. Leave Malanox, maybe head into Bilgon or Solren. We might even make it over the Dead Desert to Desert's Maw. Whatever you need, you got it. You're all I have left."

The thing about my dad is he doesn't really do feelings. He's more of a show-your-love-by-feeding-and-clothing kind of a father, so his words turn me into a statue.

He grabs my shoulders and shakes, a little too roughly. "Talk to me, Scarla. What is it?"

Clearly, my being frozen to the spot in surprise isn't helping calm him down. "I'm fine, Dad. I'm wonderful." Now that I'm back in a lit space with other people, my fears have melted away, and my joy has come pouring back. "I just wanted to tell you that everything is great at the castle and...."

Dad lets his hands fall from my shoulders. "And what?"

"And..." A massive grin fractures my face. "I'm in love with Zaden."

Saying the words aloud feels like celebrating solstice, my birthday, and Malanox Fair all in one day. I do a little spin on the spot, then smile at Dad expectantly.

He's a stern man but has a gold heart, and there's no uncertainty in his smile. "You look happier than I've ever seen you, berry."

I throw my arms around him, and this time he grabs me quickly and squeezes tight. "I am," I say, with his hair tickling my nose.

Saying it aloud to Dad makes it real and gives me the confidence to tell Zaden. But not yet. You couldn't pay me a thousand pieces of copper to walk through those mines alone again without a torch, so I wait out the end of Dad's shift and join the line of miners returning home after a hard day's work. Every person except me carries a flaming torch, and although the conversation is limited, several people are singing the whole time. The journey is quicker than my way in and almost cheerful.

Dad practically begged me to stay the night, so I do. This could be the last night I spend in the Undercity, so sentimentality has me agreeing. We've worked all day, so we can't return to our hub; we need a night hub. I used to sleep in Leo's corner if I needed to catch Zs at night because trying to catch Zs in our night hub while everybody else is awake is as annoying as you'd expect.

"Not this one," I murmur with a lurch in my gut as Dad walks toward Leo's old hub. Instead, we duck into the next one and sleep on an empty pallet near the hub's entrance, hoping we're welcome.

It's odd sleeping among dozens of families again, and even weirder how lonely I feel without Zaden. I miss the warmth of his long leg pressed against mine and the way he murmurs my name like a promise.

In the morning, I can't wait to get home and plant a big fat kiss on Zaden. But Dad is awake before dawn, and it wouldn't feel right to sneak away, so I join him for breakfast in the main cavern. A line of people waits for water, so we start in the dining area by the kitchens. The squawk of chickens is just audible over the hum of voices and the clatter of cutlery. We eat bran pancakes with ground melons, then I kiss my dad goodbye.

"You should tell him," Dad says.

"Tell him what?" My thoughts are already on Zaden, so I don't need to ask who, just what.

"Tell him you love him. Regrets grow from inaction, and I don't want you to die with regrets."

"Geez, morbid much? I'm not planning on dying anytime soon."

Dad's face is serious, with that faraway look he gets when he's remembering Mom. "Life is shorter than you could ever imagine. And with more twists than you could ever imagine. More unexpected surprises. Like when your mother departed."

I frown. "The dearly departed. I always thought that was an odd way to describe death."

Dad blinks at me. "Do what you have to do, and do it today. That's all I'm saying."

I mull over those words as I cross the cavern toward the exit. The hides are pinned open because it's dawn, and folks are streaming outside to set up the market or off to harvest food and resources.

I don't see Sadie before I bump into her. She spins around with a snarl on her octopus face, her wild tentacle hair waving around. "Watch where you're going, skank."

I feel like laughing at her aggression, which is an odd

response. The old me would arc up and slap her for talking to me that way, but I'm happy to shake it off. "Sorry, Sadie. I didn't see you there."

"So now you're a skank and a liar," she snarls, and a couple of her big hairy friends close in.

Around us, the market is in full swing, and Hightowners have already gathered to buy coal, muffins, and arts and crafts. Nobody notices a few Undercitysiders squabbling, and even if they did, they wouldn't bat an eyelid.

"I'm not lying," I say, but my foolish love grin is still plastered across my face, and Sadie clearly doesn't buy it.

"Well, me and Ralph and Petie here reckon you are." The three step closer, narrowing the ring around me like a tightening noose.

I can't help it, I laugh. I just don't feel threatened by their childish games, and I have bigger issues to worry about than trading insults with Sadie. I have a man to get back to.

The funny thing is, now I'm actually equipped to deal with these guys—I could dispatch them all in moments, either using my fighting skills or my Gaze—I find I don't want to.

Repulsive Ralph is on my left, flopping his oily bangs out of his face and looking shorter than ever. I step around him and dash away, calling over my shoulder. "Maybe another time, okay guys?"

The expression on their faces is priceless. If I could bottle that and take a sip when I'm feeling down, I'd be happy the rest of my life. But as it is, there's someplace I have to be, some castle I have to enter, and some male I need to lick.

Scarla

The pink fingers of dawn are burning away into blue when I arrive back at the castle.

I flick my hair before remembering I've cut most of it off, then wink at Rodney, one of the sterner guards with imposing black eyebrows and a furry black caterpillar living on his upper lip.

"Hi, Rodney. Do you have any big plans for the day?" He's manning the castle doors and barely affords me a glance, but I swear the corners of his mouth almost twitched. Truly, it's a miraculous morning.

With this idiotic grin still plastered on my face, I swan into the grand foyer and up the stairs, heading down the corridors to find Zaden. My belly swirls like soup being stirred as my feet prance along. I'm about to tell Zaden that I love him.

I don't even care if he stumbles on his reply, but I don't think he will. I imagine he'll stare at me with those magnificent emerald eyes, then take my hand in his. *"I love you too, Scarla. Be mine forever."*

Bleurgh. If anybody could hear my thoughts, they'd gag. I don't know how I'm not hurling up my breakfast all over these stone floors at having to endure my own saccharine thinking. But there you have it—today, nothing can bring me down.

My thoughts are flying as fast as my feet. Zaden and I can be together until I die, then I will give him Gaze on my deathbed.

When I'm a little old lady, who's lived a long happy life, I'll lie in his arms and breathe my last sigh. That little spark of vestigial magic will leave my body and enter his, the same way it transferred from old Fra Perkins to me moments after her death.

The thought of dying peacefully in Zaden's arms makes me smile. That should be enough for me. But I'm greedy, and I want more.

And maybe I could have it. He needs Gaze to return to heaven, and if I lead a decent life, I'll go to heaven too. And we can be together forever in the immortal realm.

I clasp my hands before me and leap into the air like I'm some five-year-old girl dreaming of becoming a princess.

Thank the Maker nobody can see me. Imagine Sadie and Repulsive Ralph witnessing this. I would die.

I never imagined this was possible. A year ago I didn't believe in angels, and now I'm planning to spend eternity with one. As soon as he inherits Gaze from me, he'll be able to find the gates to heaven and join me there. He will achieve his centuries-long goal of returning to his birthright, and we'll get to spend forever together.

As long as I make it into heaven.

I frown, wishing I'd paid more attention to the mechanisms of getting in. But I know that if I'm a decent person who does good things throughout my life, I'll earn a ticket.

A laugh escapes me, sounding jollier and lighter than my usual dark chuckles. "I'll just ask my personal angel how it all works," I say aloud, loving the sound of *my personal angel* floating in the air.

Zaden's voice carries from around the next corner, and my legs coil, ready to throw myself into his arms, knowing he'll catch me. He has never let me down, never lied to me, never told me a single untruth. Which is more than I can say for anybody else in my life. And exactly why I love him.

But before I launch into a sprint, Mini Xerxes' whiny tone reaches my ears, and I realize they are walking together, deep in conversation.

Dammit. The one person who could bum me out today is Sir Xerxes the Mini Fuckwit, and I don't want to spend a single moment of my precious happiness on him, so I take a quick scope of my surroundings.

This is one of the smaller hallways on the second floor, with a series of tapestries of underwater scenes. In my mind, this is the water hallway. I've explored this place enough that I know all the hiding places and access points to the castle's inner maze.

One such secret door is behind the tapestry depicting a massive fish leaping out of the ocean, a creature even bigger than an ox, so giant it must surely be fantastical.

I duck behind the hanging carpet, forgetting to hold my breath against the vinegary smell, and dive into the maze, leaving the door ajar so I can hear when they've passed. With any luck, the Mini Dick will leave Zaden alone so I can corral him.

It's dark in the inner maze, but the stone glows dimly under Gaze so I'm not afraid. The hidden hallways run inside every wall within the building, a network of crisscrossing alleyways that serves as a rat run. And a handy eavesdropping spot.

I barely use them these days, now that I'm allowed to come and go as I please, but they were my favorite part of the whole place when I was still a prisoner and needed to be able to move undetected.

And, clearly, they still have their uses even now.

Zaden and the Fuckwit have paused near my hiding spot, and their hushed tones grow louder. "Why do you keep the bitch around?" Reginald's thin voice makes my skin crawl. "She's a liability."

I'm so glad to be a fly on the wall for this conversation. My palms itch with excitement as I wait to hear Zaden bitch slap the Fuckwit for saying that.

"Never speak that way of Scarla," Zaden snarls in a voice of terrifying calm, and my heart sings. Man, I love that guy. "You are lucky to have a place in my castle at all." *Yeah, you tell him.*

"Just get rid of her," Mini Xerxes says, and I wonder that he has the nerve to be so bold with Zaden. Surely he's noticed how close the angel and I have become. Reginald might not be the smartest noble, but he can't be that stupid, right?

The warning edge in Zaden's tone has my soul soaring. "You know very well I will not tolerate you speaking callously of Scarla." I press my hands to my chest, grinning and setting up a small chant in my head.

Smite him smite him smite him.

"I just—"

"No," Zaden interrupts. "I need her to control Gaze, or I can never return to heaven."

My smile falls at that. Obviously I know that, but our relationship has moved so far past that that it takes me a moment to understand why he's saying it.

Then I sag in relief. He's telling his bloodbond what he wants him to believe. The last person I want privy to my personal business is Xerxes the Mini Asswipe, and clearly Zaden feels the same way.

Still, the Sir is a super douche, and I wish he would disappear. His voice makes me want to punch him in the face. Again. "She is the most irritating person I've ever met," Mini Xerxes says, and I can hear the sneer in his voice. "One day, I will lose control and tell her that her mother still lives so I can see the shocked expression on her face."

What? I turn to stone, as cold and hard as the rough wall my forehead is leaning against. What is he talking about? Why would he say Mom's alive? He must be making it up, spreading gossip. But he did say his brother told him all my secrets, so perhaps he thinks he's speaking fact.

My breaths come fast and shallow as I wait for Zaden to deny it, needing to hear the words directly from his mouth.

I've always had a false memory of my mother packing a bag and kissing me goodbye before leaving in the dead of night. But that was nothing more than a fantasy that my mind created to account for the fact that she died so suddenly. Nobody leaves the Undercity in the dead of night, except me.

But that image flies into my brain, the picture of Mom with a tear-stained face leaving like a thief. The scene is summoned by Reginald's hateful words, and I wish it was true, but I can't lie to myself.

My mother is dead. If I had any idea that she wasn't, I would search for her until I found her, even if it took me a hundred years.

My breathing is as light as a gadfly's, and my body just as weightless.

Say the words, love. Tell him he's wrong.

Zaden lowers his voice to a growl, and it takes me a few

moments to understand what he's saying. "You know I can't tell her her mother is alive, or she would leave to go find her. I need Scarla by my side. If she dies while she's off looking for her mother, I might have to wait another five hundred years to find somebody with Gaze. If you breathe one word of the truth, I will kill you like I killed your brother, and my bond to your bloodline be damned."

At first, the scowl in Zaden's voice makes me think he's defending me. His words blend together in my mind like a haze, floating and flying and drifting around one another while I try to make sense of them.

Mom is alive. Is that what he's saying? Did Zaden just say that my mother is alive? But she can't be because she died seventeen years ago when I was eight. Everybody knows that. My mother is dead, I know it in my bones. If she was living, I would feel a tug in my heart leading me to her because she is family.

Zaden speaks of bloodline bonds as a curse, but to me, they are everything. My mother, my sister, my father. Family is everything.

The only thing I ever found in my life that could rival the strength of my bloodline bond is my relationship with this Maker-be-damned angel.

He and Mini Xerxes have long gone, their footsteps receded into nothing, but I stay cramped in the hidden maze listening to Zaden's words on repeat.

I can't tell her her mother is alive, or she would leave to go find her.

I need her to control Gaze.

Why would he say that? It was more than just a line to keep the Mini Shit in the dark about our relationship. His words ring with truth, resounding through my head like a gong that will never stop pounding. A death knell to my hopes and dreams and the end of what I thought was love.

I can't pull apart the knotted lines of truth and figure out if Zaden has been lying to me or if he's lying to Xerxes.

Surely to Xerxes. I can't be stupid enough to fall in love with a male so scheming and manipulative that he would lie about my own mother's death. Can I?

Am I foolish enough to believe the lies of somebody I considered my closest friend?

Leo flits through my thoughts like a guilty truth, a dark spot in my past, a shadow of lies. Yes, I believed Leo, believed his lies, believed his integrity. And he played me like a fool all along.

So, undoubtedly, I'm stupid enough.

But Zaden is different. I love him in a way I never loved Leo, with every fiber of my being, ready to lay down my life for him, ready to sign up for eternity in his embrace.

My Gaze flicks off, and the darkness around me is complete, the stone against my forehead cold, and the air tastes like ash.

Scarla

Fuck it. I'm not going to slink around in this inner maze like some kind of fucking inner-maze-slinker.

I slam open the hidden door and march out, tangling myself in the stupid tapestry covering the exit.

"Maker be damned!"

I stomp along the corridor in the opposite direction from where Zaden and his right-hand-Fuckwit went, which puts me on a path to the angel's tower in the castle's northwest corner. But there is no way in hell I will confess my love to him now. Not after he admitted he's still using me for Gaze—although that part may have been a lie for Xerxe's benefit. But the part about my mom being alive?

That felt like the truth.

So much for him never lying to me. So much for his honesty being the primary reason I'm in love with him. So much for everything.

I make an about turn and march back the way I came, heat rising from me like steam.

The only place I can use this violent energy coursing through my body is in the training yard, so I go there. The guards at the castle door look at me expectantly, probably awaiting a smile or greeting, but why should I? Most of them don't bother replying, let alone grinning back.

I appear to have surrounded myself with assholes without noticing.

A few guards are already working out and glistening in sweat when I reach the training yard, but I march right up and stand between them, glowering, practically daring them to strike me.

"Get out of the way, Scarla, unless you want a sword to the gut."

My hands fly to my hips, and I stare down Jonah. He is one of the men who uses my first name, like I implore them all to, although most still call me *milady.* He's maybe two or three years older than me with a freshly shaven chin and a straight no-nonsense nose. He matches me for height, and his eyes are sky-blue and startling. In my anger against Zaden, I don't know if I want to punch Jonah or kiss him.

"That's exactly what I want," I say, not budging an inch. If Jonah attacks me while I'm unarmed, he'll lose face and every ounce of honor. But I kind of want him to because that would give me an excuse to bellow out my rage and tear him down with Gaze.

After a couple of intense moments, where Jonah's jaw sits firmly and his lips curve in a smirk, I put my hand out to the side and address the man behind me without turning my head. "Give me your blade."

I am rewarded by the press of a warm metal hilt against the palm of my outstretched hand, and I grip the sword, feeling its heft.

Jonah is still smirking, and I follow the outline of his jaw, his bunched muscles, his ready stance. I could take a couple of steps forward and shove my lips against his to taste him, feel his hard body pressed against mine.

Or I could beat him to a pulp.

Indecision has me statuing, and Jonah makes a move before I do, stepping to the side and feinting one way before swooping in a wide arc from the other.

I meet his sword with my own, a decisive blow that has my shoulder jittering in its socket. My fury at Zaden pours through my sword arm with clang after clang in a series of brutal attacks. I've trained just as hard with blades as with my fists, and my skill is growing daily.

I press my advantage and gain ground while Jonah shuffles backward, trying to make sense of my furious approach. The edge of his spine light blurs before every movement, allowing me to anticipate and block.

Fear and surprise play across Jonah's face as I continue to land blows on his sword, and I like it. I like the shock, I like the confusion.

I like the fear.

Jonah works for Zaden, a male who oppresses the people of Malanox, a leader who doesn't care for his citizens, an angel who lies to his lover. To me.

Jonah holds up his hands in surrender and lays down his sword. I throw mine to the ground in anger and kick out at Jonah, landing a heavy blow to the side of his knees. The man crumples to the ground, and I kick his gut. I breathe heavily and stare at his unmoving body for a long moment, waiting for the guilt to hit me.

But it never does. The only emotion I have room for in my overheated brain is anger.

I should feel bad for kicking this man after he surrendered... but he should be thankful I left it at that. With the weapons in my arsenal, I could have killed him by now.

A small voice in my head tells me I need to be good. If I want to get into heaven, I need to do good deeds on earth, which doesn't include the vicious slaughter of my training companions.

Dammit. I don't want to want to get into heaven, but I do. I haven't given up on Zaden completely. I need to understand what's going on in his stupid head so I can get back to loving him. Or hating him. I just need to know which.

"Somebody woke up on the wrong side of the bed this morning." I whirl at the sound of Zaden's voice, and when I see him calling from the far side of the training pitch, my traitorous heart leaps. A smile wants to dance on my lips, but it falls dead as I force myself to remember the conversation I overheard him having with Mini Xerxes.

He said my mom was dead. And I need to know if that's a lie. Because if he lied to me about that, then the whole foundation of my love crumbles.

"Are you okay?" Such a benign question, but the answer would take me a thousand days to compose if I wanted to do it properly.

I don't. I shrug and look away, searching for the next man to fight.

But Zaden doesn't let me get away that easily. He's crossing the yard with a tender look in his glittering green eyes that should melt my knees, but I lock them and stay rigid, stay firm, stay true to myself.

He's so tall. When he stands next to me, I have to crane my head up to see past his broad chest. He lays a warm hand on my shoulder, a giant paw that makes me feel petite, though I am far from that. "It's not like you to be so savage with the men," he drawls. "Tell me what's wrong." Dammit. Damn him and damn his kindness. "Join me for lunch. I missed you last night."

I still can't meet his eyes because I missed him too, but now I don't know what to think.

"Okay," I finally agree. "Lunch."

He lets me leave then, and I walk off to shower and change before the midday meal. I wouldn't usually agree to dine with somebody who just backstabbed me to my worst enemy, but I need to.

I need to confront Zaden and find out the truth.

I need to know if my mom is alive.

Scarla

I stride into the dining hall with a newly washed body, a new pair of pants, and a new attitude.

If I'm going to charm the truth out of Zaden, I need to do it with a smile. My skills aren't honed enough to beat it out of him, so I'll have to lure it out of him instead.

He scrapes out his chair and rises to stand when I enter the room. He's wearing a close-fitted green shirt the color of his eyes, made from a soft fabric that molds to the contours of his chest, and low-slung black pants. He looks Maker-be-damned delicious, and it's all I can do not to step in and run my fingers up his perfect fucking body.

Especially when he smirks at me like that. "Scarla. You look divine."

It's true, I made an effort. Dark gray pants that hug my hips and a white cheesecloth shirt with a deep V that dives past my cleavage, with lacing holding the two halves together.

"Thank you. I assume you pay compliments to all your captives?"

Okay, so much for being charming; I guess I'll just go with childish and insolent, my usual repertoire.

"Not at all," Zaden smiles, pulling out my chair like the perfect gentlemen. He leans forward as I sit and whispers the

169

last part into my ear. "Often I go for whips and chains."

How did he make that sound sexy? I picture myself entirely at his mercy, tied up in the dungeon, splayed against the wall completely naked while Zaden stands before me, watching as my breasts heave with every inhaled breath. Heat pools between my thighs, but I school my expression. "I suppose that punishment helps them behave?"

Zaden takes his seat at the head of the table, just around the corner from me. He leans in, resting his elbows on the table. "Oh yes. I know how to make people behave," he growls, and again my body interprets it as a sexual advance. Stupid body.

I regret wearing this damn top now. Every time I glance down at my plate, I catch sight of my cleavage, and my skin tingles. It's doing more to arouse me than to distract him.

"And if they don't behave, they feel every inch of my disapproval." He whispers the last word like a caress, and my belly tightens.

A servant walks past and uses silver tongs to transfer a steaming bread roll from her hamper onto my side plate.

With a wicked smile, Zaden uncurls his sensual magic, a ribbon of purple-black smoke flowing from his body. He directs it around the serving woman, barely missing her by inches, knowing full well I can see the smoky tendril, and brushes it against my lips.

It feels like being tasted, a slow drugging kiss that lingers on my tongue and leaves me wanting more. Still with that wicked glint in his eyes, which are darkening into black, he directs the ribbon of sensual energy down the side of my neck, tracing the line where my shirt meets my skin and plunging down my back.

I gasp, and the serving woman glances up at me anxiously.

"Is everything all right, milady?"

"Yes, yes," I breathe, wishing she would go away.

Zaden's smile is pure devil, relishing my discomfort. He circles my waist, teasing me with the lightest of touches, while this poor servant is next to me. "That'll be all, thanks," I whisper, talking to both Zaden and the maid.

The woman dips a curtsy and, thankfully, walks away. She passes through the Margrave's tendril of magic with a little surprised "Oh," then scurries away. But Zaden isn't so easily dissuaded.

My skin aches for a firmer touch, and my toes curl inside my boots.

I grip the table to regain my senses. This meal has quickly gotten out of hand. I stand abruptly and step back, removing myself from Zaden's sorcery.

"Do you want to run?" he growls. "I'm happy to chase." His magic pools along the ground at my feet and then wraps itself sensually around my leg like a winding serpent, slowly rising.

"Stop!"

The servants standing at intervals along the walls are well-trained enough not to jump at my barked command, but they must be curious. They can't see Zaden's magic the way I can and must think I'm mad.

Zaden scowls but lets his magic dissipate, and I sit back down and try to concentrate on my meal. The food is good, piquant with spices and caramelized oaken. "Fine, you may eat," Zaden drawls, then adds a smile. "I can take what I need from you later."

My veins course with heat at those words because my body is stupid and traitorous and hasn't caught up with the fact that we are here to interrogate Zaden, not fall subject to his sexual spell. "No, I don't think you will."

He quirks an eyebrow and puts down his fork in dead silence. "Oh really? And why is that?"

"Because you haven't been honest with me."

I'm not sure if that's true, but I need to find out, and I have to start from a position of strength. No matter what else Zaden is, he is still an avenging angel who has walked the earth for centuries. If I show any weakness, he'll never tell me the truth.

"I'm listening," he says, resting his chin on his hands.

"Do you promise to tell me the truth?"

"I always tell you the truth."

Liar.

I wipe my hands on my pants, leaving a buttery smear, too nervous to care. My heart is racing, and this time it isn't from passionate excitement but trepidation. Zaden has every reason to lie to me about this, but I need to know the truth.

I force air into my lungs and raise my chin, locking my eyes on his. "Is my mother alive?"

Zaden

The intensity in Scarla's eyes weighs at my soul, if I have one.

Not so long ago, she asked me if I killed her sister, and I happily answered with the truth. I don't know if she'll believe the truth this time.

The only thing I know for sure is that I can't lose Scarla. She's crept into my heart inch by inch until the gaping hole that aches for Elanora is healed over, and I am whole.

I can't lose Scarla. I will say anything to her to keep her safe.

But first, I have to share a truth. Something she asked me about weeks ago, before I was prepared to give an answer. But now I'm ready.

I lean back in my chair. "You asked about my bloodbond with the Xerxes family."

"Actually, I asked if my mother is alive." Her jaw twitches, but I can see she's interested in the tidbit I threw on the laden table between us.

"Several weeks ago, you asked about Xerxes." I keep my voice calm, hoping to keep the tension low. She nods, and I take that as a win. It's unlikely this story will distract her from the question of her mother's death, but I need to tell her before I broach that topic.

I need to bring her closer before I push her away.

"His great-great-grandfather, many generations ago, did me a favor."

"How many generations?" she demands, and I can see she is circling the truth. Soon she will pounce on it, even if I don't tell her.

"It was five hundred years ago," I say, and her eyes light up. "When I first came to earth. During the chaos of the Angelic Wars, Elanora stole the Ring of Roth from me, and—"

"What? The bitch! Why would she do that? That ring was your way back into heaven, wasn't it?"

I twirl a fork between my fingers, my appetite fled. "Yes. As you know, I can't remember heaven itself, but I have pieced together the key elements of why I left. I believe I was sent to earth on a mission related to the Angelic Wars. I was given the Ring of Roth so I might return home once the mission was complete. The Ring is infused with Nimbus aether and provides a direct link to the Elysian plains, which lie outside the gate to heaven. Without the ring, I cannot return."

"But..." Scarla's shoulders have crept up around her neck, making her look cramped and tense. I can scent her anger, tangy and sharp in her pores. "She loved you, didn't she? Why would she steal your ring?" The simplicity of Scarla's question showers me with needles, which attack every inch of my skin.

Scarla cannot conceive of how cruel love can be.

But then her face falls. "She stole it to keep you on earth." Her voice is lower, and a remnant of the agony I felt those two centuries ago flitters through me, but so much calmer and quieter than it once was.

I'm more concerned about how this conversation is affecting Scarla. She is pale and subdued, with none of her usual fire.

"Yes," I confirm. "She didn't want me to leave, so she took

my only means of doing so and flung it into the depths of the sea." An image of Elanora's face when she confessed her crime flashes before me. Anguish was writ clear in the lines that marred her forehead, her slanted eyes filled with dread, her silken moonlight hair in disarray.

Scarla's face isn't so different now. Sure, the features are completely changed—the silken moonbeam tresses turned copper, the dark slanted eyes now wide and brown—but the expression is identical to the one Elanora wore when I asked about the Ring.

"And what happened? Did you..." Scarla hesitates as though the words are painful for her to say. "Did you live a long, happy life together?" She knows we didn't, that my and Elanora's tale didn't have a happy ending.

"Nobody can stand against angels and expect to survive," I tell her.

Some of that fire returns to her eyes. She leans against the table, trailing a sleeve on her plate. "That isn't an answer. Don't talk in riddles, Zaden. Tell me what happened."

I wait for the wall of pain to hit me when I begin talking, but it never does. I've spent so many years trying to forget what occured that it takes me a few moments to gather my thoughts and remember the sequence of events.

I've never spoken of this aloud, but the words come easily enough. "Heaven discovered her crime and took her to the Needle of Bayrou, out in the Desolate Sea. It is a tall tower with a sharp-peaked roof that sits on a tiny island, surrounded by the foam and salt spray of the ocean. Elanora could not swim and had no hope of escape. At the Needle, she was tortured for the rest of her mortal life and then sentenced to hell."

Scarla's face is ashen, and I want to cross behind her and

pull her to my chest, but I need to finish this conversation first, and if I stop talking about this, I might never be able to restart. "That's awful," she gasps, her breaths coming fast and shallow.

I won't give her further details. Like how the angels scoured Elanora's mind to discover the exact torture that would give her the most pain. How they turned her greatest desires into nightmares and preyed on her fears. How they stretched every moment into an eternity and filled it with agony.

Instead, I simply say, "Yes."

Quiet surrounds us, cold and empty. I watch Scarla's pulse in her neck, ensuring it doesn't speed dangerously. Her anger is laced with the scent of fear now.

Good. She needs to be afraid of angels.

"And the bloodbond?" she asks, still circling the truth, trying to piece together my history.

"I sent a man to end her suffering. He entered the Needle on a supply boat, bringing food and potable water because mortals need sustenance to survive the torture." Scarla's hand is already over her mouth, but I continue. "That food was poisoned. I couldn't save her life, but I could end her torment."

I can't know if that's even true, if her suffering really ended the day she ate the poisoned bread. If hell exists—and I have every reason to believe it does—then she is undoubtedly there. My only consolation is that her torture on earth must have been worse, otherwise the angels would have killed her instantly and condemned her to hell.

Scarla looks consumed by my tale, but her mind is still whirring. She continues to surprise me with her intelligence. "And that man, the one you sent to poison her, was Xerxes' ancestor?"

"Yes. He and I made a bloodbond. He only helped because I promised to look after his children and their children, and so on, for as long as I inhabited earth. Life was desperate for mortals back then, you understand."

I can see the blood pounding through her veins, where it travels near the skin of her lily white neck and wrists. I can scent her fear and anger and hear the whoosh of her breath. But I wish I could read her thoughts because her face is blank, and she remains quiet.

Finally, she knows why I protected Xerxes for all those years, even though he was a real bastard. Why I continue to defend his brother. Their father ran from my protection, but I tracked him down and plucked his son from obscurity, restoring his position at my right hand and fulfilling my vow to his forefather.

Her voice is remarkably calm. "But you killed Xerxes."

Yes. That fact has weighed on me since I took his life. But he carved that hateful letter X into Scarla's thigh and attacked her numerous times. I couldn't let him live, bloodbond or not.

Scarla's voice is steady despite her stench of fear. "What will happen now? You told me once that the bloodbond is forged using powerful celestial magic, so there must be a consequence for breaking it."

My emotions are higher than they've been in years, and I must inject calm into my voice. This mortal has turned my world upside down, including my Maker-be-damned feelings. "Legend has it that demons from the pit of hell haunt those who break a bloodbond."

Her hand falls to her side, her mouth falls open. "Fuck."

"Indeed." I draw a ragged breath. "But there is no saying if that is even true. When I lost my knowledge of heaven, I also forget any information I may have had about hell. I don't even know if it exists, and I certainly don't know if demons do."

"But—"

"And given that I haven't been attacked since I broke the bond several months ago, I assume the legend is nothing more than a myth."

What I don't say is that I sought the other Xerxes son to bring under my protection in an effort to annul the breaking of the bloodbond, as though that might fool the Fates.

She leans back in her seat, thinking hard. "But if Elanora stole the ring, you did nothing wrong. Why didn't you return to heaven after your mission?"

Scarla imagines angels to be reasonable and fair, but she might as well picture a human toddler reigning with justice. "I fucked up, Scarla. I fell in love with a mortal woman, and I lost my ring to her."

"And that was enough to get you booted from heaven?"

And to have my very soul ripped in two. Yes. More than enough. I can't trust my voice, so I just nod.

My history has affected Scarla more than I expected. I begin to hope I've distracted her from questioning me about her mother. She pushes her plate forward and leans her elbows on the table, thinking hard, and again I wish I could delve into that restless brain of hers.

"I'm so sorry to hear the story, Zaden," she eventually says. "Thank you for telling me." I nod and spear a piece of ox calf with my fork. "But what does all this have to do with my mother?"

My fork clatters to the plate. It has nothing to do with her mother and everything to do with her. I cannot lose another woman. "Ask me your question, and I will answer truthfully,"

I tell her.

She squares her shoulders, settling her narrowed eyes on me. "Is my mother alive?"

I school my voice, hoping that she hears the truth in my response. "No. Your mother died when you were a child. I'm sorry."

And I am sorry. So much sorrier than she will ever know.

Scarla

Dad exits the Undercity at dusk sharp, and I'm waiting for him.

I'm up in my private spot above the cave entrance—I paid in one scrape and two bruises to clamber up here. And as soon as I sit my ass on my perfect butt-shaped sitting rock, memories assault me.

This is where I used to come to look at the stars, think about Leesa, or drink from my secret snowmelt. Sometimes Leo came with me, but mostly I came alone.

From here, I can see across the hovels of Lowtown and the stately homes of Hightown, all the way to the castle, a glimmering beacon in the distance. When I was little, I dreamed of being a princess and living in that castle, dancing with fine lords and dining with fine ladies.

That was before I figured out they're all assholes, obviously. Now I wish I could turn back time to when I was a simple non-vestige sitting here and scowling at the castle because I suspected the Margrave of murdering Leesa. Oh, simpler times.

Ugh. My brain can't handle this right now. As soon as I hear noise from the mouthguard, I teeter to the edge of my rocky plateau and slide gracelessly on my butt down to the ground.

Dad's one of the first outside. He spills out of the cave with men and women in dull brown clothing, rough and homespun, chattering and laughing. Their bellies must be full of grogum gruel or maybe fresh eggs on mountain-seed bread. Every one of them moves with purpose.

Pa Leeson Plucker nods his head my way. "Morning, Scarla." He has one hand on a horse's bridle, holding it still while the others climb into the wagon. I nod back.

A few others stare and elbow their neighbors, but mostly they're too busy leaping into the wooden wagon to waste precious dusk time in idle chatter.

When Dad sees me, his face splits into a grin. He doesn't pull me into a hug—he's not the physical affection kind of a father some folks have—but he's happy to see me. His wild shoulder-length hair is a copper mane around his face, completed by the bushy copper beard on his chin.

Pa Leeson Plucker nods at me. "Join us if you like, Scarla. We'd appreciate the help. But we can't linger here."

Dad leaps into the wagon, and Pa Leeson Plucker climbs into the driver's position atop a crate—everybody else is scattered on the wooden floor among the empty boxes.

"Come on, berry," Dad calls, holding out a hand to help me up.

The horse breaks into a walk, and I don't hesitate any longer. I run and grab Dad's hand just as the wagon picks up speed. I climb up and fall into his lap to a cheerful round of laughter.

"She always was a Daddy's girl," somebody calls. They're right, but I'm not sure I still am.

I climb out of Dad's lap and perch awkwardly on an empty box, hoping like Hells my weight doesn't splinter the damn thing.

Dad reaches up to touch my face but stops short. "I can't

get used to your new hair," he says. "You look damn near respectable."

I mock-scowl. "How dare you. You take that back!"

A few people laugh, which gives me an odd feeling in my belly. I'm not used to camaraderie. I'm isolated from everybody in the castle—even the servants. Molly was the only one I befriended, and she still hasn't returned from Solren.

Even in the Undercity, I never had a team job like picking blyberries or raising cattle. Shifts at the Underwing were with one or two others at most, and Fra Wang wasn't exactly an intimate friend. Or even halfway friendly.

Things would have gone so differently for me if I'd followed in Dad's footsteps instead of Mom's. If I'd trailed him between Undercity Council tasks and blyberry picking instead of loitering at Mom's heels while she worked in the Underwing. I wouldn't have inherited any vestigial abilities for a start. Fewer people die out here than in the Underwing.

I glance at my companions. Dad is one of the oldest, and I'm one of the youngest. No babies are slung at their mothers' chests, no kids are sitting on their fathers' laps. We must be headed to the Eastern Gorge. Only the hardiest and bravest farmers pick blyberries in the Eastern Gorge. There's nothing dangerous about it as such—although there's the odd sighting of a mountain lion—but it's the farthest field from the Undercity. Only accessible by horse and wagon. And if the animal throws a shoe, you're stuck. Even the fastest sprinter couldn't make it home before dusk's end.

I never thought of these people as brave, but they are. They face death every time they head outside, either the agony of burning or the numbness of freezing. All it takes is one little delay on their return journey—a lame horse, a boulder fallen across the path, a broken wheel.

Fuck. My thoughts are morbid today.

I hadn't planned to join in a chore. I intended to grab Dad by the collar and force a confession out of him. But I can't do it with all these listening ears and these brave fucking people.

Pa Plucker turns the horse's nose east, still urging him to canter. We pass through a narrow mountain pass, skirting south of the Undercity.

"We only come this way at dusk," Dad tells me. "Snow doesn't melt in time to get through at dawn."

"Right," I say, though it comes out grunty. Even in dusk, it's cold here in the mountain's shadow. Cliffs rise on either side, leaving a narrow strip of golden sky.

"Thanks for coming along," he says, fishing for the truth about why I'm back to see him again so soon.

The wagon bumps over a rock at speed, and I fly from my wooden box and land heavily, limbs askew. "Fuck." I straighten my shirt. It's one Zaden got for me, and its fine weave and subtle cream color mark me as different from everyone else here. "I need to talk to you."

His deep brown eyes—my eyes—look at me intently. He can read me well enough to understand that I need privacy. I'm grateful he doesn't push me, just nods and waits until we emerge from the narrow mountain pass.

Blyberry fields carpet the ground in vibrant purple-blue. It's breathtaking. The sweet scent of ripe berries surrounds me, and I inhale deeply, soaking it in. The horse canters a few hundred feet into the field, bumping our little wagon over the red dirt track that bisects the purple expanse. Then Pa Plucker pulls us to a halt, and we spill onto the ground.

The men and women disperse into the field without a word,

operating a well-worn process that doesn't need words to run smoothly. They fan out, evenly spaced, and begin filling the buckets strapped around their waists, picking their way back to the wagon. We only have about twenty minutes before we have to return.

I grab a spare bucket and follow Dad into the field. He twists and plucks the berries with a practiced hand, and I try to copy, but the blyberries squish between my fingers. I lick off the juice and try again.

Glancing around, I see we're far enough from everybody to talk freely.

"You lied," I say without preamble.

Dad jerks and looks at me, his brown eyes narrowed, but his hands still move smoothly across the bushes. Fat berries plop into his bucket. "What are you talking about?"

"You lied," I repeat, a terse whisper. "Mom didn't die. She left." I fumble with a berry and chuck it into my bucket, which I'm holding awkwardly by the rim.

"Why do you say that?" Dad asks, his tone as careful as his words.

I snap a whole branch off a bush and throw it to the ground in frustration. "Stop answering questions with questions. Tell me the truth. I'm sick and tired of being lied to, and I just want to hear the bloody truth. Did Mom die, or did she leave?"

Another berry plops into Dad's bucket. It's already a quarter full and filling fast, whereas mine contains just a few splattered purple splotches.

"Answer me," I demand, fighting to keep my voice low. I have no interest in becoming the source of gossip. I just want the Maker-be-damned truth.

Dad's spine straightens, and his hands still. Everything

about him goes quiet. He stares at me, those eyes full of knowledge, and I silently beg him to share it.

"She left," he finally tells me in a whisper, the words snatched away by the cool breeze.

Tears fill my eyes, and I squeeze the bucket until my hands hurt. The farmers are busy with the berries, plucking food to feed their families, intent on their tasks. They don't look up, and I'm glad for small mercies.

But I can barely remember my mother. I've spent most of my life mourning her because of my lying father. "Why didn't you tell me?" My words are quiet, and I'm not sure I even spoke them aloud.

Dad holds out a hand to me, but it's a shallow gesture. He's never been a hugger. He has no intention of starting now, and I have no intention of letting him. "I didn't want to hurt you. She left, Scarla. Your mother left. I... I didn't know how to deal with that. And I didn't want you to think she abandoned you. So, I..."

"You lied," I spit. "You thought I'd be happier thinking she was dead? You fucking lunatic. Why would I want my own mother dead?"

He flinches at my swearing, shies away from the brutality of my anger. We stare at each other, the broken remnants of a family. Mom's gone, Leesa's dead, and now this. Now all the trust between Dad and me is gone, trampled like the mangled bushes under my feet.

"Did Leesa know?"

He doesn't have to tell me—I can read the truth in his eyes. She knew Mom had left, and she lied to me too. But his nod confirms it. "Yes, berry. Leesa knew. She was older than you, so—"

"You should have told me later then. Fuck!"

The setting sun spotlights the gray in Dad's beard and hair and sets his face into craggy wrinkles. He looks older than ever and further away, like I'll never find him again. It's like the man I knew as my father is gone forever.

"Where is she?"

"What?"

"Mom. Where is she? You said she left, so where'd she go?"

The others have made their way back to the wagon, and a woman with a stoop and a loud voice yells out. "Come on, Luca. We have to go."

Dad sighs and starts jogging to the wagon.

"Where'd she go?" I hiss, trotting at his side. I can't fault him for leaving—if he stays, he'll die, and I'm not so pissed at him that I want him dead.

He climbs into the wagon and holds out a hand to help me up. "Desert's Maw," he says as our hands meet.

Desert's Maw. The city on the far side of the Dead Desert. The one nobody ever visits or leaves. And the one place I have no idea how to get to.

Scarla

The wagon ride back to the Undercity is fast and bumpy. My ass has so many bruises I could lie naked in a blyberry field and never get found.

Dad's being a dick, too. Or maybe that's me. Either way, there's not a lot of gentle chit-chat, and I can't shake the fact my mother is really alive.

I'm no longer keeping a friends list. Every bloody name on that list has turned against me. Leesa, Dad, Mom, Leo, Zaden. Liars, every last one of them. That only leaves Molly, and she's not exactly knocking down my door to hang out.

Nope. I'm switching to an enemies list. The mental tally of all the fuckers who've wronged me. And Dad's name is right at the top.

We make it to the cave mouth just as Dad's teeth start chattering. The farmers huddle together in the middle of the wagon like a pack of puppies. I'm getting a lot of side-eye for not joining them, but I'm happy being a loner.

The dusk market is mainly packed away, but a trio of figures lurks around, waiting for us. Are they here to help us unload?

No, it's Sadie and her gang of North Undercity thugs. They're wrapped up against the cold—clearly, they planned this—but I can still make out the smug look on Sadie's octopus face, her wavy brown hair fanning out like tentacles.

The farmers leap off the wagon, and Pa Leeson Plucker leads the horse inside with the wagon still attached. They'll unload in the antechamber where it's warmer, then cart the berries to the warehouse cavern while the horse gets a feed in its stable.

Dad is the last to follow the wagon inside, and he tries to catch my eye to mend the feud, but I refuse to give him the satisfaction. Like a petulant bitch, I stare at the ground until he disappears inside.

"Think you can just swagger back here and take back your place, do ya, skank? Well, me'n the Council don't accept that." Sadie's voice is as shrill as I remember. She's itching for a fight, bloody gagging for one.

I don't give her the satisfaction. "I'm not in the mood, Sadie. Don't push me." There, I gave her a warning. Now she can't complain if she ends up bleeding on the ground while her blood slowly freezes.

I walk away, but one of her goons, Petie Mackintosh, grabs my wrist. His stench of onion and coal dust makes my nose wrinkle, and I don't try to hide it. "Have a wash, Petie," I snarl and yank my arm away.

They've obviously come prepared to fight me. With long legs and a mean streak he can't scrub out, Frank wears one of the sorcered suits they stole from the Margrave's patrol. Ralph is in the other, looking like a kid playing dress-ups.

"Whatsa matter, Scarla? Are you scared? It ain't so easy to beat us now that we can stay out, right? You're nothing but a pathetic one-trick pony with a superiority complex. Why don't you turn around and face us like a real woman?"

Sadie's voice set my nerves on edge, and I should keep walking, I should just go home to the castle, but I can't help myself. I can't fucking help myself. I whip around. "Big words, Sadie. Did you take some vocab lessons at creche?"

She scowls, and I love it. Outrage creeps across her face like marching ants, and I fucking lap it up. "Watch yourself, skank. You're outnumbered four to one. And we got suits."

I change my mind about not being in the mood for a confrontation. This is exactly what I need. The beast inside me awakens, and it's hungry for blood.

"Ah yes, the stolen suits. You reckon that'll make the difference?"

Sadie laughs, and her obedient goons chuckle along. "The only skill you ever had was staying outside when things got tough. Well that's done, you hear. You're done." Shivers wrack her body, and they're getting stronger. The sun is just a thin line of red on the horizon, and she doesn't have long.

Which means I don't have long to kick her ass.

She's still talking, though her numb lips make some of the words collide. "When me'n Petie go inside, you'll still be two to one, you dumb bitch."

"Remind me," I say, stroking my chin. "That makes you the brave ones, does it? Going up against little ole me with a whole gang?"

Petie spits. "Fucking bitch. Let's finish her, Sade. Prove to the Council who's boss." His spittle turns to a glob of frost on the red dirt. I'm running out of time.

That's twice they've mentioned the Council. Sadie's dad is a councilor; I know he has run-ins with mine. But it isn't an inherited position, which seems to piss Sadie off. She must want a spot on the leadership board, which is news to me.

Petie launches at me, probably trying to warm up. His movements are as slow as his brain, and I block him easily, retaliating with an uppercut that lands him on his ass.

I grin meanly. "That was fun. Who's next?"

Petie kicks out with a loose leg, which I stomp on. He groans in pain, and the beast inside me laps it up. I should feel guilty, but I don't. I warned them not to take me on, and they ignored it. It's not my fault if they underestimated me.

Sadie keeps talking while Frank sneaks around behind me, as though I can't hear the swoosh-swoosh of his suit or see his giraffe-like movements. "You got lucky," she snarls, and I pay her my full attention, pretending I can't see her circling goon. "Let's see you take down my real fighter," she hisses.

That must be his cue. He hooks an elbow around my throat and pulls me tight against his chest. He's stronger than he looks, and his bicep cuts off my airways. Frank pulled a knife the last time I got into fisticuffs with these guys, and they definitely had the advantage. If they'd had suits, they would have got me for sure.

I don't know precisely what they would have done with me—pretty sure they're not murderers—but they would've had the upper hand. And I would've shit myself.

But today, his grip just makes me want to laugh. They might be better fighters than I was six months ago, but since then, I've been training with elite soldiers and learned a thing or two.

There are so many choices. I could stomp his foot so he buckles forward, then elbow him in the gut. Or I could go straight for the reverse headbutt. He's hurting my neck, but I reckon I could wriggle enough to clamp my teeth down on his bicep.

So many options, so little time.

I stare at Sadie, capturing her face in a beam of intensity

so she can't look away. Her grin falters at something in my expression, and I press my advantage. If she wants to see me take down her best fighter, I'm happy to oblige. "Sure," I burble through my compressed windpipe.

Then I feel for the ribbon of light running down Frank's spine. Usually I can see it, but even with him behind me, I can sense the fragile light beam. I squeeze it gently, and he collapses. His arm slides down my shoulder and falls down my back, and he lands in a crumpled puddle of suit behind me.

I don't take my eyes off Sadie. "Now," I say agreeably, "who would you like me to take down next?"

She picked the wrong day to mess with me. I barely have any fondness in my heart for my dearest friends and family, and I have absolutely none for my enemies.

She takes a step backward, her shivering now macro. "I..."

I step closer. "Sorry? What was that?" I cup my ear to drive home the point. "Did you have another request, Sadie?"

"Fuck off," she spits, and I have to admire her attitude. She still hasn't given up. But she started this shit-show and can't just beg off when she's had enough.

I stalk closer, never letting my eyes waver from her. But I reach out my Gaze to sense the ribbon of light down Ralph's spine, and I squeeze. Terror storms across Sadie's face when he drops to the ground. "You really are a witch," she breathes, and it almost seems like respect.

"I'm so much more than that," I say, stalking closer. She stumbles over Petie's prone body and lands on her ass. I punch her in the face hard enough to knock her out, and she slumps onto the freezing ground.

Petie closes his eyes when I glance at him, playing dead. I'll leave him alert, so he can drag his buddies inside or get the mouthguard to help him. I'm not a monster; I don't want them to die.

But I did want to hurt them. The monster in my chest preens with pride, and I turn to head along Lowtown Road, beaming a massive smile.

Scarla

There's a reason I can be such a bitch.

I was raised that way. Sure, Mom was the best doctor in the underwing, nurturing and caring with healing powers unlike anyone else. She taught me how to mend bones and cure fever.

But she also taught me not to care if I couldn't.

"The hardest part of being a good healer," she told me, "is not falling into an emotional pit. You'll be no use to anybody if you cry over every death. Toughen up or find a different profession."

When I was seven or eight, not long before she disappeared, she woke me from my nap in a rocky nook in the underwing. I used to hang out down there while she worked, watching her lay hands on febrile patients and bring them comfort in their suffering. My sanctuary was a small nook in the cave wall—too small for an adult but just the right size for a curled-up child. I thought it was my secret place.

Mom woke me and beckoned me closer to the bedside she stood by. Blankets draped around a tiny shape on the mattress, and it took me several moments to identify Lucille, a girl from my sleeping hub. She was my age but looked younger in that bed, somehow not occupying enough space.

Sweat poured from her, and I could see she was really sick.

Mom pulled me onto her lap. "What treatment do you recommend for Lucille?"

I tumbled my sleepy head in confusion. "What?"

She turned at me, a severe expression pinning me in place, stopping my squirming. "To be a healer, you must make hard decisions. Tell me, how should we treat Lucille? Whatever you tell me to do, I'll do."

Fear gripped me, and my muscles tensed. "But I don't know how to fix her."

Mom's fingers dug into my arms. "Make a decision."

I shook my head, terrified. "I can't. You do it. I don't know what to do. I'll kill her."

She stared at me for a long while, looking in my face for something I couldn't give her. I didn't know the proper treatment for Lucille, and I damn sure didn't want the responsibility. Mom's straight auburn hair absorbed the flickering torchlight like a black hole, and shadows sharpened her nose into a point. She looked every inch a storybook witch, and I felt afraid of her for the first time in my life.

She sank in disappointment, but her lip curled. "Fine. You choose not to treat her. So we won't treat her."

I wriggled free of her lap, sobbing, begging her to give Lucille the best treatment possible. But Mom only said, "I'll give her whatever you want. Just tell me."

But I couldn't. I sat there the rest of the long night, Mom's steel fingers handcuffing my wrist so I couldn't escape, and watched Lucille's tiny chest rise and fall. Until it stopped rising and falling.

I hated Mom that night. She let Lucille suffer and let me suffer, for no reason at all. I wanted to pinch the soft white flesh under Mom's arm until she squealed like I sometimes did to other kids. But even as a child, I winced at the idea of losing a battle, and I knew I was no match for my mother.

That awful evening has never left me. For years, I could close my eyes and still picture Lucille's fluttering breath, her waxen skin, and recall the sensation of hopelessness as I watched her die.

No doubt it made me a better healer. I learned that inaction is as good as murder. If I choose not to treat somebody, I might as well stab them myself because I'm killing them. My job is to make the best decision possible with the available information.

Mom told me later that nothing could have saved Lucille that night. She was hours from death, and our company may have eased her passing. It took me years to understand that lesson, but it was worth it.

The true lesson? Sometimes patients die. They just die. And the best thing the healer can do is move on. Leave the tears for the family, and use your skills on a sick person you can actually help.

So being a bitch is actually part of my job description. And I'm in the mood to be a proper asshole.

I step into the Malanox Castle infirmary, looking for Jonah. I knocked him to the dirt in our training bout yesterday, and I want to see how much damage I inflicted.

He isn't here. Three of the eight beds are occupied by patients, but not him.

Rosa, a cook's aide with a headache and fever, smiles at me. "Thank you for coming." She thinks I'm here to heal her, and the weight of her expectation chafes.

"Hello, Rosa." I take a few steps closer, aware of six eyes following me across the room. "Tell me, why do you work for the Margrave?"

Her smile falters as she takes in my severe demeanor. I can't say the word Margrave without tensing every muscle in my body. I can't think of that lying shit without grimacing. "Oh, I... my parents work in the kitchens."

I fold my arms across my chest. "That's not an answer."

Her ruddy cheeks grow heated, even redder than usual. "I... It's the... there aren't many options for a human like me."

I can see I'm scaring her, but that doesn't feel like my problem right now. I'll make it up to her later when I'm in a better mood. If I'm ever in a better mood.

Her phrasing is odd. *Not many options for a human like me. A human like me.* She's right. Angels have all the privilege and power, all the opportunities. Those fuckers should stay up in heaven and leave earth to us mortals.

I spent my childhood rebelling against the Undercity Council, hating the injustice of job allocation and food rations, wishing they would do more to improve our lives instead of ducking their heads and dipping their hats to the Margrave.

But it was never their fault. Expecting the Undercity Council to change is like expecting my shoes to take me across the desert. They only do as they're told.

The Cloaked Court controls everything. The cities, the resources, the sorcery. They could erect a fucking dome over all of Malanox and improve everybody's lives, but they don't.

Because they're angels who don't give a fuck about mortals.

The Cloaked Court has to go.

"Where's Jonah," I bark, and Rosa stutters a confused reply, but I don't have the patience to wait for her to spit it out.

"In his barracks," an older man with a broad nose and brown skin replies. "The guards don't mix with us if they can help it." The man's face holds contempt, and I can see it's directed at me. "And if you aren't planning on mending us, you can bugger off. You're scaring Rosa."

This man's name escapes me, but I don't bother asking. He's right, though. I have no intention of treating these patients now. I'm too worked up, too full of anger at Zaden, and I wouldn't be able to draw their fevers even if I wanted to.

Which I don't. They chose to work for the enemy, so they can live—or die—with the consequences.

The barracks is a stone building tucked behind the castle out of view from the town and river. I've only been inside once or twice out of pure curiosity, but this morning my strides hold determination and purpose.

A guard directs me along a hallway to a bunk room, where I find Jonah alone on a bottom bed.

He's bedridden from his injuries, unable to join his comrades in training. A triumphant smile lights my face. I'm not pleased that he's hurt, but I'm proud to have been strong enough to damage him.

"You look happy," he says, his gaze glued to my approach like he's never seen a woman before.

I swish my hips, bringing out the flirt. A sense of power floods me, and I don't mind exerting every bit of it I have. "You look like you've been waiting for me."

He grins and raises himself onto an elbow, swallowing a grimace of pain. "No, but I'm delighted you came."

His mattress dents as I sit, and he rolls toward me, making no effort to prevent contact between our bodies. Stubble lines his chin, and I run a finger along the edge of his jaw, feeling the roughness. It's smoother than Zaden's, which is sandpaper.

I eye Jonah critically, inspecting every inch of him. He is like a toned-down version of Zaden. My height, no taller. Muscular

197

but leaner than the angel. Sexy, but not un-fucking-deniable.

My stare rests on the cream sheet over Jonah's crotch, which is tented with an erection. Also less impressive than Zaden's but large enough to impale yourself on happily.

"Are you here to heal me?" he whispers.

I watch shamelessly as his erection grows. "I'm here to inspect the damage I inflicted on you."

That statement should deflate him, but it has the opposite effect. His cock gives a little jump. "You're welcome to inspect every inch of me," he says hoarsely.

Men are so predictable. Even this hot-as-fuck one is thinking with his dick. Zaden would kill him if he found out he was flirting with me. That would piss off the angel more than anything else I can think of.

So I lean into the flirt and drag my gaze to Jonah's eyes. They are such a startling blue that I lose concentration momentarily, wondering how my life might have turned out if I'd met Jonah before Zaden. Maybe I would have fallen for him and had his honest little guard babies instead of falling in love with the celestial asshole who turned out to be a liar and the biggest dickwad of all.

I bring my face close until the heat of Jonah's breath mists my lips. "I might just do that," I whisper, running a hand inside his cream sheet, down his chest, and over his belly, which tightens in response. "Would you like that?" I tease, hovering inches away from his straining cock.

"Yes," he breathes, leaning up to smash his lips against mine, but I move away, keeping the power, maintaining control. I never want to be controlled again.

I push aside his shorts. Jonah's face contorts in pleasure as I wrap my fingers around the base of his cock and slowly run the length of it, circling the very tip. He shudders beneath me and curls a hand around the back of my neck, which I slap away with my free arm. "No," I whisper. "You only get what you're given."

I can see why angels love this power. It's intoxicating. Jonah's entire being is focused on the slightest movements of my fingers and lips, which hover above his close enough that he can feel their heat but not touch.

My body fires in response to Jonah's pleasure, but I refuse to succumb to desire. Jonah's vulnerability is palpable. I could squeeze a little tighter and rip his damn cock off, but he isn't trying to stop me. He wants me here more than anything else in the Maker-be-damned world.

His moans are so inviting, and my core pools with heat, my skin tingling. I allow myself to press my breasts against his hard chest. He groans at the touch and locks his gaze on the place where our bodies meet, watching the fullness of my bosom expand toward him.

His cock thickens beneath my grip, and his moans fill the room. I adjust my position, taking deep breaths, focusing on my nipples moving against his muscles. He writhes beneath me, aching for more pressure between our bodies, but I pull away, refusing to give in to desire.

With a shudder, he explodes, and I direct the sticky mess toward his chest like a fire hose. His face contorts in release, sharing another moment of pure vulnerability where I could stick a knife in his chest, and he'd thank me for it.

I wipe my hand on the bedsheet and extract it. He grins at me sheepishly and fumbles toward my legs. "Let's take care of you next, babe."

Reluctantly, I stand, moving out of his sphere. "I can take

care of myself." No way am I putting myself in his power, as much as my traitorous body wants to.

With a sudden movement, I pull back his bedsheet and expose his entire body. He wears boxer shorts, which he tugs up over his limp dick with a sheepish grin. "What are you doing?"

"Inspecting your wounds. I already told you that."

"Right. I thought you were kidding."

Several large bruises bloom over his belly and legs, a satisfying blue that will turn purple and green. The skin is torn in numerous places. "Anything broken?" I demand.

"Couple of ribs."

I know I should feel sorry for having inflicted this pain on him, but I don't. What I feel is closer to pride and a sense of achievement. I managed to down a fully trained guard using only my combat skills—and a massive dose of fucking fury.

"An apology wouldn't go astray," Jonah says, smirking, expecting some banter. Maybe he's hoping this will become a romance.

I look him dead in the eyes. "You just got it." Then I turn my back and leave.

Scarla

The barracks is churning with men, obviously on a meal break. I shove my way through them, pleased that they move aside for me.

A hush falls over the crowd, and I wonder if my power extends to making a mass of grown-ass men fall silent.

But no, it's Zaden. He's appeared at the far end of the space, hulking, taking up the entire doorway even with his wings glamoured.

A frown passes over his face, and his muscles roil with potential. I stick my guilty hand—the one that tugged on Jonah's hard-on—behind my back. I shouldn't care what this lying angel thinks of me. I fucking shouldn't. But that damn hand stays firmly behind my back.

He stalks closer, mowing a lane through the men, barely seeming to notice them. "What are you doing here?" he growls.

Anger stiffens my spine. He has no right to demand answers from me. At least, not if he expects the truth.

I smile piously. "Attending to the injured."

He sniffs the air like a damn animal, scenting my lingering arousal. "I didn't realize you enjoyed it so much, mortal."

My lips twist to hold back my smile because, damn him,

I won't fall for his easy manner. "I didn't realize you were paying attention."

A frown flutters on his forehead, but he quickly clears it. "I pay more attention than you know." He stalks closer, and the remaining men scatter, leaving us alone.

Every nerve in my body wants to back away, but I force myself to hold my ground. I need to get to Desert's Maw to find my mom, and Zaden can help me get there.

Still, I can't paint a pretty smile on my face and simper to secure his help. Too much energy is coursing through my body and too much rage. I thought I loved this male, but he's no better than the other lying scumbags who populate the planet.

"You think you have me all figured out, don't you," I snarl. "The little woman with Gaze who will fall at your feet and do everything you say if you just whisper pretty words in her ear. Well, I bet you've got a few surprises coming."

My words don't penetrate his easy manner. He stalks closer, closing the gap, forcing me to crane my neck. "I'll take any bet you care to wager," he purrs. The warmth of his breath steams my ear.

My panties are still wet from rubbing up against Jonah, and heat flares through me again, melting me from the inside out. "I'm not as sweet and innocent as you think," I growl.

He grabs my chin and yanks it up, hard. "Oh, there's nothing innocent about you."

My chest heaves with fury, and I bring my knee up between his legs. "Or sweet," I spit.

A gasp from somewhere behind tells me some of the men are watching. I take advantage of Zaden's momentary surprise at being kneed in the balls to shove him away with all my force and duck out from between his arms.

Spinning away, I take quick stock of available weapons. Heavy wooden tables and chairs, plus lightweight tableware. I hurl a plate at Zaden, and he ducks. He's grinning, the asshole. "Do you dare to take a bet against me?"

Right now, I'll do anything against him. Spit, hurl, bite, fight. And definitely bet. "I bet I'll win this fight," I say recklessly. I've never beaten him before, but I've come close. And the rage pouring through me has to count for at least ten men.

He smirks, ducking another plate and a flying knife, stepping closer. "Fine. But if I win, you must take your punishment like a good girl."

"You won't win," I snarl. "And *when* I win, you have to take me to my mother."

His approach pauses momentarily, then he resumes stalking. His green eyes glitter, reflecting every ounce of sunlight pouring through the sorcered skylights. He has the intensity of a panther hunting prey, his muscles bunched and hard.

I remember those forearms planted on either side of my head and those delicious full lips pressed against mine, but I shake the image aside. I'm not here to seduce this fucking angel. I'm here to beat him.

I spin low, taking advantage of my shorter stature, and swing a chair against his shins, then dance in close and punch his ribs. It feels like hitting a Maker-be-damned stone wall, but the pain in my knuckles is nothing, irrelevant.

He turns to watch me spin and dart in, blocking every move but not parrying with any of his own.

"Attack me, asshole," I yell, overflowing with frustration, but he just keeps blocking and holding me at bay. I feel like a damn kitten attacking a tiger.

Time for a classic misdirect. I reach behind me and grab

a mug from the table behind me, then hurl it upwards with all my might, aiming at the skylight. It makes contact with a bang, and Zaden glances up to see if it's broken.

By the time he refocuses on the fight, I'm already at his throat, pressing my fingers into the bobble of his Adam's apple.

With a growl, he prises my hands apart and forces them together behind my back, holding both my hands with just one of his own. Fucker.

I'm panting with fury, and he just smirks. He leans forward and sniffs my neck. "I can scent your arousal," he whispers.

"That's your own fucking ego you're smelling, asshole. I'm the opposite of aroused."

He just grins into my neck like he can tell I'm lying. "Do you yield?"

I can barely force the words out. Somebody sniggers from the doorway, and my rage escalates. But I can't stay here with my arms trussed behind me like a bloody pig for the rest of my life. Zaden is pressed against me, pinning my legs with his, and I have nowhere to go.

My shoulders are killing me.

"Yes," I whisper.

"Say it." He licks my neck and along my jawline.

"It," I manage to spit out.

He chuckles darkly. "I can stay here all day, mortal. I'm rather enjoying myself. And we're not going anywhere until you admit I won the bet."

I'm exposed and vulnerable, my entire body open to his, with all my defenses shut down. And the worst part is, I'm kind of loving it.

"Fine, you win," I admit, needing to wrap my arms around

him and claim him as mine. But as soon as he releases me, I shove him aside. "Now leave me alone."

I walk away, but he grabs my wrist. "Not so fast, mortal. You have to take your punishment."

I spin slowly to face him. What the holy hell have I gotten myself into?

Zaden

This fucking mortal. She thinks she can treat me like trash and I'll follow at her heels like a tame puppy.

She has another thing coming.

I will punish her until she begs for mercy, cries for release. I will show her who the master is.

First, she has to wash that guard's stink off her. The one she injured yesterday, whom she claimed she just healed.

So why does she smell of his arousal? If he touched an inch of her pure flesh, I will flay him. Her healing hands on his skin must have given him an erection, and if it's anything more than that, he will die.

Still holding her wrist, I pull her toward the castle.

"Where are we going?" she asks, and the uncertainty in her voice is my balm.

She won't get the satisfaction of an answer from me. She doesn't need to know that the scent of that mindless guard—a human man—torments me. That his musky odor disgusts me. That if I don't leave the barracks now, I'll slaughter him in his bed.

That if it wasn't for her mortal sensibilities, I'd have already destroyed him.

Scarla doesn't need to know that she inhabits my mind and

206

that her every mood and whim affects me.

And the last thing she needs to know is where her damn mother is.

"Oh, you're back to ignoring me, are you? So fucking immature."

Anger flares in me, but I refuse to rise to her taunts. I drag her into the castle and down the central staircase, satisfied when she stumbles a few paces to keep up.

Blue light reflects off the underground pool, marking glowing waves on the rock walls and ceiling. This is where I first saw Scarla naked, and I still can't shake the image. She stood here, with hatred and shame mixing in her gaze, daring me to look away.

She pulls back against my grip. "What are you going to do to me?"

Fear clouds her brow, and for a moment, I like it. I fucking love it. She *should* be afraid of me. I was forged in the primordial fire of the stars, and she is a mere mortal, a gadfly, insignificant. Humans die before I bother to learn their names.

But this one is different. She's Scarla. The fleeting span of her life makes it more valuable, like diamond. In comparison, us celestials, with lives as long as eternity, are as common as coal.

Perhaps I really am a monster. Maybe that moment of joy that lanced me, riding on her fear, makes me as despicable and evil as she always thought.

I force gentleness into my tone, but the Maker only knows how I find it. "I'm going to bathe you."

She flinches but covers it with a false smile. "Bloody Hells below. He speaks." Even when she's at my mercy, when I could hold her underwater for a moment too long and extinguish her spark forever, when she's vulnerable and nothing she does could stop me, she never backs down. She seems unaware of her own fragility, like she doesn't know how close she is to death at every moment of her fleeting life.

"Careful with that tongue, or I'll put it to good use." I send a swirl of magic around her. A pulse of arousal wets her panties, and the scent makes my cock jump. She lets out a little, "Oh," which is sweet and sexy enough to sustain me for days.

But she's not getting away with it that easily. "Now, I believe you owe me your punishment."

I release her wrist, and she immediately juts out a hip, trying to take control. "Isn't spending time with you punishment enough?" she demands, half teasing and half serious. I have retracted my magic, but the salty-sweet scent of her core is growing stronger, and my body can't help but respond. Every inch of my skin tingles just from seeing and smelling her. We're not even touching, although the air between us is hot.

Her defiance is utterly sinful, and I could come just by talking to her.

"You will do as I say for the next sixty minutes. No push back, no refusal, no denial."

"No way."

I'm on her instantly, pinning her delicate wrists behind her back and leaning into her neck. Water laps against the cave walls. "Do not deny me, Scarla," I growl, and she shivers in response. "Pay. Your. Debt." I wait for her to push back, knee me in the balls, or headbutt my forehead, but she doesn't.

She submits, saying, "Yes, Margrave," and the moment is delicious. Her words drip with sarcasm, but I don't care.

For the next sixty minutes, she's mine.

"Strip," I command, and a rebellious fire lights her eyes, but

I can tell she wants to. She can't help the smile that twitches her lips and the lightning that strikes her body. And the smell, that glorious smell. "Slowly," I demand.

"Yes, Margrave," she says, wriggling her hips as she lowers her pants, letting them pool on the rock at her feet and exposing lacy peach panties that are softer and more feminine than anything she usually wears.

My breath hitches. Her thighs are toned and muscled from hours of battle training, yet creamy and silken from a life in the shade. And the small peach V at their apex is intoxicating.

"And your shirt," I bark, though my voice is already hoarse. She bites her lower lip and locks her wide brown eyes on mine, knowing she has me completely entranced when it should be the other way around.

She slowly unbuttons her light blue shirt, one hole at a time, never releasing me from her stare. But I can't drag my eyes away from the flesh she is revealing, painfully slowly. Her breasts pop out from her shirt like a whore's, and I want her like that, bent over and submissive, one tit in each hand.

Before she has finished unbuttoning, I pull the peach bra cups down to release her goosebump flesh. She startles at my touch and arches her back toward me. I can't resist claiming her nipple between my fingers before I step back to continue watching.

She moans a little, disappointed at the space between us, and I strike that up as a victory. This is supposed to be about me being in control, but I'm having a hard bloody time maintaining it.

Finally, the last button is undone, and she wriggles out of her shirt, fully aware that her breasts are jiggling with every shimmy as she lets it fall to the rocky floor.

She stands before me in her lacy peach underwear, with the bra cups wedged beneath her breasts. Reflected blue light from the underground pool washes across her skin. I could stare at her all day. My clothes are still on, but my cock doesn't know it—it's jumping and straining with no dignity whatsoever, unaware of the power play between Scarla and me.

She shifts her weight to stand on one leg, highlighting the curve of her waist and hip and the shapely dip of her leg. "Now what, Margrave?" she asks sweetly.

I want her to lose control of herself like I almost am. To launch herself at me, strip me, and beg me to fuck her. But she's better at this resistance thing than I am. "You haven't finished your last task yet," I growl. "Strip."

A pulse of desire stabs her core, and my muscles jump in response. She wriggles out of her panties, revealing her soft curls, then reaches behind her to unclasp her bra, sticking her Maker-be-damned perfect tits right in my face.

"I can't get this," she lies. "Can you help, milord?"

"Turn around."

She ignores me and shimmies closer. "I'm sure you can just reach around from the front."

I'm sure I bloody can too, but if those breasts go anywhere near my chest, I'm a goner. "Turn," I demand.

She pouts but does a one-eighty and shows me her back, which is just as smooth and flawless as her front. I unclasp her bra with one hand, and she leans forward so it can drop.

Less than an inch separates my jumping cock from her ass, and I know she's wet enough—I can smell her. I could free my cock and be inside her within a second, thrusting my anger and lust into her sinful body.

But first, she has to pay for losing that bet. And I must

prove to myself that I can resist her for longer than five damn minutes.

"Into the water," I snarl. The guard's scent lingers, mixed in with her musk and my own salty oils, and she needs to wash him away.

She sashays in slowly, pretending to yip at the cold when we both know damn well she barely feels it. Reflected torchlight glitters on her thighs and ass, sliding up her body as she enters the pool.

She turns to face me without being told, standing hip-deep in the lapping water. Her nipples are hardened pips, dark and inviting, and every inch of her skin is pebbled from the cold. It would feel like silk.

"Submerge yourself," I say.

"But—"

"Do it!"

She drops instantly into the water, and a flare of pleasure strikes me at her obedience. I love her strength, but I like my own too.

Finally, the guard is erased completely; the only scents left are hers and mine. She stands again in the hip-deep water, droplets dancing on her skin and dripping from her hair. "Can I ask you a question?"

Her copper hair is darkened with water and flat against her head, making her brown eyes bigger and more irresistible. I can't refuse her. I nod.

"Who is the Cloaked King?"

That throws me. I was expecting a question about her mom. Or whether she could have a towel. Or would I please fuck her.

"I don't know," I answer truthfully. Nobody knows his identity—that's how he keeps his power. Otherwise somebody would kill him for Inflict and take his throne. I've told her this already.

A lock of wet hair falls on her face, and as she brushes it aside, light reflects off the different curves of her body, which is damn distracting.

"Okay, I believe you."

"Good, then let's get back to—"

"Where is Molly?"

I can barely resist rolling my eyes. Scarla is obsessed with this one damn maid, and I don't know or care where she is. "In Solren, living life to the fullest," I say. The maid is nobody special—just one human woman among millions, leading a nothing life. I'll never understand why Scarla fixates on this particular person and not on another. "There are plenty of other maids here."

She narrows her eyes at me, and I can tell I've said the wrong thing. I wish I could make Scarla understand that she is the only remarkable mortal, and the others are interchangeable. Then she'd spend less energy on individuals who don't matter.

"Where's Bwadu?" Scarla asks, tilting her head to the side.

I have no Maker-be-damned idea who Bwadu is, but I'm not stupid enough to admit it. "She's taking care of Molly," I lie, regretting letting this conversation get out of hand.

"And where's my mom?" Scarla asks.

The last thing I will ever tell Scarla is where her mother is. I need Gaze to stay here. And, most irritating of all, I need Scarla to remain here by my side. I've developed an annoying fondness for her company that I can't give up. Ever. I will not lose her.

"Question time is over," I scowl, adding enough anger to my words to make Scarla think twice. I remove the glamor from my wings and spread them wide behind me, so they drag on the floor and brush the low ceiling. The black feathers absorb the light.

Their drugging effect is instantaneous, and Scarla whimpers.

"Come here." I beckon with one finger, and she obeys immediately, drawn to the sensual pull of my feathers. She is dripping wet, cold on the outside and hot on the inside. She reaches out a hand to stroke my wings, and I allow her to.

We both shiver with desire. Her fingers stroking my feathers is almost as good as her tugging on my cock. The sensuality is overwhelming, and magic sparks from her hands to my very essence. I throw my head back and fall into the sensation for a moment, filling myself with the whisper of her touch.

But I can see she is losing control too, so I snap my wings away. "Don't orgasm yet," I growl.

"Why not?" she demands, gripping me through my pants.

I turn her around and bend her over. "Because you're mine."

She leans into a rock, finding purchase with her fingers in a crevice, panting in anticipation. Her whole body expands and retracts with every quick breath, making the torchlight slide over her skin like a caress.

I release my cock and tease its tip against her ass. "Do you want me?" I whisper.

"Yes."

"Tell me."

"I want you. Please. Now," she whimpers.

I slide into her, letting her silken warmth drip down every long inch of me, filling her until she gasps. Even entering heaven can't feel as good as this. The pressure around me has me almost bursting, so I pull out, then ease in again. She takes my full length with a moan that has me throbbing.

213

"More," she groans, and I know she would do anything I ask her in this moment.

"Stay with me," I whisper into her ear, then nibble her lobe.

"Always," she says on a moan, and I almost explode. All the power in the world that I have over this woman is nothing compared to the power she has over me.

I reach around and clasp my hands over her breasts, squeezing gently. She bucks into me. "Harder." I clutch tighter, pinching the nipples, and the swell of her flesh against my fingers has me moaning in symphony with her.

I thrust into her in a steady rhythm, biting my cheek to keep control. Her salty scent is my entire world; I could spend eternity nibbling on her neck. Her back is pressed against my chest, easing some of the pulsing need in my skin, and I keep one hand on her breast while I run the other down her belly and hip.

I can't get enough of this woman. "Tell me you love me," I whisper in her ear, and she tenses slightly but doesn't answer. Again I thrust, and she presses her ass against me, meeting the challenge every step of the way. I want to keep her forever and share my soul with her, but I need to hear it from her first. "Tell me you fucking love me," I growl.

She heard me. She Maker-be-damned heard me, and she's ignoring me. I bite her ear and put a hand on her jaw, squeezing. "Do you love me?"

She bites her tongue, which looks as sexy as hell, and I turn her face so I can claim her lips, kissing with all the passion in my heart. Fire ignites between us, electricity that lights up the entire cavern, and I know she can feel it too.

So why is she so damn stubborn that she can't tell me? This infernal power play between us is too much—and I refuse to lose.

I pump harder into her, kissing her full lips and crying out in pleasure. But if she refuses to give me satisfaction, I'll withhold satisfaction from her.

Letting myself go, I release into her, combining my essence with hers and becoming one with her. But she hasn't climaxed, and I don't intend to let her.

"That'll do," I spit out, hating that I love her more than she loves me. Then I stride from the room fully dressed, leaving her alone, naked, and still panting with desire.

Scarla

Well, that was hot. Who would have thought that being ordered around by a bossy angel could be so intoxicating? I daydream about it all night long and well into the next morning... probably because he left me so unsatisfied that I can't think of anything else.

I breakfast in my bedchamber, sitting in my window and looking out across the gently curving river and over Hightown. The mountain I used to call home rises in the distance, but it feels less like I belong there with every passing day.

Dad lied to me for years about Mom dying. Leo lied to me about who he was and what he wanted from life. Even the Undercity Council, which I plotted to overthrow and dismantle, seems unimportant now that I know they are puppets dancing to the angels' tune.

Zaden's words whip through my skull, riding the tornado of my thoughts.

Do you want me?

Stay with me.

Do you love me?

That male is so all-encompassing that I can barely hold a thought in my head when I'm with him. It took every ounce of energy not to fall at his feet and declare my devotion, and the electricity sparking between us didn't help.

But his arrogance kept me in check. *Tell me you fucking love me.*

No, I'm done dancing to the tune of others. Dad the liar, Leo the betrayer, Xerxes the Fuckwit, Mini Xerxes the Mini Fuckwit, Count VanDyke the power-hungry angel.

And Zaden. The male I loved with all my soul for a brief shining day, but who lied to me about Mom. Just like the others.

Abby minces into the room, a terrible replacement for Molly's liveliness. She takes my plate and clears her throat.

"Yes?" I bark, annoyed at her meekness.

She wipes a hand on her cream apron. "Milady, some of the servants are sighing again, and we think they might have the sickness."

"So give them Wilton's Dale," I snap. "I'm not the only one who can chew a herb and stick it in somebody's mouth." I've given up asking her to call me Scarla because she seems incapable of forming the sounds.

"No, milady." She curtsies but hovers like a damn mosquito.

I sigh and look out the window, not bothering to look at her while I speak. "What else? I can tell you want to say something, so just bloody say it."

"It's... we're out of Wilton's Dale, and you're the only one who knows where it grows. Could you go to Penngrove Forest and pick some more? The servants would be ever so grateful." Her voice is tinny and thin, entirely lacking in substance.

I lean my head against the window and watch a leaf flutter along the stream, ducking and eddying in the currents. Soon it will be obscured by a curtain of steam as the day heats up. "Are these the same servants who willingly work for the angel who oppresses the people of Lowtown and the Undercity? The same servants who take no steps to change anything in their damn lives but expect me to drop everything to scurry around and pick up the pieces of their pathetic health? Are those the servants you mean?"

I know I'm being a bitch, but I don't care. I'm sick of being the good, helpful one who solves other people's problems. They should know by now how to identify the damn herb that saves so many of their lives. The fact that nobody bothered learning is infuriating.

I think back to Mom's first lesson about healing: be a bitch. Don't care too much about your patients. By refusing to go to the forest, I'm doing these servants a favor—maybe now, they'll get off their asses and figure out how to obtain Wilton's Dale. It'll probably save an entire generation of freaking servants.

I sigh. Maybe I'll go to the forest tomorrow, but I'm not going today.

Abby bobs, and I can see she has no clue how to handle me. "Yes, milady," she murmurs. "I suppose those are the same people."

Heat flows through the glass and directly into my forehead, warming my skin to the point of discomfort, but I don't move. "I'm sure they'll figure something out," I say dismissively, waving my hand.

She stares at me in disbelief. They're all so used to me jumping to help them, but I'm done dancing to the tune of others.

I should feel bad. I know I should. But I can't muster up the energy. Until I find my mother and ask why she left, I'll never be able to show kindness again. It's like I'm stuck in deep snow, and until it melts, I'm not going anywhere.

Abby leaves, and a tiny part of my soul goes with her. I can't help but feel like the person she farewells is more of a monster than the one she greeted.

* * *

I'm going to visit Jonah again. I'll apologize for being so weird yesterday, then maybe I'll feel like a better human being and go collect some medicinal herbs. Plus, he might have a lead on how to get across the Dead Desert to find my mom.

He's in the common room of the barracks. The mess hall, I guess. Most guards smile and nod as I pass—one woman claps her hand against her thigh as though I'm a musician at solstice who played my part well.

But Jonah grins. I scrape out a chair and sit at the table beside him. Wooden tables dot the room, each big enough for a small family, and the two guards sharing Jonah's scurry away when I sit down.

A pang of loneliness hits me right in the gut. I don't want to be isolated from everybody or perceived as different. They think I'm some kind of princess, but I'm just a lost girl trying to pretend I know what the hells I'm doing.

I frown. "Hi, Jonah."

He winks. "Nice to see you again, Scarla."

It's so lovely to be called that. Not milady, not mortal, but my actual damn name. "I heard your family's from Desert's Maw?"

He shifts in his seat, wincing in pain, but doesn't back away from answering. "Yep. Originally."

"How can I get there?" The only person I know who's ever

crossed the Dead Desert is Leo, and he's always been cagey about how he got there. Not because I didn't pump him for information—I tried.

Jonah shrugs. "You can't."

An obvious lie. "Clearly, you can. People do. I'm just asking how."

"Why do you want to go?"

"None of your damn business. I just want to know where to book the carriage," I joke, knowing it won't be that easy. Nothing travels north from Malanox.

He shifts again like I'm making him uncomfortable. I'll make him a shitload more uncomfortable if he doesn't answer me straight. "I've never been myself. I was born here. Only the Nashanti know how to cross the Dead Desert."

I lean forward and tuck a lock of copper hair behind my ear. "The who?"

"The Nashanti. The desert people. They have a network of hidey holes and tunnels and secret ways. The only way across is to find a Nashanti guide."

"How do I find one?" I demand.

"No idea. Sorry, Scarla, I'd tell you if I did. Really. We're friends, aren't we?"

My mouth twitches in a smile. I believe he's told me everything he knows, which is much more than I knew five minutes ago.

To get to Mom, I need to cross the Dead Desert, and to cross the desert, I need a Nashanti to guide me.

I lean on my elbows and take a deep breath, preparing for the hardest part of this chat. "Look, I'm sorry about yesterday. And the day before."

He thumps his fingers against the wooden table like he's

playing a drum. "Knocking me down in front of the lads was bad. They'll never let me forget that."

"Why not?" I know exactly what he means. Because he got bested by a woman. But I'm more powerful than him, so why in Hells below shouldn't I knock him on his ass?

His rhythm on the tabletop falters. "Oh, because... well, but... but you don't have to say sorry for yesterday. Thanks, actually."

He winks again, and my stomach curdles. I came to apologize for my weird power play, for aggressively wanking him with no emotion or even proper consent, and hope he'd forgive me. After breaking his ribs, I came in like some kind of psychopath, slipped my hand beneath his sheets, and then left without even saying goodbye.

And he's thanking me?

"Whatever." I shove back the chair with my knees, scraping out a screech of wood against stone, and stand, leaning over Jonah on the table. Irritation rakes along my scalp. "If the Margrave finds out, he'll kill you." That comes out sounding like a threat, but it's supposed to be a warning. "So I suggest you keep it to yourself and don't tell any of your buddies that you got a hand job from the lord's girlfriend."

Jonah blanches. His blue eyes dull, and he visibly retracts into himself. His jaw is rounder than I recall, and his shoulders hunched.

This conversation has run wildly off the rails—it's jumped the tracks and crashed off a cliff. I planned to apologize and warn him, but instead I threatened and scared him.

"Okay, sure. I didn't realize you were... Sorry," he says, stumbling over his words.

Why is it easier for me to scare people than befriend them?

Back in the Undercity, Leo was the charmer and I was the bitch. Here in the castle, it's just me, el bitcho. Jonah is one of my favorite people—he was even making his way onto my friends list—but now he knows me for the sociopath I am.

Maybe I should just lean into it. I smile menacingly, surprised at how naturally it comes. "Doesn't bother me either way," I whisper, like his death would mean nothing to me.

But actually, I'm dripping in guilt... wearing remorse like a fucking gown. Touching Jonah so intimately feels like a betrayal of Zaden, even though he betrayed me first. Just thinking about it makes my gut churn and my hand feel dirty, like I turned my back on the stars when I ran my hand down Jonah's belly.

Bloody Hells below, that angel is killing me. I can't believe he left me high and dry yesterday, panting for his attention and un-fucking-satisfied. It's time I showed him what's what.

Scarla

I storm straight out of the barracks and up to Zaden's chambers. The tower guard withers under my snarl and steps aside, and I shove open the door without knocking.

Zaden's unbuttoned cream shirt flutters against his contoured chest as he turns from his bookshelf to look at me. The sharp V below his hard stomach drops into low-slung black pants. The whole damn lot of him glistens in the brilliant ray of sunlight coming in through the window.

He raises an eyebrow, a full-blown celestial smirk.

"Take your shirt off," I demand, and his smirk deepens.

"Did you win a bet I've forgotten about?" he drawls.

I stride to the foot of his bed. "I've had enough of your shit. Just do as I say for once."

He stares at me for a long moment, and tension sparks between us. So much damn electricity, it's like the Maker manufactured this angel especially for me.

I have no idea what he'll do. He's weighing up his next move, considering my emotional state, probably smelling my damn feelings or something.

Finally, he moves, shrugging out of his loose shirt, which flutters to the stone floor. "Yes, milady," he mocks.

"Don't fucking call me that. Call me Scar," I roar. The name

Scarla seems too cutesy for my mood, but Scar is perfect.

"Yes, Scar," he says, with some of his mocking tone gone. It's hot as Hades. This dominant male who could smite me with a mere thought—one of the few beings in existence who could beat me—is doing as he's told for once.

"Don't look at me. Eyes on the floor," I snap, and, through some miracle, he obeys. I stalk closer and run my hand around his chest, feeling him shiver beneath my touch. "This is payback for not letting me orgasm yesterday," I whisper.

Honestly, I don't know if I'm furious or just playing a role, but I'm loving the power. "On your knees," I say, and he throws me a mischievous glance, loaded with fire, but kneels at my feet. I cup his stubbled jaw and yank his head up, though he's not far off my height, even cut off at the knees.

I smash my mouth roughly against his, grinding my lips and sucking on his, not caring if I hurt him. His jaw is so rough and masculine that I don't ever want to let go. Compared to him, I'm tiny and feminine, and I like the novelty of that sensation.

"Today is all about my pleasure," I growl, and heat sparks inside me, igniting my skin. From this angle, I can see all the way down his body, but his pants are blocking my view.

I step back. "Remove your trousers then resume that position," I order, then I stand back and watch the show. His black pants catch on his huge cock, and when he tugs them off, I swear I feel it as though he's rubbing me in just the right spot.

Already, I'm aching for his touch. Right there, between my legs, my need is pooling and hot.

He kneels, and I come closer, grabbing his jaw again, letting the heat build in the inch of air that separates our bodies. He groans as I kiss him and bite his upper lip. Now I can see him properly. His huge cock juts out like it's reaching for me, and it jumps when I whisper in his ear. "Good boy."

"I can hear your heart hammering," he tells me, his ears in line with my chest. I nearly brush against him with every shallow breath. But I resent the nod to emotion, the implication of feelings, the involvement of the heart.

"This isn't about my heart," I growl. "This is purely physical."

But that's a lie. Otherwise I wouldn't feel bad for touching Jonah. I wouldn't care that Zaden left me unsatisfied yesterday—I'd just have finished off the job myself, under my blankets or in the bath.

No, this is about Zaden and me, but I can't admit that. Not to him. Not to this lying scumbag of an angel who's kept me from my mother.

"In that case," he purrs, picks me up, and throws me on the bed, landing on top of me, caging my head with his hands. "I'll do as I please." He shoves a knee between my thighs and presses, pushing my pants and panties up against my core, making everything wet.

I can't help but moan, but then I push back against his rock-hard chest. "Get off me, asshole."

He smirks, and I want to slap that bloody grin off his face. "Yes, Scar."

I scramble to my feet, trying to get my breathing under control. His layers of perfection glisten before me, all hard planes and firm contours, muscle sculpted from rock.

One minute he's pinning me down, showing his strength, and now he's back to his obedient dog routine? I'm getting whiplash from his mood changes.

I slip out of my shirt and pants, and his hungry gaze watches my every move. He's standing like a soldier at ease, with his hands clasped behind his back, but the muscles in his arms twitch, and I can tell he's struggling to stay still.

Smiling with power, I rush to him like a magnet and wrap my fingers around his silken cock. He groans, almost a roar, and I release him in a flash, earning a moan of frustration. Gotta say, I do not mind behind his puppet master.

"For fuck's sake, Scar," he spits out. "Touch me."

I bend down and place the lightest of kisses on his tip, smelling his musky scent, thrilling in my power over him. I whisper so the heat of my breath caresses his cock, but nothing else. "Will you take me to meet a Nashanti?"

While I have him under my control, it's the perfect time to get what I need from him. He must know some of these desert people, so he can damn well introduce me.

"What? No. I'm busy."

Despite myself, I laugh. He's earned a lick, so I run my tongue from his base to his tip, long and slow. I can feel his eyes burning into my back, my ass, the curve of my hips as I bend down.

Then I smack his cock with my palm. "Wrong answer." He growls and loses his composure, reaching for my waist. I slap his hand away. "No touching until you promise to introduce me to a Nashanti."

"Why?" he snarls, gaze roving over my breasts.

"You know why." With deliberate slowness and my eyes locked on his open mouth, I run my hands over my body to make him squirm. Not at all because it feels fucking sensational.

"No. Desert's Maw is too dangerous."

I reach out and tweak his nipple, hard. "I can take care of

myself."

He moans. "Bitch."

"Asshole," I spit, and his lips curve.

I see it in his eyes a moment before I feel it. He pounces at me like a freaking mountain lion and pins me against the wall, slamming me hard but cushioning my head with his palm. "Playtime's over," he snarls in my ear, sending gooseflesh shooting down my legs.

He grips me by the ass and lowers me over his cock, which slides inside me like oiled steel, filling me completely. A shriek escapes me—a Maker-be-damned shriek. I'd be embarrassed if I wasn't so drenched in desire.

"Do you like that?" he purrs.

"No," I snarl, and he chuckles darkly.

"Then I'll stop, shall I?"

I curl one hand behind his neck and grip his bulging bicep with the other. "Don't you fucking dare."

His muscles bunch and release as he moves me up and down, meeting me with hip thrusts and screwing his face in desire.

I fucking love this male. I fucking hate this male.

His fingers dig painfully into my hips, and I grip his bicep tighter, watching it flex.

The fire inside me burns brighter with every thrust, every moan, every flex until it explodes, throwing sparks all through my body and as far as the heavens. My muscles shudder, and I collapse against Zaden as he groans and thrusts into me one last time, releasing his control completely.

He holds me close, and I relax against him, breathing, sagging, happy. My inner rage is extinguished, my demons sated.

I smile happily into his perfect golden skin, resting against his chest and listening to his heart. Maybe I'll keep cuddling him like a monkey for the rest of my life, my legs around his waist and my arms tucked under his, wrapped in our musky scents.

But he ruins it. "Don't go to Desert's Maw, Scar."

I sigh. "I need to see my mother. To ask her why she left and if she's working for some higher purpose I can help with. I need to make my life count." I disentangle my limbs from his and drop to the floor.

"It's too dangerous."

"Not for me. If I can beat your guards, I can beat anyone."

He holds my stare for a long moment, arms loose and limber by his sides. Our future, his and mine, depends on his answer. I wonder if he knows it.

If he lets me go, it proves he cares. He doesn't just want me for Gaze, but he cares about me. My wants, my needs, my life. I'll give him all the time he needs to make the right choice.

He shakes his head. "You're not going. I can't risk losing you."

My heart breaks. It shatters into two pieces—one lodged in his chest like a dagger, and the other dripping and bleeding in my own.

That's it. It's all about him. He can't risk losing me and his precious Gaze. He doesn't actually care about what I want.

"Fine." I retract my emotions from the room, dress quickly, and take my lacerated heart out into the tower.

But there's nothing fine about it.

Scar

It isn't difficult to get to Angel VanDyke's castle in Solren. It's as simple as snapping my fingers and ordering a coach—Zaden's footmen and guards respect me, even if he doesn't.

The journey is long and uncomfortable, and when we take the spiral road up to the city's sealed section, which is elevated above the rest of the town, I know we're almost there. The jostling carriage finally pulls to a stop.

"Wait for me here," I command.

"Yes, milady," the footman says, and I just nod, beyond caring to correct him.

The palace rises white and gold in the middle distance, a magnificent ode to elegant excess, serene against dusk's gaudy pink streaks. Before I can get there, I need to pierce the shimmering protective dome and get through the two sets of castle walls.

My stride is steady, powerful, and my magic hums in my veins, ready to rise to my defense.

At the first wall, a guard wearing the Count's dark gray uniform with the slash of indigo down the sleeve steps in front of me. "Halt. Who goes there."

I smile and cock out a hip. "Relax, dude. It's just me, Scar.

VanDyke's expecting me," I lie. I can't quite force myself to spit out my full name, though I know that would sound more official. I don't want to be associated with my mother, who ran away from me. And I feel more like a Scar than a Scarla.

"You're not on the register," the man grunts, but his muscles relax minutely, and I can tell I'm winning him over.

"You do remember me, right?" I try for a joyous smile, but I'm not sure I have it in me. This guy won't be joining my friends list any time soon. "I left here in a glorious battle, right after being held prisoner." I stick my hip out the other way, pleased that he glances down at it. "Now, why would I willingly walk back into the castle if I wasn't invited?"

He looks me up and down. "Well..."

"Alone," I add in a conspiratorial whisper. "So please let me through while you sort out this error in your register. I need to be inside before dusk's end. And if you find out I was lying, then feel free to stop me on the way out."

I sashay past him with a winning wink, hoping he doesn't bar my way. His partner glances up from his card game as I walk through the arched gateway and assesses me as I pass but makes no move to stop me.

The no man's land between the two sets of walls is a ring of vibrant grass with a row of colorful poppies set against the inner wall. It smells fresh and rich, like Penngrove Forest. A gardener is on his knees in the soil by the flowers, pulsing with a deep green light the color of a lush forest. He must be a Grower.

It must be wonderful to have a vestigial power that can only be used to improve the world. So benign and helpful. Nothing but pretty flowers and life-giving trees—no bloodshed or politics for him.

It's a pure vestigial skill, so to inherit it, I'd have to wait patiently by his side until he died. Perhaps I could marry him and live a quiet life among the greenery. Even then, I might miss the moment of his passing, and it would have all been for nothing.

Dark vestiges don't need such patience—they're rewarded by instant gratification. Frankly, I can see the appeal.

I crunch along the cobblestone path to the inner wall. The second set of guards is not so easily fooled as the first. Three stand at attention outside the arched stone gateway, their indigo-slashed livery mirroring the sky's shards of pink and purple.

"You have no business here," the middle man growls. He is grizzled, with bushy gray eyebrows and a kind face.

"Neither do you, Pa," I say sadly, unsure what prompted the words. He is here to defend an angel with his life—an angel who doesn't care if this kind-faced man lives or dies.

"Turn and get on your way. You have no Angel of Malanox to help you this time." His words seethe in fury, and I wonder if he knew some of the guards Zaden killed during our escape.

Who am I kidding? Of course he knew them. He must have trained with them, dined with them, lived with them. They were his family.

I sigh, resigning myself to becoming an uncaring monster. Because the truth is, I can't bring myself to give a shit. Perhaps a flicker of discomfort traverses my heart, but the solid truth is that these men choose to serve Angel VanDyke, and no amount of wishing otherwise changes that fact.

"Let me pass," I say steadily. Obviously, flirting won't work here.

"This is your last warning," the kind-faced man growls.

I can see he means it, so with a resigned sigh, I strike. I gently squeeze the ribbon of light at the top of the guard's spine, and he instantly collapses.

His two partners follow. One moment they are standing, and the next, they are arrayed on the lush green grass like discarded puppets. The guy on the left landed on his nose, so he'll wake up sore and bleeding and have a good story to tell his mates.

I stride through the inner gateway, thrumming with power.

My celestial knife is in my hand. Two men run at me, and I kick the first in the stomach while putting the other to sleep with my gentling Gaze. The first guard soon joins him on the grass.

It feels unfair that I can narrow their spine ribbons from a distance without putting myself in danger. But I'd be stupid not to. A sea of dark gray and indigo-slashed uniforms runs at me, and I fell each man with a thought and a moment's concentration.

But somebody is behind me. I spin and kick out low, my boots wiping him off his feet, and a moment later, he is sleeping.

Breathing heavily, I uncoil to my full height and resheathe my blade. It doesn't have a speck of blood on it.

Men litter the grass. They will wake soon, but I'll be long gone.

I spy five Growers attending the gardens, which are even more luscious here in the palace's inner sanctum. Spectacular. Envy spears me in place for a few moments while I watch their simple, beautiful work, wishing for their lives instead of mine.

But my burning ambition for change would never be satisfied tending to the lawns of monsters.

Leo greets me outside the palace doors. "You make quite

an entrance," he remarks with a lopsided grin, motioning to the fallen guards littering the grounds behind me. His breath hitches as he takes me in properly. "You look beautiful, Scar."

Regret and longing fill his expression, but I am fresh out of pity.

I examine him closely. His familiar red hair, which brought so much color and life to the Undercity, is smoothed flat and greased into conformity. His pallor is the dull, sickly green of an old bruise, making every effort at joy look contrived.

"You look ill." I brush past him and sweep into the entrance hall. He always followed my lead, and I don't intend to change our dynamic just because he's playing a little lordling.

"No, I'm well. Thanks for asking," he says, following me in.

"I didn't," I say flatly, looking around.

The floor is a sea of white marble veined with gold, and vast white pillars grow to the distant ceiling, which depicts mortals adoring a golden angel. Subtle. Elegant gold-edged sofas with cream velvet are the only nod to comfort, but they look as if they've never graced an ass, human or otherwise.

No sign of VanDyke.

"I said you look sick because you have the murky glow of an evil vestige."

Leo clears his throat, but his smile doesn't falter. He just chuckles, like we aren't discussing the fact he murdered somebody to get his vestigial power. "I prefer the term mirror vestige."

I chew my lip, unshuttering Gaze to see if VanDyke is anywhere in the palace. A bright orange blob shimmers through the stone of the walls, somewhere off to my left and several stories up. "And I prefer friends who aren't murderers, but the Maker doesn't care what we want."

"You've killed too, Scar."

VanDyke's orange glow is on the move, weaving through corridors and growing bigger, coming closer. I snap my attention to Leo. "Skitter beetles don't count."

He raises an eyebrow. "And the guards out there?" He motions toward the gardens, where I left dozens of men on the ground. "Are they no better than skitter beetles?"

Interesting. He doesn't know I left them alive. Every single one is still breathing and will wake up later with nothing worse than a headache and maybe a broken bone or two.

But I don't bother correcting him. There's no point. I have zero interest in impressing Leo or having him think well of me. And, frankly, I don't deserve the credit.

I would have killed those men, every last one, if I wasn't worried about my place in heaven.

A dark chuckle escapes me as I realize I'm no better than a murderer. Just a cowardly one, too scared for my own future.

Leo misinterprets the sound and leans in as though we're co-conspirators. "There's still hope for us, you know. We still want the same things."

"No," I say flatly, "we don't. You want to control me, and I want to be free. I'd say it's pretty hard to reconcile those. Unless by the same things you mean opposite things."

He smiles as though we're bantering, like back in the old days, and I suppose we are. But it feels different. My heart feels flat, which I believe is because half of it is embedded in Zaden's chest like a dagger, and only the bleeding dregs are left inside me.

But it doesn't feel like sorrow or loss. It feels like nothing. Like my body is hollow, the place where my soul should be is just an empty tree trunk that was killed by lightning.

VanDyke's orange glow is bobbing closer, so I get to the point. "Leo, if our friendship ever meant anything to you, you have to tell me how to get to Desert's Maw. My mother is still alive, and I know she must have left for a reason. A really good fucking reason. So I need to find her and help her."

To Leo's credit, he swallows that mountain of information with dignity and only sputters briefly before snapping out of it.

"She's alive?"

"Yes, in Desert's Maw. How did you get there? And don't tell me you slept in foxes burrows because I don't buy it. You went with the Nashanti, didn't you?"

Leo's brown eyes grow wide, and his freckles stand out against his cheeks. "I...Yes. How do you know about them? And what's your mom doing in Desert's Maw?"

Emotion other than anger enters my voice, but I still don't feel it in my bones. It sounds like desperation, so maybe it is. "She left her family to go there. Her husband, her two young daughters. She must have had good reason. Something better than her whole life. I know she's fighting to change the power imbalance in the world, I just know it."

Leo's eyes are earnest. They transport me back to the Undercity when he was my most trusted friend and would believe me, even if nobody else did. I give in to the temptation to lean forward on my toes to inhale his grainy scent, but it's gone. He smells of greasy hair oil now.

"How do you know?"

"I can just tell. It's a bloodbond, I suppose." It doesn't matter how I know, it just matters that I find her. Even if she's sitting in a bucket of shit and sucking off lords for cash, she's still my mom. I shift impatiently. "So how can I find the

Nashanti? How did you find them?"

Leo glances around as though he doesn't want to be over-heard, then leans close. "It's a family secret."

"You always said I was family," I counter. I'm happy to play the friendship card if it gets me to Desert's Maw.

"Yes, but I didn't arrange it. My dad did. He worked for years to sort it out, proving himself reliable to the Nashanti, performing secret tasks for them. Just to get me to Desert's Maw."

I search for the tic in his jaw, his telltale sign that he's lying. But he isn't—his face is as smooth as the marble floor, and his brown eyes are wide with sincerity.

"Why?" I demand, but we're running out of time for lengthy explanations. VanDyke is getting closer. Impatience flutters in my veins.

"Dad wanted to start a trade route with Desert's Maw. He figured he could set himself up as a merchant and buy one of those big fancy houses in Hightown. But when he went lame, he shifted the plan to me."

I cut him off. "Greed, I get it."

Leo frowns. "Ambition. Dad just wanted more for himself in this world. Same as you and me."

I fold my arms across my chest. "The difference is that I want a better world for everyone, not just me."

Leo shrugs, like there's no difference, and opens his mouth to speak, but we're running out of time. "How did you get home?" I hiss.

"I Coerced some Ashanti to bring me home. But I'm not in contact with them. I can't help you, Scar. I'm sorry."

"Coerced?"

He twists his lips, and finally something close to shame

shutters his eyes. "That's my mirror skill. Coercion." He shrugs again. "It's not foolproof, but it's helpful at times."

Understanding grows in my belly like a shrub. Leo's sudden buddy-buddyness with the Undercity Council after he returned, his mysterious meetings with Pa Loonta. How he borrowed that Maker-be-damned horse to come rescue me.

"Fuck," I breathe.

"Yeah," he agrees.

Van Dyke's glow is almost life-sized now, and when he arrives, I don't want to be sitting in the foyer like I'm waiting for admittance, so I sweep into the adjoining reception room.

This is where I last saw the Cloaked King after being forced to join him for dinner upstairs. The foul, stocky man dripping in dead animal fat who inflicted me with pain.

A fitting place to exact my revenge on VanDyke. I finger the dagger hidden under my jacket. The short, dead straight blade with the intricate hilt and the glowing emerald. Zaden's finest gift to me and one he may end up regretting.

I don't want to use it. I'm still hedging my bets about that bloody angel Zaden, and if I kill, I will never get into heaven.

But I'm not stupid enough to pretend I don't have it. It's the most potent weapon in my arsenal and the only one of any use against an angel.

Leo follows me into the reception room. "You shouldn't have come back," he murmurs. We both know VanDyke still wants to control me. To control Gaze. His aspirations of overthrowing the Cloaked King are admirable—I kind of want the same thing. But I don't want to install myself as his replacement. I just want to dismantle the whole damn thing.

"I'm not planning on staying," I say.

VanDyke glides into the dining hall in full cherubic glory, like he just stepped out of a painting. White-blond curls frame his symmetrical face, and his ivory robes sweep the marble floor. His straight white teeth are perfection, a nice contrast against his fine rose lips. But a faint Z-shaped scar mars his rosebud cheek, and I shimmer in satisfaction at seeing it, evidence of Zaden beating the crap out of him.

The angel throws his arms wide and speaks like honey over butter. "Scarla, darling. How wonderful of you to return."

Power pulses from him, and fear constricts my throat for a moment. No matter how strong I am against mortals and vestiges, I will always be at the mercy of angels. That fact sticks in my gaw like a pigeon bone.

Leo steps forward. "Let her go," he says sharply, and a pulse of his sickly green glow wraps around the angel. "She will return when she is ready and give us Gaze." Leo's voice is laced with Coercion, deep and commanding. Even though I can see the magic, I'm still compelled to agree with his excellent points.

If VanDyke could see his Coercion, he would resist it. But without knowing Leo's using it, he's vulnerable.

Not for the first time, I'm amazed at how much power Gaze grants me. I chalk up resistance to Coercion, though I can see my resistance is shaky at best.

VanDyke crosses to me and runs a finger down my cheek. I slide my fist around the hilt of my blade beneath my jacket, waiting for the moment to strike.

"Yes," the angel purrs, "I believe she will. You'll come back and see me when you're ready to die, won't you, darling?"

In just one quick motion, I could stab this asshole in the heart and wipe that self-satisfied smirk off his face. I glance at Leo, who pleads with me silently to go along with his Coercion.

I force my eyes to crinkle. "Of course." Surely a deaf man could hear the lie in my words, but they seem to satisfy VanDyke.

I stride from the castle without a backward glance. I have retained my life and my clean soul, but I'm no closer to getting to Desert's Maw. My hopes were pinned on Leo, but he was as useless as ever.

There's only one place left I can think to try.

Scar

Bwadu told me she lives on the Rim. I don't know much about Solren, but the Rim has a reputation that extends even as far as Malanox. Rumor has it that the Rim is a run-down couple of streets where the city's rejects gather. Crime, murder, disease—these words populate my thoughts.

Putting two and two together, I figure the Rim must run near the Rim Road. The sealed section of Solren is on a circular platform where the elite live. It is lifted above the rest of the city, like a massive round dais in the middle of Solren. The only access to the raised sealed city is via the Rim Road. As the name suggests, the Rim Road follows the circumference of the seal and marks its boundary.

The Rim Road spirals up from the lower city, completing a full circle and ending fifty feet higher than it started. The Rim is tucked in beneath the layers, underneath the sealed city and still protected by the seal's power.

It doesn't take long to find the access point. The sealed city is only about twenty-five blocks across, and I know where the Rim Road reaches level with it. I spot some rough stone stairs that take me down to a maintenance passageway.

An odd sliver of buildings, tucked beneath the sealed city, squeezed in beside the road, which curves up and around us.

Archways support the rising road, each with a dwelling covered with grimy boards.

Who would choose to live here?

But there's more to it than the naked eye can see. My Gaze can see the outline of tunnels pulsing below my feet, a warren of alternative routes into the city. It seems that not everybody enters the sealed section through the official checkpoint at the Rim Road's base.

This is the dingiest place I've ever been and the most overtly dangerous. But I'm not scared. Not one cell of my body is afraid. I'm strong and feel like I could take on the world. I'm more motivated than ever to take down the angels, seeing this disgraceful evidence of how little they care for the mortals they rule.

I stride along until I get to a boarded-up archway that glows under Gaze. The dim lights of vestiges shine through the walls, so this must be the right place.

A man wearing the gray overalls of a maintenance worker slouches against the wall, stinking of alcohol. But his muscles are toned, and his posture too alert. Plus, he has the vibrant blyberry blue glow that some of Zaden's soldiers have. The strongest ones. It's the blue I associate with strength. Although this man's is muted, like the blyberries have rotted, oozing and seeping... a sick version of blue.

He must have the mirror of strength. What does that do? I should have grilled Zaden on all the different vestigial powers and their mirrors, because I'm woefully unprepared for this, and I can only blame myself.

What is the opposite of strength? Weakness, I suppose. But why would you kill somebody to become weaker?

As I step forward, I have my answer. I grow weaker with

every movement until I can barely muster the energy to breathe.

I give in and stop. I take a step back, out of range of his power, and energy floods my body again. His vestigial power doesn't make him weaker, it weakens others.

"You there," I say.

His quads tighten, but he doesn't look up, still playing the part of the drunk worker.

I don't have time for this. That part where we play games and dance around each other until he grudgingly respects me and lets me in. So I cut to the chase. "I need to see Bwadu."

That gets his attention. He drops the slouch and straightens, meeting me eye-to-eye. "Nobody sees the General."

General? I didn't know Bwadu was a General, but I can't say I'm surprised. That explains her lethal poise and intimidating presence.

But what does she lead? An underground rebellion of some kind, obviously. Perhaps they're planning a coup against the angels, just like my mother. If I can find Mom, then we can join forces and work together to—

I'm getting carried away, but hope flares in my chest nonetheless. I consider incapacitating this guard just by pressing that narrow ribbon of light behind his neck, but that doesn't seem like the best way to kick off a friendship.

And I'm sure that's what it will be. We're on the same side. We'll fight together in the end, I just know it. So I don't want to cause any more bloodshed. I aim for pleasantries instead. "I met General Bwadu in Castle VanDyke. We were both prisoners, and we escaped together. I guarantee she will want to see me."

The guard sucks his teeth. "Wait here."

He disappears behind the boarding, and the lingering effects of his power leave with him until I feel myself again, powerful, unstoppable.

I wait an eternity. A leaf blows presses against the upper edge of an archway, held by the same wind that flicks copper hair into my eyes. Suddenly, the leaf pops up over the edge and onto the roadway above. No carriages pass at night, so the leaf won't be trampled under hooves. I imagine it floating upward on a draught and flying over the outer city, freezing and crumbling like rain over the homes.

Fatigue drags at my limbs moments before the guard reappears. I can see why he gets door duty—nobody would want to hang out with him inside. What a total bummer of a power.

He leads me inside the warren of tunnels. We descend some stairs and then double back, presumably passing beneath the maintenance tunnel and deeper into the sealed city. The walls are rock in some parts, wood in others, like we're walking between buildings and dugouts.

Eventually, we come to an open room, broad and long but with a low ceiling. Tables, chairs, and a ragtag bunch of folks lounging about. Several of them are vestiges, most of them not. I'm surprised to see a heap of people with gray hair and even a couple of kids. This isn't the army I was expecting.

Everybody turns around when we enter, and the room falls silent.

A slight man steps forward. A dragon tattoo runs up his left cheek from his lips to his hairline, but it's nothing compared to the scowl on his face. "What do you want?" he demands.

I ignore him for the moment and scan the crowd, looking for Molly. I can't see her, but dozens of shapes lurk in the shadows, an uncountable number of observers.

A young woman with a solid yellow glow cowers behind an

older woman who is clearly her boss. She scolds her young apprentice, who turns beetroot and mutters something that is probably an apology.

I ignore the man with the dragon tattoo and step between the old woman and her protege. "Show her more respect," I command. "She has the strongest healing power here. Much stronger than yours."

The crowd gasps as though I've just pulled off the best party trick ever. They should see Leo cry milk.

Dragon man grunts. "Lucky guess," he drawls.

It's easy enough to prove my usefulness, so I point to the man with a strong green glow. "He's your best Grower." I indicate a man with a weak orange glow. "This one's a Faunus." The man looks confused, so I explain. "You're good with animals. You probably find creatures are drawn to you, but it isn't strong." The man nods. Several people glow with the vibrant blyberry of Clout, so I point them out as the strongest fighters.

The room practically bloody applauds when I'm finished.

As though I've passed some test, Bwadu emerges from the shadows. The dragon man bows to her. Clearly, Bwadu is the true leader here.

I step toward her, but an arm bars my way. I sigh my impatience. "We need to talk."

Bwadu is leonine, strong, and every inch a warrior. Her dark skin reflects the candlelight in flashes as she stalks toward me. That curling leaf tattoo on her left temple flickers orange. "You may speak freely."

I look around. So many ears here, and I don't trust any of them. What I have to say could get me killed by a pissed-off angel in a heartbeat—angels love a good smiting. I shake my head. "Not here."

Bwadu exchanges a glance with a slim, dark-skinned woman whose eyebrows are joined by a horizontal black tattoo. A cord of intimacy pulses between the two women, a current of conversation that I can't follow but only observe. They share a closeness I can only imagine.... One I thought possible with Zaden at one stage, in my naivety. Jealousy tightens my chest, but I can't draw my eyes from the tenderness between Bwadu and her lover.

The other woman nods slightly, granting permission for Bwadu to leave.

The General takes my hand and leads me out a door into a smaller space. She fiddles with a hook, and a leather curtain swooshes into place, separating us from the larger room.

"This is a nice setup," I begin, feeling foolish for commenting on the decor.

Bwadu gives me the look my comment deserves. "It's a place to be," she says, like that makes any sense. She really is a mysterious woman, and I can't get a handle on her. Even with my months of training and growing, I'm still intimidated.

"You're leading a rebellion," I say, and she slides into a seat with feline grace, motioning to a sleek leather-backed chair opposite her. I sit. "Among other things."

She nods, and the trace of a smile lights her face. "Oh yes? You seem to know a lot about it."

Somebody brings two steaming mugs of tea that smell and look like muddy water, hands them to Bwadu and me, then leaves.

The thread of tunnels around us pulses with faint light, and I take a few more guesses. "You smuggle things into the sealed city. Things the elite want but can't openly allow. Like..."

Actually, I can't think of anything the rich people couldn't get with a snap of their fingers.

"Like opium," Bwadu finishes for me. "Or siblings."

I almost choke on my tea. "What?"

"People whose brother, sisters, nephews, aunts haven't been allowed into the sealed section. I can get them in."

"For the right price."

Bwadu shrugs, not shying away from the truth. "I need to fund my real work." She's skirting around the rebellion. She must be General of something, after all.

"You use the underground tunnels," I declare.

Bwadu raises a black eyebrow. "You're a fast learner. Or an excellent guesser."

I sip my herby brew, trying not to grimace at the taste. I won't tell her about Gaze detecting the magic imbued in the warren of passages. She doesn't need to know the full extent of my abilities.

"Is Molly here?" I nod toward the other room. "Out there somewhere?"

She thinks for a moment. "No."

Disappointment spikes my gut, and I slouch. Molly is the only person left I can trust. The only person I can love. And she's still missing. I was sure she was working with Bwadu, but I was wrong. Fuck.

Bwadu folds her arms across her chest. "But I can find her. Or find out what happened to her," she adds darkly

I refuse the implication, not entertaining for a moment the idea that something terrible happened to my best friend. My only friend. "Thank you," I murmur.

"She is my ally, as are you. I will not leave her in need." Bwadu's glare is matter-of-fact, so my thank-you seems out of place, too small. "Is that why you sought me out?"

I chew my lip. "It's one reason. I also need to get to Desert's Maw to find my mother. I think she's fighting the angels' rule, and I intend to help her."

If that shocks Bwadu, it doesn't show on her face. "Stay here and fight alongside us."

I knew it. They really are fighting the same cause as me—well, apart from the fact I'm sleeping with an angel. "I'll come back. I promise. But first, I have to see my mother. I need to meet with the Nashanti."

Bwadu's dark eyes swallow the light. "The Nashanti must not be dealt with lightly. If you make a bargain with a Nashanti, you must honor it. They will hound your bloodline for generations if you fail to."

Bwadu explains that the Nashanti used to dwell on ships many generations ago. They made an agreement with an ancient people, the Strethu, to come ashore and trade. While they were on land, the Strethu betrayed the accord, burned the Nashanti's ships, and then forced them into the desert.

The Nashanti made the desert their own, settling deeper into the land, burrowing beneath the red dirt, and building new lives. But they never forgot the betrayal of the Strethu. It took generations, but they eventually killed every last descendant of the Strethu, wiping the entire race from the earth.

"Do not make a bargain with the Nashanti that you don't intend to keep."

I shudder and promise never to betray the desert folk. If I can ever find one. Bwadu cannot make an introduction because she steers clear of the Nashanti. My trip here was a Maker-be-damned waste.

I haven't finished my tea, but Bwadu rises to her feet in a

smooth motion and plucks the mug from my grasp. Obviously our meeting is over. "If you make it to Desert's Maw, seek my sister Mahari at The Jagged Tooth. She will assist you."

I clamber to my feet, way less gracefully than the General. "The what?"

"The Jagged Tooth is a tavern. Tell her you're my friend."

If she's as fierce as her sister, this Mahari will probably stab me before she chats with me. "Will she believe me?"

"Give her this token. Tell her I gave it to you."

Bwadu holds out her hand and drops the token into my open palm. When I see what she's given me, I know something for a fact. If I ever make it to Desert's Maw, I will get myself fucking killed.

Scar

The coach takes me back to Malanox. I swear the coachman hits every pothole on purpose, probably giggling like mad at my increasingly sore ass. We make it across the Hightown bridge just at snowfall, and by the time we pull up to the castle forecourt, thick snowflakes are covering the flagstones.

It seems weeks since I crept out of bed to apologize to Jonah in the barracks, but it was just this morning. Or yesterday, I suppose, since it's after snowfall, marking the official beginning of a new day.

I yawn and stumble upstairs to my bedchamber, but sleep doesn't find me. It's as elusive as my Maker-be-damned mother. After several hours of turning about on my mattress, which doesn't feel so soft tonight, I give up and slip into my new blue shirt and black pants. Might as well use the time usefully.

The dim glow of magic in the walls lights my way along the corridors and out to the training yard. It is a sorcered space, but I imagine I'll have it to myself at this time of night anyway.

Snow falls thick and fast, blinding me, but I know the way and don't falter. It reminds me of those midnight walks I used to take as an escape from the Undercity, filled with wonder at the world's beauty and looking for any chance to soak up the solitude.

But tonight, the peace and calm of those walks are missing. All I sense is a tangling of fate, like ropes twisting around my legs but I keep walking, oblivious, until I inevitably fall.

Under cover of the training yard, I pick up a wooden sword and practice my drills, swipe, dart, lunge, until a light sweat coats my limbs. I need this release of tension and mindless focus even more than my poor body needs sleep. The thud of my feet against the ground in hypnotic, soothing, and my deep breaths fall into the same rhythm as my strikes.

A movement from the periphery snags my attention, and I spy Zaden mirroring my moves with his own.

He'd better not come over here and demand to know where I went and why I took his carriage. Or I'll swap this wooden sword for a real one and slice him open.

He doesn't approach. He just runs through his own training moves, sliding over the hard ground like water over a rock. Even training alone, he's graceful. I can't help comparing his movements to Jonah's. Zaden is fluid grace, a dancer, compared to Jonah's miner-like stomping.

Maybe he comes out here every night and trains alone? Perhaps he sneaks out while I'm sleeping, works up a sweat, then slides between our sheets before I wake.

I move to another corner and pick up a bow and arrow. This isn't my weapon of choice, and frankly, I suck worse even than Leo at archery, but I need to test Zaden.

Sure enough, he follows suit, choosing his own bow plus quiver.

Yep, he's definitely tailing me. Protective asshole.

I can't put it off any longer. I march up to Zaden, his dark bulk growing larger until he looms above me. His short hair is somehow disheveled, and his stubble looks extra rough.

"Scarla," he says, and the sound of my name on his lips almost undoes me.

I straighten my spine with steel. "I'm going to Desert's Maw, with or without your help."

His lips thin, and I can't help but notice his sword is still out, an ominous dark shape in his hand. Very much within reach.

Dammit, I wish I was taller so I could see him eye to eye. I edge my voice to make up for my lack of height. "But I'd be much more likely to survive if I have it. Your help. Otherwise I'll waste your precious Gaze by dehydrating in the desert with nobody around to benefit."

Zaden's jaw ticks like I'm pissing him off by implying he only cares about Gaze. Good. I want to piss him off.

And I mean it too. I'll walk across the bloody desert until my feet bleed and my kidneys collapse.

"Fine," he growls.

My heart beats. "Really?" I can't keep the delight from my voice. "Thank you!"

He just scowls. "It's a long journey."

"How long?"

I realize I have no idea how far it is, how broad the desert is, how big an ask this is. I think it took Leo three weeks to cross, although he's always cagey on the matter. So I guess that makes it way farther than Solren. And not in the friendliest of terrains.

Zaden sheathes Jonshu with a clear ring of steel. "Long enough."

I huff. "That's not an answer."

"You don't deserve an answer," he seethes.

He's angry! At my leaving? At my fury? At how I ran away to

Solren without mentioning it? Don't know, don't care... except I do, of course, which pisses me off even more.

"Okay, fine." I won't allow myself to get sucked into his emotional turmoil. He can have his little hissy fit, it doesn't bother me. As long as he takes me to Desert's Maw.

"We leave at dawn sharp," Zaden says, then stalks away and disappears into the swirling snow.

* * *

Sleep eludes me, and I spend the rest of the night imagining Mom's face when she sees me, trying to picture Desert's Maw, and basically attempting to contain my nerves.

As the sun peeks over my mountain home, I stumble out into the castle forecourt. Zaden is already there. He nods at me once and beckons me closer. He manhandles me into position, and I'm too tired to object. His hands on my shoulders are rough and warm as he rotates me, so my back is pressed against his chest. I wonder if he's thinking about the places where our bodies meet or if he's too full of seething rage.

Zaden clips me to his front in a harness, so he doesn't have to cradle me on the long trip to Desert's Maw.

I feel like a parcel being delivered to Hightown. Or a baby suckling at my (terrifying) mother's teat.

"Ready, Scar?" he murmurs into my ear, his warm breath sending tingles down my legs.

"Yes." But I'm not. I want to call the whole thing off, crawl under my covers, and let somebody else deal with all the crap in the world. I'm terrified of how my mother will react to seeing me. Whether I'll recognize her. If she's even alive.

My stomach drops as we launch into the sky with powerful

beats of Zaden's midnight wings, soaring over the vertical sheet of steam evaporating from the river and northward over the desert.

The Dead Desert is a place of myth. So far below me, it looks like a benign red plain with bundles of lost leaves tumbling in the wind.

But I know it's so much more. Legend has it that the desert used to be lush forestland with wildflowers peeking out among meandering streams, rife with life. Until a sorceress was imprisoned in a stone cottage, her evil spread through the land, killing everything it touched.

I scan the ground, looking for signs of the witch, wondering if she was a vestige too. She must have been mighty if her evil affected the landscape, turning the lush green forest into the dead red land beneath me.

There's no sign of ancient rivers or an old stone cottage. No indication that the legend about the Dead Desert is true. Only endless reams of red dirt and no relief from the eternal flatness. Impossible to believe anything could live down there, let alone an entire tribe of Nashanti.

The dead land flies beneath us as the sun grows hotter. The angel's wings cast moving shade over me and the red soil below, the only visible movement.

As the burn deepens, the sun reflects so brightly off the sand that it seems to glow white hot, turning from deep umber to a brilliant, lustrous silvery-gold that strains my eyes. With no buildings or structures or mountains to diffuse the sun's glare, it is truly blinding. I wonder that Zaden is able to keep going, because with his heightened senses, the blaring light must be truly horrifying.

Well, I won't mention how damn uncomfortable the glare

makes me—he doesn't deserve to feel smug and superior, Instead, I just close my eyes against the glow, dimming the light enough to save my eyes. Maybe I'll wear a blindfold on the return journey so the damn reflected sunlight isn't so painful.

Despite it all, the bubbling nerves and the baking heat, my head nods and I fall into a fitful slumber, lulled by the steady motion of Zaden's beating wings.

My last thoughts are of Desert's Maw. It's north of Malanox and more temperate, with a longer dawn, longer dusk, and less extreme temperatures. I've heard dawn and dusk last two hours each, so perhaps people spend longer at the markets.

That's the extent of my knowledge of the foreign city, and tendrils of fear squirm in my stomach. But I push them down and force myself to relax as I fall asleep. After all, it's probably no different from Malanox.

Scar

Well shit, was I wrong.

Desert's Maw couldn't be more different from Malanox or even Solren. The streets are already busy, though the sun isn't touching the horizon yet.

Zaden lands awkwardly on a wide brown boulevard, stumbling a few paces in fatigue. I wait impatiently while he unbuckles the harness, scowling at the stares we are attracting.

A family of two harassed mothers wearing yellow dresses and a cacophony of trailing children bumbles past us, and I wonder at seeing folks out in the plain day.

But it really is cooler here. Dusk's fingers spread farther and longer than back home. Living here must be paradise.

"What's that?" I demand, pointing out a series of arcing stone steps around a lowered semi-circular platform.

"An amphitheater for showing plays."

"Plays?"

When he tells me they're like stories, but with people acting out the different parts, I almost shove him in disbelief. I can't picture it. How would they act out the tales about mountains spewing fire that runs down over villages or how the seas rose up in fury and drowned out the fire?

Zaden's probably spinning me bullshit. Again. He probably

thinks it's funny. Like that time he told me my Mom was dead.

But my anger doesn't rise like I expected. So many strange and wonderful sights surround me that I don't have room in my body for fury.

But there are hints that Desert's Maw isn't the paradise I first thought. Grim expressions haunt most people's faces, and their clothes may be spun from brightly colored fabrics, but they're torn and dirty.

Zaden rests a hand on my shoulder, and I sense his weariness.

"Go find us a place to sleep," I tell him.

His wings have disappeared again, but folks are giving us a wide berth, kicking up brown dirt in a circle around us as they pass on an arc.

Zaden nods. He looks so tired. Regret tightens my chest, and I have an impulse to cradle his stubbled jaw in my hands and drag his face down for a kiss.

"Go," I urge. "I'll wait right here. Promise." I settle my ass onto a bench seat, which seems to exist outdoors for that very purpose. I'll never get used to that.

He sees there's no disagreeing with me, and he strides off toward the town center, away from the desert. As soon as he disappears around a corner, I march off in the opposite direction, scanning the crowd as I go.

There. That man trailing soiled root on his foot and stinking of mulled wine is the one. I'd vote him most likely to stab me out of all the people I can see, so he'll probably know where to find The Jagged Tooth.

He does.

I follow the direction of his knotted hand, thankfully away from where Zaden headed. That smelly man must have been a beggar.

Desert's Maw is famous for its beggars—they're about the only thing I know about it. People who don't work but just lie around all day waiting for food. It always sounded lazy to me, and as a kid, I wanted to grow up to become one of these magical beggars who didn't work a day in their life. But this bloke looks like the Maker's snot, and I don't think he's living his best life.

I might have to rethink that life goal.

But his directions are flawless. I felt The Jagged Tooth would be an underbelly establishment, and it seems like I'm right. A sign of a broken incisor swings gently above an ox-hide door, and I push my way through.

Inside is warm and smoky, and sultry music caresses me.

A stout man with trees tattooed on his oversized forearms, which are crossed over his chest, stands in my way. "Pain or pleasure?"

I falter. Is this some kind of entry test? "Pleasure, obviously."

He looks at me like I'm an idiot, which I suppose I am. "It ain't obvious to everyone, sugar." He hooks a thumb over his shoulder at a bunch of bodies squirming in a red-rubber-lined pit, their faces contorted in pain, clearly having the time of their lives.

"It's two gold pieces for pleasure," he says.

I don't have the money. But like hells I'm choosing pain.

He reads my hesitation. "It's five gold for pain. Free to go sit by the bar and watch."

I tilt my head, reading him. He's got a lot of muscle, but it's all for show. But he isn't being a dick about me being clueless, so I throw him a smile. Everything is free in the Undercity, provided by the community fund. I'm not in the habit of paying for things. "That's me, then."

The Jagged Tooth is divided into two distinct halves, separated by a long, narrow bar. The side the doorman directs me to reminds me of the pleasure hubs in the Undercity, but with less flesh, fewer muscles, and not a single boob. Tables are dotted about in the smoky haze, occupied mainly by groups of laughing friends.

I slide onto a stool by the bar, overlooking the room's other half. It is sunken into two pits, one lined with red rubber and the other with purple velvet. Pain and pleasure.

At first glance, it's hard to tell which is which—faces in both pits are contorted, and bodies are writhing, and moans and screams come from both. But that one bloke tearing his fingernails down the red rubber walls leaves bloody trails, so I'm guessing that's pain.

The barman slides a glass of something clear before me. His long pale hair is swept back in a braid, and his right eye is sewn shut but tattooed with an eyeball, making me double-take.

I hold up a hand. "Nothing for me, thanks." I don't have a copper piece on me, and this place is clearly more expensive than it looks.

"On the house," he tells me, then winks. "It's just water."

My throat is parched after our flight, and I gulp the drink greedily. "Thanks."

The man rests his hands on the counter and watches me, ignoring the other customers trying to get his attention. "First time here?"

So much for blending in. I must have *tourist* stamped on my forehead. "Yeah. What's with people paying to get hurt?"

Clearly, somebody is using Inflict on the poor bastards in the pain pit—that much I can understand. But people are paying a fortune to experience it.

The barman slaps the counter. "You get a life experience. Pain beyond compare. And you come out of it without a scratch. What's not to like?"

There's a shitload not to like, but I'm not here to argue. Instead, I play up my flirt and bite my lower lip. His gaze follows precisely where I want. I even twist a strand of my copper hair, though it's not really long enough. "You seem like you know what you're talking about," I purr.

His jaw ticks, and I might be pissing him off, but maybe that's his sign of interest. "Yep."

"I need help." I pout slightly, feeling like an idiot, but he leans forward and rests his elbows on the bar.

"What's up?" he asks.

"I need to find someone called Mahari. Do you know her?"

The barman straightens up and glances behind me but shakes his head. "Sorry, no. Good luck with that." He moves away so fast that it's clear he knows exactly who I'm talking about. And that glance he stole over my shoulder tells me she's here.

But I don't mind waiting. I'm sure I've got her attention now.

I take the opportunity to observe. It's not every day you wind up in a bar in Desert's Maw. Something nags at me, and I can't dismiss it. Something is wrong, and it's not just the masochistic dicks lunging about in agony in the pain pit.

Inflict. I can't see it. Somebody is inflicting pleasure and pain on the paying customers, and I can't detect it.

Shit. Am I losing Gaze? I search about and see several vestiges in the room. A Grower with a dark green glow is

259

rubbing her ass against the purple velvet in the pleasure pit, and behind me, a couple of Healers at a table are shining bright yellow through the smoky room.

So why can't I see Inflict?

I keep watching, searching for the tendrils of magic that must be there, connecting the customers with the Inflictor.

Finally I see her. A woman, perched on a stool off to the side, wearing a red jumpsuit, looking bored out of her brain. She looks like she might leap up to wipe a dirty table or mop a spilled drink.

Unassuming. Innocent. Disguised.

If anybody discovered her identity, they could kill her for Inflict because it's a mirror vestigial skill. So she hides from detection because knowledge is power.

But also, power is power. I could murder this woman and obtain the dyad if I wanted to. A myriad of options is available. Walk right by her and wring her pale neck. Gently squeeze the ribbon of light behind her throat from across the room. Wait for her outside until after closing and strike her with my knife.

So many options. I could become the Cloaked Court's first Queen.

But ruling a bunch of assholes holds no appeal to me.

Nothing much holds any appeal right now except finding Mom.

Plus, the most annoying, girly, princessy part of me still doesn't want to kill anyone... in case I end up in heaven with that irritating fucking angel I seem to be in love with.

So I keep observing, straining to see the Inflictor's magic, staring at her hands which are stubbornly idle in her lap. I sip my water, increasingly irritated that I can't see it.

Finally I notice the floor. Thin veins of magic creep from the

Inflictor across the floor, blending in with the violet vines and flowers that pattern the carpet. The same vibrant violet color snakes towards both pits of revelers, but the shapes the magic traces along the carpet differ.

The pleasure seekers receive thin, feathery magic, which weaves down into their velvet pit like an ancient tapestry, moving sensuously and slowly.

The pain seekers receive whips of violet, thicker and sharper but the same vibrant hue. Even to my trained Gaze, the effect is subtle, nearly invisible against the dark floor and walls of the pits.

I think back to when the Cloaked King inflicted pain on me in VanDyke's palace. I couldn't detect his magic at all, and I wonder if it slunk across the stone floors, creeping along the cracks between pavers.

Maybe I wouldn't have detected it then, even if I'd known where to look. But I've worked hard at my magic in the intervening months and improved greatly. I promise myself that next time I see the Cloaked King, I'll detect his magic too.

Then I'll reveal him and remove the veil of secrecy he hides behind, stripping him of his power. I'll take him and the Cloaked Court down together. That vague idea seems to have formed into an entire plan while I was focussing on finding Mom.

Perhaps she'll even help me achieve it.

An ebony-skinned woman with a high brow and a warrior's stare slides onto the stool beside me. Her thick black hair is shaved against her scalp on one side, and long and loose on the other. "I heard you asking after Mahari," she says by way of introduction. "What do you want with her?"

The woman has the harsh, guttural accent of Desert's Maw,

but her face and composure are so like her sister's that I know her instantly.

I lean an elbow on the bar, aiming for casual. "Do you know her?" I figure I might as well play along with her little game.

Mahari's eyes narrow. "Maybe I do, maybe I don't."

I hide a smile. "You'd probably recognize her if you ever saw her. She looks identical to you. Same prominent cheekbones. Same don't-fuck-with-me stare."

The woman scowls, clearly not enjoying the game as much as I am. "Who are you?" she demands.

"My name is Scar Rosedarter Healer."

Mahari cuts me a sidelong glance. "We don't use Southern names here. Go by Scar." She seems unsure whether to strike or befriend me, but I'll take anyone's advice as long as it's useful.

"Your sister sent me."

"Athara?" she asks over the moans and screams from the pit.

I wonder if that's another test. "No. Bwadu. She... she has a leaf tattooed over her left temple." I hope that will be sufficient to identify me as a friend because I really don't want to show Mahari what her sister gave me.

The warrior's eyes narrow. "Anybody could tell me about her tattoo. It's on her bloody face."

I take a breath. Fine. "She told me to give you this." This is the part where I get killed. I reach into my pocket and retrieve what Bwadu gave me to convince her sister I'm legit.

Mahari's eyes are trained on my outstretched hand. I open my palm to reveal nothing. A big fat nothing. How Bwadu thinks showing my scrawny white hand will convince Mahari I'm for real is beyond me.

After a heartbeat, the imposing woman throws back her head and laughs. The barman raises an eyebrow, making me think it's an unusual sight.

I scowl. "Do you want to tell me what's going on?"

Mahari nods at the barman, who brings her a tall glass misted with green fluid. He slides one my way too and mouths, "On the house."

Mahari takes a sip and sighs. "When we were kids, Bwadu and I made a pact. We'd get rich enough and powerful enough that we would want for nothing. Nothing. That was always the signal that we'd made it."

"Nothing." That's a stupid fucking signal and way too subtle. Mahari could have missed it and instead drawn the dagger I can see stuffed down her boot. But I still need her help, so I take a sip of the frothing green drink to keep my cool. It's good. Damn good. Slightly sweet and very refreshing, with bubbles that make my nose itch.

Mahari slaps her knee. "So, I guess Bwadu's doing well? Does she have anyone special?"

The question jolts me. This fierce woman before me doesn't look like the sentimental type. I think back to the slim, dark-haired woman whose eyebrows were joined by a thick tattoo and who seemed to share an intimate bond with the rebellion's general. "Yeah," I mutter. "She's got someone."

Mahari takes another sip of her green juice. She turns around and surveys the room behind us, but I can't drag my attention away from the pits. "So, you've found me. What do you want with me?"

A curvy woman in a blue jumpsuit in the rubber pit arches her back, and I hold back a wince. "I need your help to find someone." I sigh. I might as well be honest. "My mother. Her name is Rose Pennydarter Healer." I glance at Mahari. "Just Rose, I guess."

Mahari nods her head in time to the sultry, slow music. "Well, Just Scar. I think I know where to find her."

Scar

A shadow moves at the edges of my vision as I follow Mahari out of The Jagged Tooth.

I have a sneaking suspicion it's that sneaky damn angel, who should be off finding us somewhere to sleep instead of trailing me like some sneaky, psychopathic nanny.

But I can't catch sight of him.

"Something wrong?" Mahari asks.

"Nothing," I say curtly. Who knows how she'll react to the Margrave of Malanox following us around? The Jagged Tooth strikes me as an underbelly, resistance type place, not a hangout for celestials. And I can't imagine she spends time there because she wants an angel bestie.

My sense of direction is excellent, but even so, I'm soon lost. The streets of Desert's Maw make no sense to me, with roads intersecting at strange angles, too sharp or too wide. At one point, we take three lefts in a row but end up nowhere near our starting position, like geography works differently on this side of the Dead Desert.

Even the material underfoot can't make up its mind, switching between brown dirt, small pavers, and lengths of bamboo. It's a miracle I haven't twisted an ankle yet, between watching my footing and keeping an eye out for Zaden, who I know is trailing us.

The most striking thing is the color. Back home, everybody wears a variation of brown or gray. The only exception is the stripes of color on the livery worn by rich people's guards. A sign of wealth.

I always put so much freaking effort into dyeing my shirts blue with blyberry juice to alleviate the visual boredom.

But here, even the poorest people are brightly dressed. Yellows, oranges, greens, purples. It's a riot of color.

"Stop gawking," Mahari sneers. "You'll draw attention."

I snap my eyeline forward but keep peering out of the corners of my eyes. "How do you dye the clothes those bright shades?"

She cuts me a sidelong glance. "Red is from lac insects. Yellow is from chromium, a mineral we find down by the inland sea. Blue is from blyberries, I think, and green is from some weed or other. I don't know. Ask a dyer."

A dyer! They have an entire job devoted to making these fantastic colors. I must meet and interrogate one. Not to mention the inland sea. A body of water so large you can't see the other side. Unfathomable. Truly, the world holds many wonders.

And how big is this bloody city? It's very late dusk, and we've been walking for ages. We'd better reach our destination soon, or we'll be caught out at nightfall. If we were back in Malanox, night would have fallen long ago, and Mahari would have frozen solid enough to use as a bat.

"Here," she breathes, with a sense of wonder I haven't heard from her before. Her dark eyes reflect dancing lights, and I turn to see what holds her attention.

Large strips of red and blue ox hide are layered to form a circular building with a peaked roof. I've never seen such a flimsy—or beautiful—structure. Even VanDyke's cream and gold palace pales in comparison with the vibrancy and warmth of this place.

"What is it?" I breathe.

"It's called a tent," Mahari tells me, her breath fogging in the cooling air. "A big top." She turns her head to look at me, grinning like a kid at the Malanox Fair. "Welcome to the circus."

The space must be sorcered because the temperature inside is perfect.

A man wearing a red hat so tall it could hide a child greets us at the door. "Roll up, roll up, come see the purple lions, if you dare. Watch flowers grow from seeds in moments. Be astounded by the Resplendent Rose! Roll up, roll up."

At the mention of the Resplendent Rose, I cut a glance at Mahari, who quirks an eyebrow and lifts her chin ever so slightly. "Yes, we've already rolled up, buddy," she says to the man, who hasn't stopped spruiking. "We're not going anywhere until morning."

The man in the tall red hat doesn't drop his grin or falter in his patter. "After you've had your fill of the wondrous delights, find a bed to relax for the night. Choose the quiet room, or the ghost room, if you dare."

A giggle escapes me. A fucking giggle. But I can't help it—this is like solstice and a massive orgasm rolled into one. The air is tinged with incense and anticipation.

As we're moving into the throng of people, many who seem to have come in costume and wouldn't be out of place in a Solren ball, tittering and chatting and gawking, the man in the tall red hat begins his patter again to the next customer, and I swing my head.

267

"You're the last for the day, good sir, as night has fallen. Welcome to the circus."

Zaden. I *knew* he was following us. I shake my head imperceptibly, giving him serious *don't approach us* vibes. If he spooks Mahari, he could mess up everything.

Thankfully, he peels around the other side of a cage holding a mountain lion that has clearly been dyed purple. Still, I've never seen a lion before except in drawings, and it's magnificent. Large, muscled, and preternaturally still, assessing the crowd like prey.

The room gasps when a man wearing diamond-patterned tights in red and yellow enters the lion's cage. He pulses with the bright orange light of a Faunus, indicating an affinity with animals. Well, I'd damn well hope so. You wouldn't catch me going near that beast.

The deeper into the throng I push, the harder my heart pounds. Sweat forms on my brow as I look for Mom. Every wonder I see makes the question more prominent in my mind: is my mother just a cheap circus trick, like the purple-painted lion?

Ever since I learned she was alive, I imagined she left home for a noble reason. She must have had some awesome reason to abandon her husband and girls, right? Right? Like saving the Maker-be-damned world. Not performing to gawking tourists.

My breathing comes faster, and I wipe the sweat from my brow. The incense is too strong, cloying. A hand squeezes my arm in reassurance, and I look up at Zaden's broad face smiling lightly at me, then he washes away in the crowd. I hate how much strength I take from that one tiny gesture.

But she isn't here. Each section of the vast big-top tent has a different wonder, mostly vestiges, but she isn't one of them. No sign of the Resplendent Rose.

A magnified voice booms through the tent. "Ladies and gentlemen, prepare to be amazed. I invite you to watch the central space." The ox hides in the tent's center, which I imagined to be some kind of roof support, fall away, revealing a circle around ten feet across.

The circle is separated from the rest of the space by a transparent material, and I can't see anything special about it.

The voice booms again. "Behold the Resplendent Rose."

The crowd parts for a woman wearing a tiny skirt, a black and pink striped corset top, and auburn hair piled on her head with pink feathers sticking up. She looks good. Sexy. Not like a mother, and certainly not how I remember *my* mother.

But it's her. My throat bobs, and I try to swallow but fail. Something is stuck in my gaw, and I want to spit it out but I'm too polite. Too fucking polite.

Mom saunters to the edge of the inner circle and smiles broadly, flourishes a long slender arm, and somebody hands her a chicken.

Tension simmers through the crowd, and I feel like I'm a step behind. I have no idea what's happening—or what's about to happen—but everybody else seems clued in.

Mahari grips my forearm, and I sneak a glance at her face, which is tight with anticipation.

Mom must be about to do something extraordinary. Something that warrants all this attention. Something that can impact the future of the world. Despite the short skirt and the chicken.

She pushes through the transparent hangings and into the central circle, still holding the damn bird.

The necks around me crane up, looking at the ceiling, and I join them. The roof over the central circle falls away, opening it to the night sky. The crowd gasps and then stares back at the Resplendent Rose.

She holds the chicken in one hand and raises her other in triumph. I watch in horror as the bird stops moving and slowly freezes, its eyes bulging out and its feathers solidifying into arrows.

Mom shifts stances, striking poses, smiling and waving as the animal dies. It's the first time I've witnessed Quiet, temperature resistance, because I can't see my own glow. She vibrates gently with sweet pink light, the color of sunrise, holding each pose long enough for the crowd to gasp.

To prove the animal is entirely frozen, the Resplendent Rose smacks it against the floor, and it fractures into a dozen shards.

The crowd explodes in riotous applause and wolf whistles, jumping up and down at the magnificent woman who can withstand the cold.

But I can't move. I'm frozen as solid as that damn chicken. My mother isn't a superhero, gathering support to overthrow the hierarchy and demand more rights for the underprivileged. She doesn't care about making change and improving the world. She didn't leave her family, leave me, to follow a cause.

She's a fucking circus clown.

Scar

Hello Mother, I'm your daughter.

No, that sounds like shit.

Hi Mom, nice skirt.

Even worse.

Well, hi there. Why'd you abandon me to become a fucking clown?

Yeah, maybe I'll go with that last one. I spend the next few hours figuring out how to approach her, but instead of finding suitable words, I find anger and hurt growing in my chest.

Finally, after most people have wandered off to find somewhere to sleep, including Mahari, I get up the nerve to tap her on the shoulder.

The Resplendent Rose spins around and looks at me blankly. Up close, her face is plastered with make-up, splotched on unevenly, but still seems exotically glamorous. She stares at me, an uncertain grin on her face, waiting for me to talk.

I clear my throat, willing her to recognize me. Doesn't happen. So I take a deep breath. "Hi, Mom."

Her face holds the grin for an instant while she catalogs the possibilities, and she eventually figures out who I am. "Scarla, is it really you?" She squeals with delight, drawing a few glances from the thinning crowd.

Her accent is weird, a mix of the guttural north and the lilting south. The combination makes her sound like she's still performing, like nothing about her is real, and I struggle to believe anything she says.

"Darling, I'm so happy to see you," she purrs, as though I've just returned from a trip to the market. "Come and give your mother a hug."

I trot over obediently and submit to a squeeze, but her scrawny arms hold no warmth. I can't shake the disappointment of her life. Incense clings to her hair, and a feather from her hairpiece tickles my nose.

"Angel feather?" I ask, though it has no erotic appeal. But I'm aching to turn the conversation to the ruling class and how she plans to overthrow them.

She just titters. "I wish!" She holds me at arm's length. "Look at you, berry. You've grown so big."

Fury pulses through me, and my jaw clenches. "What did you expect? I was a child when you left. Now I'm an adult. Adults are bigger than children." My words are tight, and I'm struggling to loosen my tongue, relax my face.

Resplendent Rose giggles again. "Of course they are, berry."

"Don't call me that," I snap. Only Dad calls me berry. She lost the right to call me that when she walked out the door.

She pouts. "You're angry." Her jolly facade drops for a moment, and I glimpse a sadder woman beneath it. "Leaving you was the hardest thing I ever did, baby," she says. "But look around. This world is full of color and motion and life. The Undercity was killing me. Life was so dull."

I bristle with rage. "I'm so sorry we bored you." The ribbon of light inside her spine quivers, tempting me to brush it with my magic. I shake away my violent urge and try to see the world through my mother's eyes.

But all I see is a veneer of fun underpinned by trickery and fraud. The purple-painted lion. The frozen chicken. The vestiges using their powers to strip people of copper pieces.

The Undercity may be dark and grim, but the people are authentic and kind, and all the resources are freely shared.

Mother's face is haggard for a moment beneath the makeup. "You didn't bore me, berry. I just needed more from life."

She just needed more. More than her community, more than her job healing people in the Underwing, more than her family.

More than me.

Her lazy regret is no match for my raging fury. My muscles bunch and I adopt a fighting stance on instinct alone. My fists curl, and I'm glad at the fear that registers in her eyes.

How dare she abandon me just to showcase her powers to strangers? How dare she throw a dark blanket of mourning across my childhood on a whim? How dare she stand before me with tears in her eyes and tell me she needed more?

Power coils within me, ready to strike, and only the gentle caress of Zaden's magic down my back prevents me from unleashing it. His soft touch calms my body, soothes my muscles, tempers my rage.

Instead of killing her where she stands, I take a deep breath.

Suddenly, I wonder if she has Gaze. If she can sense Zaden's magic too. I lean in and snarl, hooking a thumb over my shoulder at Zaden. "Can you see him?"

She glances at him. "Yep. He's pretty hard to miss."

"No," I hiss. "I mean, can you really see him?"

Mom tentatively pats me on the arm like we're making up. Like we're over the little hump in our relationship, the part where she abandoned me as a child. "Yes, darling. I can see him. You could see those muscles from the moon."

She says that last part louder, aiming for approving laughter from the room at her fantastic wit.

Zaden is behind me, whispering in my ear, his hot breath warming my neck. "She doesn't have Gaze, Scar. Trust me, it's rare."

True. He sought it for centuries.

His forest lily scent calms me further, and I step away from the murderous cliff I lingered at and calm the beast in my chest. I can't help it. I stroke his bicep from shoulder to elbow, taking courage from his presence.

But the moment of tenderness is over instantly, and I turn my back on him despite the hitch of disappointment on his face. He lied to me too.

"Come and let me get a good look at you," Mother says. I narrow my eyes but straighten my back, like if I display perfect posture, she'll love me. "You're so beautiful, Scarla. Really, I'm so proud of you."

The beast inside me snaps, braying for blood, and I pull away from Zaden's touch. "You don't know anything about me. How dare you be proud of me? What does that even mean? You're proud that my hair is the same copper shade as Dad's? You're proud that I have two legs and two arms? Or are you proud because I left my whole fucking life behind to come and find you, believing you must be working toward something bigger because why else would you leave me? Or are you proud that I'm a little bitch who can't stand the sight of her own mother?"

The words are like poison leaving my body, and I feel better for saying them. Shouting them, really. And the hurt in this woman's eyes only feeds the monster in my chest.

She doesn't have the right to be hurt by my words. My

whole life has been overshadowed by her departure—her "death"—by her single action that defined my childhood. And she claims to be hurt by mere words?

Perhaps if she'd used a few more words herself, we wouldn't be in this mess. Dad would have fallen over himself to keep her happy, I just know it. He would have hollowed out the mountain if it had made her smile. He would have felled the Margrave's army single-handed. He loved her. The way I thought she loved us back.

"Did you ask Dad to come with you?"

She cocks her head, trying on a brave smile. "What?"

"Did you ask him to come to Desert's Maw with you? You said your life was dull and colorless, and you needed to live somewhere else, so did it occur to you to ask your husband if he wanted to move here? You could have brought us all with you if you needed more."

She blinks at me like I'm speaking Pombalese, or like I suggested she take her family to a nice hotel on the sun.

"Right," I say, breaking the eye contact, learning everything I need to from her silence.

She didn't ask him to join her. She didn't mention her plan or try to figure out how to keep her family together. She just sneaked away in the night like the coward she is.

"Dad's right," I spit. "You are dead. You couldn't be more unalive if I ripped your guts out myself."

She flinches at that, and the beast in my chest snarls right back.

"I... Sit down, have a cup of tea, and I'll tell you everything. Then maybe you'll understand." The Resplendent Rose gestures at some forlorn slouch chairs that look nasty and old without the gawking crowd.

I sit. This is the last chance I'll have to hear her story, so I grit my teeth and plonk my ass in the shapeless chair, trying not to slide off the side of the damn thing. "No tea, just talk."

Rose settles into the slouch chair opposite, and Zaden stays standing, taking up guard behind me. Does he expect an attack? I don't know, I can't read that male anymore. But his presence at my back is comforting, like he's looking after me. A stark contrast to my mother.

"You know Bill Bradson Farmer, how his family has always had a connection with the Nashanti." She's talking about Leo's father. And no, I didn't know their family had a connection with the desert people. I didn't know they existed until yesterday. But I bite my tongue and let her keep talking because if I interrupt, I might never stop shouting, and then I'll never hear the story.

"Go on," Zaden growls, startling me. I'm glad he's prodding her because I'm biting my tongue so it doesn't lash her. But I need to hear this tale first.

"Well, I arranged a meeting through him, and the desert people got me across to Desert's Maw. It was such a horrid journey, you wouldn't believe the difficulties. We scurried from hovel to burrow to cave, and I can't tell you how many times we almost got caught outside in the burn. Honestly, you'd never guess how those people live."

With every syllable, my sympathy for the Resplendent Rose dwindles, and it already started from a low base. She isn't telling me how hard it was for her to leave; she's telling me how clever she was to arrange it.

I interrupt her tale of woe. "And when you got here? What did you do?"

She's bright and airy. "I was amazed. I mean, you've seen

276

it here. So much life. So much color. So much nicer than Malanox."

Zaden growls behind me, a soft warning rumble that Rose doesn't seem to notice. She carries on about how lovely the town was, but how difficult it was for her to meet anybody to give her work, and how she struggled to fit in.

She went from bar to bar searching for employment and finally landed her dream job with the circus. And isn't she clever. And isn't it wonderful for her unique talents to be appreciated. And isn't she persistent and a hard worker who deserves the best.

And isn't she a self-centered bitch whose lipstick bag is deeper than her caring streak.

Zaden

"We're leaving," Scarla announces, taking her mother and me by surprise.

Rose splutters, indignant. "But... but you've only just got here. Stay awhile."

"Nope." Scarla strides across the tent, weaving around the caged displays. The room looks tatty without the crowd, without the excitement and anticipation holding the frayed edges of the curtains together.

"Will you come back tomorrow?" Rose calls, trotting after us. "Where are you staying? You can stay here with me, you know."

"Not happening," Scarla yells over her shoulder.

"But... but it's cold out. You'll freeze."

That stops Scarla. She turns to survey her mother, her beautiful face frozen in a sneer. "Pay me a copper piece, and I'll let you watch me go." She resumes walking, and Rose doesn't follow this time.

Outside, Scarla simply says, "We're leaving, angel. To Malanox."

"I figured," I mutter. Frankly, I'm exhausted from flying over the desert and need to recharge my energy. I dutifully arranged lodgings for us before tracking Scarla down to The

Jagged Tooth, and I want nothing more than to crawl into the tiny bed in the tiny motel with my tiny mortal and sleep.

Honestly, I was looking forward to it. It's the first time in years I've looked forward to sleeping outside my castle. Centuries, maybe.

But the look on Scarla's face brooks no argument. We are flying home tonight.

"I need food," I growl.

She cocks a hip. "You just downed three seeded bread rolls and half a chicken."

"Flying takes energy, woman."

"Well, woman's a step up from calling me mortal, I suppose. But I'm sure you'll figure out my name soon. And yes, I know flying takes energy, I just didn't realize you were so greedy."

I slap her ass. "I've got to carry you around too."

She almost smiles... so close. But her regard shutters again. I raid the harness pockets for the oatcakes and water bottles and restore my energy as best I can without a solid six-hour sleep.

I don't mention the prospect of demons chasing us across the desert. I have no reason to believe they will, other than a general sense of foreboding that I haven't been able to shake since I killed Bastien Xerxes and shattered our bloodbond.

After a long dramatic sigh to prove how amenable I'm being, I clip her into the harness at my front, her long body pressed against mine. It's hard not to think about our escape from VanDyke's palace and the flying sex that followed. But tonight's escape feels very different indeed.

We lift off, rising quickly through the dark night. We are at the outskirts of Desert's Maw, so we are over the Dead Desert in mere moments, swapping the twinkling lights on the ground for twinkling stars above.

Scarla is pressed against me. Every updraft, every shift in the air currents, shifts her ass against my cock, and my semi-solidifies into rock. My arms are free, and I run them down her silhouette, feeling the indent of her waist, the swell of her hips. Even the scrunching of her pants under the harness reminds me of what else she keeps in there.

My cock throbs. This is going to be a long trip home.

She snarls over her shoulder. "Put it away, angel." I guess she isn't in the mood.

But there's not much I can do, so this throbbing steel bar sits between us for the remainder of the journey.

My wings beat steadily, and fatigue stays at bay. If I keep my pace languid, we'll make it back without having to stop for a rest.

Scarla's mood is clearly sour. She almost killed her own mother, which is saying something after how she carried on about her being alive. When Scarla adopted the killing stance and looked at Rose with cold rage, my chest tightened in fear. I had to calm her somehow and stop her from murdering her mom.

Although the Maker knows the woman deserved it.

But I couldn't allow that. I need Scarla to join me in heaven. And I may not remember much about the place, but I'm pretty sure murder isn't a ticket in.

For so long, my goal has been to find the gateway to heaven. For so damn long. And it still is, but my motivation has changed. I no longer just want to return to my rightful place, driven by pride. Now, I need heaven to spend eternity by this mortal's side. She would just wither and die here on earth, leaving me alone again.

Still selfish, but changed. When did that happen? This mortal's like a Maker-be-damned virus, infiltrating my system by stealth.

"About time," she snarls over her shoulder. "That thing was poking me in the back."

My cock jumps again at the sound of her voice, but it's true—my erection has eased because feelings for this mortal go way beyond the physical. I love her.

I just need her to figure it out. To stop meddling in petty earthly affairs and realize we just need to be together. She can find the gate to heaven with Gaze, and we can go there. Together. Forever.

She needed to see her mother. I can understand that. Sort of. I suppose her feelings for that woman were akin to mine for her... but without the sexual element. Or perhaps it felt like a debt, like the bloodbond I owe to the Xerxes line. So I can understand why she needed to see her.

I was hoping that would be Scarla's final earthly mission, that she could look beyond the mortal realm for her next adventure.

But I sense none of the calmness and finality I expected. Seeing her mother has only riled up Scarla even more, invoked her passions and stoked her fire. I admire that and would support her fully if it wasn't interfering with my forever.

Damn mortal. Why won't she ever do as she's told?

I sigh because, whether I like it or not, that's exactly my favorite part of her.

I heard her talking with that woman, Bwadu's sister, about overthrowing the Cloaked Court. I heard her discussing it with her mother too. She keeps her voice low as though that would stop my angelic ears from hearing, and as if I would even care.

My mortal can wipe the Cloaked Court from the face of the earth, and I wouldn't lift a finger to stop her. She'd be doing me a favor. That Court is nothing but a thorn in my side. Worse even than the insects I'm forced to govern. The Cloaked King beckons me to the ball more often than the earth rotates about the sun and punishes me with exquisite pain if I resist.

I hate him. I care nothing for the other Fallen Angels. I only care for Scarla.

My wings fatigue as the night wears on, but I keep beating them steadily, not allowing myself to change the rhythm. Thick snow blinds me, and I consider flying above the clouds, but the air is thinner up there, and I haven't the energy or breath to combat it.

The snow doesn't affect Scarla at all. Fire runs through her veins, growing hotter with every passing hour. My magic senses it and responds like a frost beetle to a flame. I can't ignore it, pulsing through her and around her, growing stronger.

It is her desire for action made into liquid fire. Her drive for change courses through every cell of her being. It is, I pray, her last earthly mission, after which her attention will return to me.

Finally, we land at Malanox in snow as deep as my knees. Our feet have barely touched the ground, I've barely unclasped the hooks that harness her to me, when she whirls around to face me, her wide brown eyes alight and her copper hair wild and messy. "Is there anything you need to tell me, angel?"

A quip springs to my mouth. "I need to tell you where we keep the hairbrush."

But it was the wrong thing to say, and her eyes turn cold. "I need to know. Are there any more lies you told me? Tell me now. This is your last chance." Her words are forged in the primordial fires, edged with celestial steel.

I sense that she is setting me a test, and if I fail, I will lose my forever with her. I must pass. I must tell her what she needs to know.

But honestly, I don't know how to answer her. A thousand years on this planet have taught me nothing about how humans think.

What is this mortal's definition of a lie?

Am I lying every time I pass her without admitting how I long for her? Am I lying when I refuse to acknowledge how she haunts my thoughts, my dreams, leaving me no time to myself? Is it a lie to greet her in the morning with hello instead of I love you?

If so, I've lied to her a dozen times. A hundred. More. Every moment I spend in her presence is a lie because I'm not prostrating myself before her and begging for her love.

But she doesn't mean that. She's talking about killing her sister. Letting her mother live. The two major sins I've committed against her.

Her brown stare impales me, and I tell her the only truth I can. "No. There's nothing else."

Nothing in her stance or gaze tells me if I passed her test. Perhaps she doesn't know.

She just turns and stalks away.

Scar

I kiss the single glowing emerald on my blade's hilt, then strap it to my thigh. Not because I intend to use it, but because it's my only defense against angels, and I'm about to go swimming in a sea full of the motherfuckers.

Tonight is the Cloaked Court meeting and associated ball. I'm all frocked up in a frilly pink number that I'm wearing ironically, though I doubt the rich assholery will notice. The dress cascades to my ankles like an overblown wedding cake but is tight and sexy up top. My frills will make people lose their appetite, or my cleavage will poke their eye out. I'm happy either way.

Zaden smiles as I descend the curving stairway. He's waiting for me, like some kind of gentleman. Weird. "You look... interesting," he comments.

I almost laugh. But the tension simmering inside me these past few days won't subside. "Thanks, I think."

He scoops my hand into his and escorts me to the carriage. "I take it you haven't suddenly developed a taste for the gentry's fashion but are wearing this as some kind of materials-based protest?"

I bite my lip to stop the grin. "You know me too well."

"I don't believe that's possible." He holds my hand while I

climb into the carriage. "I wish to know you as well as you'll allow."

He looks at me oddly, and cold pierces me. I sense he's holding something back that would affect how I felt about him. Another lie?

I steel myself against his charm. He is, after all, equipped with the wit and words of centuries on earth, and I don't know if I can believe any of them.

I feign sleep for the entire journey, although the damn carriage keeps slamming my ass and the side of my head like a demented teacher. But at least Zaden has gone back to his usual brooding silence.

When I asked him to tell me the truth, if there was anything else he needed to say to me, I meant it. That was his last chance to fess up. The last possibility of any future between us.

But I don't allow myself to believe him. Yet. I can't. Everyone I ever loved has lied to me, betrayed me, destroyed my trust, and I don't have any faith left to give.

We finally arrive in the sealed section of Solren, right outside the palatial building in the middle of a hand-carved courtyard where we attended the last ball six months ago.

Bwadu must be here somewhere. She agreed to bring me news of Molly—perhaps even Molly herself. Seeing my friend's brown eyes and that dancing mole on her upper lip would bring me so much comfort. She is probably my last, uncomplicated friend in the whole world. But I can't see her anywhere.

Angels and vestiges dot the courtyard, a steady flow of blurs and glows heading in through the massive ornate doors. Last time, I was overwhelmed. This time, I know exactly what's happening.

285

I can identify each vestige's skill based on their color, and their power based on its strength. There's a light green Charmer, the hue of a fresh leaf but with very little power. Here's the vibrant blyberry of Clout, a vestige with supernatural strength like several of Zaden's guards. The strong dark green of a potent Grower, the weaker tree-bark brown of a Grit. Even the feverish pink of a Keen, which I've only seen once or twice.

So many skills, so many suck-ups. Each here to grovel to the shiny angels.

I drift inside and away from Zaden, needing my own headspace to undertake my plan. Identify the Cloaked King, then expose him.

He isn't anywhere. I met him at VanDyke's palace over dinner, but he wore a mask. Still, he was short and round and dripping in animal fat, although I suppose that last part isn't permanent.

He isn't here. He isn't fucking here. I prowl the entire room, seeking my prey. Last ball, I was petrified I'd trip over and embarrass myself. Now, I couldn't care less. And my muscles are lean from months of training, coiled, ready.

Music swirls through the room, soft and string-based, carrying the song and scent of flowers to every patron. I work the space too, smiling as I swan from angel to angel, looking for my mark. We've arrived earlier than last time, and the Cloaked Court hasn't yet convened. Bright angels are dotted among the revelers, and I approach each and every one. Even the overblown cream-and-golden cupid that is VanDyke, who simpers at me like we're best buddies.

No sign of the King. But he must be here. He's the one who convenes the Maker-be-damned Court.

A tall angel with a deep yellow glow, like so many have, smiles warmly at me when I approach him. "Good evening, young lady. I haven't had the pleasure of meeting you yet." He offers me a slim hand, lithe and bronzed like the rest of him.

He tries to bring my hand to his lips, but I shake it firmly instead, refusing to be compartmentalized as a mere female. "Pleasure isn't the word," I say silkily, then retract my hand.

His pale gray eyes darken, and his smile deepens into a predatory grin. "Would you care to join me outside for some fresh air?"

"There's nothing I'd like less," I say sweetly, and his eyes darken again. I turn to walk away when my toes curl and my nipples harden into peaks. A flush runs over my chest, and my skin becomes sensitive, aware of the movement of air across my exposed neck, the closeness of all these other bodies.

Inflict. Somebody is inflicting pleasure on me. A quick glance confirms that nobody is using standard angel lust magic, so this is Inflict.

"Are you quite sure about that," the lithe angel murmurs, his breath in my ear igniting a fire between my clenched thighs.

"Oh," I say breathily, responding to the pleasure despite knowing precisely what is happening.

I run my fingers down my neck to distract him while I look down. Sure enough, fingers of violet magic snake across the floor in feathered tendrils, connecting me with the lithe angel.

It's the Cloaked King, and he's wearing a glamor.

I look into his light gray eyes, which sparkle with the promise of delight, and lean into him. It takes no effort to inhale his scent deeply and let my lust show. "Take me outside, angel," I murmur, and his grin licks his cheeks.

He grabs my wrist, and a flush of sinful pleasure runs up my arm, trickling into my armpit and around my back. I feel like sex incarnate as I swing my hips, sashaying across the floor, feeling the heat of bodies and the flow of my own arousal. Perhaps I'll screw him before I expose him.

We head through the crowd toward the intricately paneled glass doors leading to the balcony. An ebony-skinned woman wearing one of those dresses with trailing sleeves, a blue monstrosity with almost as much silk as my own, catches my eye. Candlelight reflects off her prominent cheekbones, although the tattoo of a leaf over her left temple is hidden by makeup.

Bwadu. I was expecting to see her outside. Kudos to her for scoring a way in. She leans forward, kisses me on the cheek, and whispers into my ear. "I found Molly. She's dead."

Her voice is flat and cold and erases the last trace of pleasure in my body. I can't get enough breath into my lungs, and for a moment, I wonder if an angel has sucked all the oxygen from the room. "How do you know?"

Bwadu gives me a flat stare but doesn't dignify that with an answer. I have no reason to doubt her. With a smile fixed on her face, she keeps talking, holding me close. "She never escaped Van Dyke's palace. Your pet angel heard her screams and left her to die."

My pet angel? Zaden. She must mean Zaden. My brain is fuzzy, though I haven't taken a sip of mulled wine. Zaden. Something about Zaden. "What?" I manage to say, though my lips feel cold and numb.

"When your pet angel came to his buddy's castle, he heard Molly being tortured. And the bastard left her to die."

"But he told me he saw her escape." I say the words, though I know they're stupid. But I remember it so clearly. In the

SCAR

servants' corridors in the palace, I saw Zaden, who appeared like a God, glowing with greatness and beauty. He kissed me and cared for me—cared that my neck had been hurt. My words brought him out of his killing fury.

But I refused to escape without Molly. "*She's fine*," he told me. "*I saw her being set free.*" But he never saw that. The opposite was true. He heard her being tortured and still lied to my face.

Then, back at Malanox Castle, he offered to join me while I asked the servants if she'd returned. Probably to keep track of their answers, to keep track of me. Mother-effer.

A dim part of me knows he only lied to protect me—because he wanted me to flee Van Dyke. But I don't care. I don't fucking care. He doesn't get to decide what's best for me, like I'm a damn baby. I'm a grown-ass woman, and if I want to run into a proverbial fire to rescue my best friend, he'd better come and help me, or he can piss right off.

Bwadu's fingers grip my upper arms tightly, and I realize she's stopping me from swaying. The music here is too damn loud, it's swamping my senses, and I need to get outside. "Okay," I mutter stupidly, then wrench myself free.

A moment later, I'm outside, gulping the cool air and trying to figure out what happened. Zaden lied to me. He treated me like a child and overruled me. And last night, when I asked if there was anything else he needed to confess, he lied again.

Fury bubbles through me, growing like a beast, raging to be set free. I grip the marble railing overlooking the gardens, but the lights in the trees all blur into a mess. My breath comes fast and shallow, fueling the creature within.

A sound behind me, the whoosh of noisy chatter and laughter from inside at the opening of a door, the ensuing silence after the thud.

I release the railing, and my fingernails dig red moons into my palms, dripping blood. Red blood on the white marble floor.

But the pain is nothing. I don't even feel it. I just smell it. Rich, iron blood leaking from my body.

I turn. The lithe angel with light-gray eyes stares at me lecherously. His lips move, but I can't hear his words—the maelstrom of roaring in my ears is too loud.

His magic weaves across the floor, the violet snake of another male trying to control me. His pleasure doesn't pierce me. All I feel is the rage and the beast inside me that needs feeding.

The Cloaked King steps closer, and I let him.

Come closer, little king.

He's panting, sneering, claiming his prize, but the beast within me wants sustenance. I raise my pink skirt, revealing my thigh, and the leering king follows my movements. I pull the dagger from the sheath, the celestial blade that can kill an angel.

If he recognizes it, he gives nothing away. But he gurgles when I plunge the dagger into his chest and twist upward, leaning into it with all my weight.

The King's gray eyes widen in disbelief. His glamor falls away, leaving the bloated male leaning against me, sweating and grotesque. Without emotion, I push him away, and he thuds onto the marble, mixing his red blood with the splattered drops of mine.

The Cloaked King is dead.

Scar

The Cloaked King's lifeless body sprawls on the marble floor, one arm caught beneath his back.

Blood leaks from the wound in his chest, and I can't look away. I've knocked out plenty of guards, but those fights are always clean. Not like this messy, gruesome wreckage.

I should be scared. I just feel guilty. But all I have is the roaring beast in my breast, baying for blood. More blood. Everyone's blood.

His body is bloated and pale, and the sneer on his face has disappeared along with his life, leaving a blank mask that provokes no emotion in me.

He deserved this death. For centuries, he reigned over the Cloaked Court, which made everybody's lives a misery—except the angels' themselves. But even they were subject to the Cloaked King's Inflict, scared to ignore his summons, whipped into submission.

Not anymore. This despot is finally gone; he will never raise a hand against Zaden again, nor stand by in apathetic silence while beggars struggle to survive.

No wonder I don't feel guilty. Why should I? I have rid the world of a terrible angel and made it a better place. If my methods are violent and my place in heaven is denied, so be it. I'll go to hell with a grin on my lips because I'm a fucking martyr. Selfless. Putting the people on earth ahead of my own future in heaven.

Man, being selfless has never felt so good. Power thrums through my veins and ripples from my body through the air. Like a stone dropped from the sky, my influence and actions will ripple throughout the world.

The Cloaked King is leaking blood onto the marble, a dark pool that snakes through the grout between tiles. He must be shrinking, losing volume, spreading himself across the balcony like this.

Something else pours out of him too, a violet haze the exact color of rooshen spores. Spores that are poisonous when breathed in but curative and delicious when brewed into tea. Spores that are rare, growing beneath one in a hundred thousand silken oaks, the stuff of legend.

A lot like Inflict. Pain or pleasure, poison or cure.

The violet smoke drifts from the Cloaked King's mouth, his final exhale. It hovers in an uncertain cloud above his corpse, seeking its next host. This haze of magic moves deliberately, like a living, sentient being, not subject to the whim of the warm breeze.

It assesses me. I get the distinct feeling it is looking me up and down, taking in my blood-stained pink gown, the glittering knife still in my hand, weighing up my deeds and actions, calculating the worth of my soul.

I wipe the celestial blade clean on my dress, leaving another dark streak of blood, and return it to the sheath on my thigh. Straightening my shoulders, I stretch out my arms and inhale, breathing deeply, filling my lungs.

The violet smoke invades my body like a worm, diving

down my throat and into my organs, spreading tingling cold throughout every cell of my body, all the way to my outstretched fingers. It is a physical entity that violates me right into my soul. The hair on the back of my neck stands on end, and gooseflesh streaks down my legs. My body is inhabited by a foreign being, a power much stronger than I am.

Deep breaths, remembering to fill my lungs, stamping my feet, wiggling my fingers. And we are one. The new power is part of me, and I don't know how I ever lived without it. It completes me, filling a gaping hole inside me I never knew existed.

It is euphoric. I throw back my head and roar at the sky, a deep guttural sound that soars over the garden, over the sealed section of Solren, past the Rim Road to the outskirts, and all the way to heaven itself.

Now, even the Maker knows my name.

I am the Cloaked Queen. The dyad of Gaze and Inflict are mine, and none can compete with me for power. Not even those asshole angels enjoying the ball inside. Nobody is stronger than me.

Power and joy mingle within me, filling me completely. I am the Cloaked Queen.

And I will not hide my face.

The pathetic, broken male at my feet was too scared to reveal his identity to the other angels. Too frightened they would kill him for his precious Inflict.

Not me. I don't give a shit if I die tonight or any night soon. There is nobody on earth that I love and none who loves me. Just some betrayers and liars I once knew.

So I'm going to show these assholes who I am and make

them grovel at my feet. I will change the world, then I'll die. And in the meantime, I'll make some fucking chaos.

Scar

I stride into the ballroom, pulsating with power. It trails me like a cloak, caressing my skin and following in my wake, ready to do my bidding.

Inside, angels are gathered in the central dome, glowing spots among the dull humans. Every single one of the bastards has a superior sneer on his or her face, and I can't wait to take them down. I'll take them so far down they're groveling at my feet on the filthy marble floor.

The gentry wearing the latest fashions swirl around me, trailing floor-length sleeves and oversized jackets. They largely ignore the angels gathered in the room's center, giving them a wide berth and casting the occasional glance their way. These people don't have my advantage of being able to see the shimmering dome, so perhaps they give it more leeway than necessary.

Not me. I beeline for the glowing dome, thrumming with the Cloaked King's power. My power. Zaden never said that Gaze and Inflict interacted with one another, but they clearly do. Not only do I sense the King's new power, but my own Gaze is heightened too.

I am unstoppable.

I circle the dome, walking a lap of the center, trailing my

fingers in the glimmering bubble and watching sparks fly where my flesh meets the sphere. Testing the waters. The last thing I want is to march into the globe and rebound flat on my ass. First, I need to weigh up my enemy. My fingers leave a sparkle but penetrate without pain or repercussion.

Most of the glowing assholes ignore me, but Zaden's eyes are locked on me as I circle him, the brilliant green emeralds darkening with danger. He shakes his head at me, a silent warning to stay away. He probably thinks he's protecting me again, but he doesn't know what I do. I am the Cloaked Queen.

Count Van Dyke watches me also from beneath his curling eyelashes. He wears an oversized golden jacket and cream pants that match his wavy locks. His smile is wolfish, and I can see his beady little brain calculating how to capture me again. But that Z scar on his cheek will forever remind me—and him—just how fallible he is.

The true power of the dyad dawns on me, and a grin spreads across my face. I truly am invulnerable. Nobody can take my leadership from me because Gaze can only be inherited through death by natural causes, and Inflict only through murder. None of these glowing assholes can steal my dyad.

With this knowledge shining as brightly as any angel, I step through the dome into the sealed center. Into the room's heart.

A dozen angelic faces snap toward me, carved in cruelty. The female nearest to me smiles wickedly, her amber eyes darkening, her matching amber aura deepening as it readies to attack.

To her right, a man with long black hair swept into a ponytail and a dark brown face that is pleasingly round, holds up a hand before anybody strikes me. "Explain yourself, mortal," he commands. "Who let you into the council span?"

Arrogance drips from this male, pooling at his feet and spreading across the marble.

I don't need to answer him. From now on, I answer to nobody. I ignore him and address the gathered celestials. I will give them one chance to submit to my rule willingly, which they will fail to do. Then I'll force them and enjoy every moment.

I throw back my shoulders and stand tall, projecting my voice clearly. "Humans shall be treated as the equals of angels," I declare.

Zaden's emerald eyes shoot warnings at me, but I ignore them too.

Count VanDyke puts his arm around me, resting it casually across my shoulders as though I am his little girl. "I apologize for my friend," he says with a flash of white teeth. "She doesn't understand how things work here. I'm still teaching her. You won't find any problems with her again."

Zaden bristles at Van Dyke's touch, his eyes darkening to rage. I shake my head at him minutely, a silent warning to back off. I can fight my own battles.

But VanDyke's arm across my shoulders feels like a slimy worm, and his casual ownership sends waves of fury through my body.

Time to flex my muscles. I close my eyes and reach within myself, falling into the swirling streams of Gaze and Inflict. They swirl together inside me like liquids that cannot mix, each repelled by the other. Gaze's goodness and Inflict's evil circle one other like liquid animals, perfectly matched in strength. I pull a thin violet strand from the stream of Inflict and close my eyes, trying to shoot a dart of pain through VanDyke's arm.

I push. With every ounce of concentration, I will Inflict

to flow from my shoulder into VanDyke's hand, but nothing happens. Nothing happens. Nothing bloody happens.

Shift. Fuck.

The beautiful angelic faces contort in derisive laughter, showcasing flawless necks and perfect teeth.

The female with the amber aura drawls, "Let's have her killed." She snaps her fingers, and a dozen armed guards with bright green stripes march through the crowds and stand at attention at the central dome's perimeter.

Black Ponytail holds up a hand. "Not the guards. That'll spoil the fun. Let's release her into the garden and hunt. I haven't hunted a mortal in years."

These fuckers still aren't taking me seriously, and I cannot make my Maker-be-damned Inflict cause even a splinter of discomfort in VanDyke's possessive arm.

Zaden crosses to my side in a moment and punches VanDyke in the jaw, a crunching uppercut that leaves the Count on the floor. He snarls at the other angels, pulsing with obsidian rage. "Scarla is under my protection. Nobody hurts her, or you answer to me."

The angels micro-step backward, seeming to pay Zaden heed. Small domes appear over several angels, which must be protective shields.

Some of these celestials are expecting a battle.

And I'm happy to oblige. But I won't do it from behind a man. I take a step around Zaden.

The amber-eyed female nods to her guards, who all unsheathe long swords. Perhaps the angels don't want to dirty their hands—or don't want to get on Zaden's wrong side.

If this female thinks she has me trapped here, she can think again. Gaze is so intense within me that it takes a mere moment to pinpoint the ribbon of light in each guard's spine.

This time, I don't just squeeze the ribbon of light. I rip it in two.

The guards fall to the ground, dead. Completely lacking in life, and I did that. I don't have time for regret—perhaps I never will. Maybe I've moved so far beyond Scarla Rosedarter Healer that I'm no longer capable of remorse.

It doesn't matter. What are half a dozen more murders? I've already committed the biggest sin, I can't get more condemned than I already am.

Each guard falls with a clatter of metal on wood, and the crowd gasps.

The gentrified humans at the ball are no longer pretending the Cloaked Court isn't convening—they watch us with wide eyes, as though they've paid a hundred gold pieces for the privilege.

But I can't deal with angels like I do with mortals. Some of them have glowing ribbons of light, but those ribbons soon flare into massive light balls with no apparent weakness. They're fucking sun gods.

I'm screwed.

Then I remember watching Inflict creep across the floor in The Jagged Tooth. It doesn't come from my eyes the way Gaze does, nor can I force it directly into the body part I want to hurt. Inflict works differently.

I refocus on my swirling whirlpool of violet Inflict, trying to command the slippery magic the way I command Gaze. It resists, falling from my grasp time and again until I hold tight and force it out from the soles of my feet.

It pours from me, shooting across the marble and into every one of the angels before me. Best of all, it sneaks under the protective domes they've erected and penetrates them all.

Each and every one falls to their knees, faces contorted in agony. I have no filter. There is no limit to my fury or edge to what they deserve, so I don't hold back.

Behind me, Zaden murmurs my name. "Scar, don't." It is an empty, soulless murmur, and I don't have time to process what that means. He should just be thankful he isn't writhing in pain at my feet like his buddies.

If he thinks I'm unfair to use Inflict, he's got another thing coming. "It isn't cheating," I snarl at him, throwing back words he once said to me. "It's just another weapon in my arsenal."

Giddy power fills me, and I wonder if I'll ever stop torturing these assholes.

Scar

The angels have been brought to their knees.

VanDyke is crumpled in a heap at my feet, his perfect face contorted in pain and his blonde curls disheveled. His magnificent gold jacket will be dirty and torn, and I'd like to see him hold a sneer after this.

The other angels are just as disarrayed, crouching and wincing. Somebody is emitting a high keening sound, and all of them are fallen. Fallen so much further than they ever thought possible.

Euphoria swells within me, lifting me higher, filling the room with my presence.

I hold the angels-in-pain tableau for several minutes, aware of the sea of faces staring at us from without the central dome. The only sound is that high keening, which I've sourced to a lanky angel curled in a ball and clutching his knees, his shaggy brown hair curtaining his face.

I like watching them squirm. After the torture they've inflicted on humankind for centuries, they deserve it.

But I want to hear the angels grovel, so I release them. I relinquish my hold on Inflict and let the whirlpool of energy within me simmer down to a gentle swirl.

The celestial beings at my feet sag in relief, and the world is right for one beautiful, shining moment.

Everything I have worked for has led to this single instant in time. Finally, I am in a position of power where I can change the world and tear down these haughty celestials from their ivory thrones.

But the moment shatters in a burst of activity. VanDyke is the first to attack me. His blue eyes harden and narrow, and a shot of pure orange light strikes from his outstretched hand and pierces my chest. It feels like an arrow in my heart.

I stumble back a step, struggling to figure out what's happening, when a ray of turquoise light slams into my left hip.

Other angels see my weakness and join the attack, shooting spears of luminescence at my body.

I stumble again. Pain pings through my nerves, every inch of me alight, burned by lightning, and it's my turn to be tortured.

Every last angel has clambered to their feet now. The male with the long brown ponytail stares at me with an ice-hard glare, and I lurch backward as his ice-blue lightning lights me up.

I fall, but Zaden catches me as I collapse, hissing something into my ear.

Hell cannot be worse than this. My body is alive with suffering, every particle screaming in terror, and the truth is as unshakable as the agony.

These are angels. I am a mortal. I never had a chance.

I'm dimly aware of applause from the gathered humans. Fucking applause. They clap their oppressors and cheer their martyr's downfall. Maybe they are as stupid as the angels think.

But I am no martyr. No hero. Just a failed peasant girl who thought she could be Queen and is about to die to a damn round of applause.

At least I'm going out with a light show. Nobody else can see the spears of light flying at me or appreciate their malevolent beauty. But I can, and it's the last thing I'll ever see.

Zaden slams down a shield around us, a translucent purple bubble I've never seen before. He's still hissing in my ear, but I can't make out the words. Then he lifts me in his arms and pushes through the jeering throng of gentle folk and out the ornate front doors, down the broad stairs and onto the paved streets of Solren.

The last things I see before I pass out are his black eyes staring at me in fury.

Zaden

Scarla is heavy in my arms, as though the weight of murder drags at her soul.

I stride through the streets of Solren, carrying her like a babe. But she is the opposite.

She is a woman who should know better.

My carriage is nowhere to be seen, so I have to take her up a narrow alleyway between two tall buildings. I will kill that driver as soon as he shows up. I will slice off one of his testicles and stuff it up his ass, leaving the other one intact so he can have children and tell them never to disappoint me. I will remove his nose from his face to teach him to have the horse ready when I need it.

I need to get Scarla home. I need to get her away from those angels who would enjoy nothing more than to torture her for decades. I need to get her safe.

My stride eats up the pavers, and I take lefts and rights through the maze of inner Solren, carrying my precious cargo far away from that ball.

The moment she began circling the assembled council in the center of that ballroom, I knew something was wrong. Her face shone with wrongness, with evil. I may not possess Gaze, but I can read Scarla like a greenbird reads the wind.

Everything about her posture, the way her hand danced behind her in the air like she was trailing it through water, the glint of diamond anger in her eyes, all of it was wrong.

I should have stopped her then and there. I should have prevented her from entering the dome. I should have tackled her to the marble floors.

But I didn't, and now she'll pay the price. We will both pay the price.

A scuffling noise to the west has me darting into shadows like a damn rat. I can't help the fear that billows through me. I still expect demons around every corner, coming to extract their measure of revenge for me breaking the bloodbond with Xerxes. When I took his life, I sent ripples through the celestial sphere and woke the demons of hell. Now I'm just waiting for them to strike.

Scar stirs in my arms, blinking up at me with a blank, sweet face that I recognize. Then it hardens, the soft curves of her cheek grinding in determination, and she pushes cold hands against my chest, struggling to get free.

I place her down gently on the cobblestones, and she stumbles for a moment. I grab her, of course. I will always catch her when she falls.

"You're a fucking idiot, Scarla," I growl, spitting in anger. "The Cloaked King keeps his identity secret for a reason. You don't dangle power in front of angels and expect them not to devour it. You should have kept your identity a secret."

Not to mention that she shouldn't have gained the dyad in the first place. But we'll deal with that later.

That hungry look enters her face again, and her eyes narrow. When she speaks, her voice is commanding, and I almost fall to my knees to obey her. "There is no Cloaked King," she declares.

"I am your Cloaked Queen, and you shall kneel before me."

I glance around to make sure nobody is near. My teeth grind so hard my jaw hurts, but I manage to spit out a furious response. "You're not listening, Scar. If you keep going on with this shit, you'll die. Do you understand me? Those angels will fucking kill you, but not before they have tortured you until the end of your days. They will feed you barley and pumpermelon to keep you healthy so they can have their little fun for decades. Then they'll laugh about it for the next few centuries, the little mortal girl who thought she could be Queen. You need to run away and hide, Scar. This isn't a joke."

Moonlight strikes her copper hair, ringing her face in amber fire. "This isn't a joke, you're right." For a moment, I think she's going to give in. I need her to give in. She has to survive because if she dies, then the last of my morality goes with her. I have no reason to be kind or good if Scarla doesn't walk the earth.

But she treads on my hopes and crunches them beneath her heel until they lie dismembered and bleeding on the cobblestones. "I will never hide," she says in a voice ringing with power. "I will never run. I will lead the angels, or I will die trying."

"Then you will die," I snarl. "An undignified and agonizing death. How will that help your little cause?"

Her full lips thin into a wicked slash. "My little cause? Can't you take any part of me seriously? You call me an insect, tell me to run and hide, and now you're saying my life's work is a little cause? Well, maybe you're right about that. Maybe it will only impact the lives of a few thousand people who happen to live at this time in history, which is nothing to someone as grand as you. The cause may be little, but it's mine."

I reach out to grab her shoulder, but she's too quick and ducks out of the way. "You're missing the point," I growl, bristling in fury. "I will support you in your cause. I will make it my life's work to achieve whatever you want done in this world. But I will only do it if you live by my side. Because I cannot survive without you, Scar. I cannot survive another loss."

My words echo off the buildings around us and trail down the empty streets. She knows what I'm talking about. She knows I'm thinking of Elanora and the centuries that losing her stripped from me. She knows that my soul will not survive if she leaves me.

But she doesn't soften. She doesn't step toward me and rest her cheek against my chest. She doesn't lift her mouth in a smile.

She steps backward and plants her feet squarely. "I don't care, angel," she says. "This isn't about you. This is about me."

My heart fucking breaks.

Scar

Absolute certainty. That's all I need. Is that too much to ask?

Absolute certainty that overthrowing the Cloaked Court from within is the right move. Absolute certainty that killing the Cloaked King and those guards was worth it. Absolute certainty that losing my place in heaven was a good trade for peace on earth.

Absolute certainty that Zaden and I could never be together forever.

Zaden's face is pinched, his stubble pronounced against his golden skin. Even in the gloom of evening, tucked among these tall stone buildings, his emerald eyes twinkle, brilliant spots of purity.

Staring at his anguished face, my certainty crumbles. It dissipates into a fine powder and blows away on the gentle warm breeze.

Zaden loves me. And I love him. And the only reason we can't be together forever is that I will never get into heaven now.

Fuck. FUCK. I wasn't supposed to kill the Cloaked King. I was going to expose him and destroy the Cloaked Court.

What have I done? The word murder floats through my mind. Yes, that's what I did. I killed. And wielding the blade felt as natural as breathing.

Zaden reaches out to take my hands in his, and because I'm too weak to resist, I let him. His hands are enormous, warm, making me realize how icy my own are. He squeezes them too hard, painfully gripping them in his rough fingers.

"Walk away from the Court, Scar," he tells me. "I have spent centuries searching for you. The stars watched me as I waited alone, biding their time until you were born. Your birth, your life, give me a reason to exist. You can't know how great and terrible eternity is, the exquisite loneliness of forever. But infinity with you would be joyous.

"Be by my side forever, Scar. We can shape the world into whatever form you desire, as long as we do it together. I am yours, mortal. Forever. Will you be mine too?"

Shivers rack my body, and he squeezes my hand even tighter as though channeling warmth into my body. So this is how being cold feels? It's empty and lonely, like Zaden's vision of eternity.

Tears stream down my face, and I can't stop the quaver in my voice. "I love you, Zaden."

His face relaxes, shedding tension like a second skin, and his angelic aura glows so brightly I have to squint.

He tugs me toward his embrace, and I want so badly to go. To nuzzle into his neck and press against his hard warm chest, to rest in that easy place.

But I've been selfish for too long. Losing Elanora broke Zaden's heart, and it took him centuries to repair it. I can't do that to him again.

"We can never be together," I tell him. "You have forever ahead of you, while I only have a handful of years."

I don't say it, but the crease in his forehead tells me that we're both thinking it. I might not have years at all—if those angels get hold of me, it could be more like hours or days.

He shakes his head, and his green eyes darken. "I don't care about that, Scar. We'll find a way. Just come with me, and I can keep you safe. I'm an angel, woman. I can make anything happen."

But we both know that isn't true. He can't change the past. He can't resurrect those guards or the Cloaked King, can't erase my soul of sin. And he can't bend the Maker to his will.

His stone face and granite jawline melt into wax. "Please, Scar," he begs. Tears glisten in his eyes. I didn't even know angels could cry.

For so long, I wanted to see this man weep, the man who killed my sister.

But now, I can't watch for a moment longer. "Goodbye," I whisper, then I wrench my hands free, jerking painfully and leaving my lover grasping.

I turn and walk down the street, trying not to break into an undignified run to get away faster, trying not to spin and beeline for my angel's arms. But I force myself to walk away, and every step I take cleaves one more shard from my heart.

* * *

Hi there, thanks for reading! I love Scarla so much, and although this one broke my heart a bit, it was also super fun to write.

For the latest on new releases, follow me on Amazon. I write steamy fantasy romance with bad men and badass women.

Chapter 49

FREE BOOK

Sign up to my newsletter to receive a free novella, A Mortal of Caprice... It's never a good idea to catch the eye of the fae king.

A Mortal of Caprice is set in a magical fae realm, and still filled with kickass women and sexy men. Only this time they're fae. Yum. It is the prequel to a steamy fantasy romance series.

* * *

If you enjoyed reading, I'd really appreciate you leaving a review. Reviews are like gold to indie authors like me, truly.

* * *

Now, what are you waiting for? Go get your copy of *Mirror*, the final book in the Fallen Angels trilogy.

Xxx Zara

About the Author

Zara has a pretty sweet life – hubby, kids, and a kick-ass Dyson hairdryer. But that doesn't stop her from inventing new worlds and having steamy affairs with her book boyfriends. Angels and demons and fae, oh my!

Lucky Zara, she gets to spend hours with those sexy beasts every day. The rest of the time she's working in health, negotiating with her kids, and beating her husband to the remote.

But mostly it's angels.

Come along for the ride with Zara and her feisty heroines. You can provide the mulled wine.

You can connect with me on:
- https://zaradusk.com
- https://www.facebook.com/zaraduskauthor
- https://www.tiktok.com/@zaradusk

Subscribe to my newsletter:

✉ https://zaradusk.com

Also by Zara Dusk

He's fated for heaven, but she's doomed for hell

My sexy Angel and I are on a collision course with fate. While he marches towards the heavens in search of the elusive Ring of Roth, I am shackled to the infernal realm, cursed to an eternity of fire and brimstone.

But I won't go down without a fight. I will overthrow the cruel Angels who reign above us.

But with the new power thrumming through my body and recent betrayals burning in my memory, it's hard to remember my noble motives.

All I can focus on is revenge.

The stage is set. The pieces are in motion. The war for justice is about to begin. But no matter the outcome, I can't shake my fears for a future without Zaden. Eternity in hell is nothing compared to eternity without him.

FREE PREQUEL NOVELLA

I'm a mortal in a fae realm filled with marvels, like weather that's influenced by the king's mood.

But life isn't all forested streets and magical forests. There's the fact that everybody here treats me like garbage because I'm not fae. The bratty kids I teach in Human Studies are the worst.

When a student is kidnapped, I must tell the fae king.

Judging by the dark clouds in the sky, the king is already in a foul mood. But when he sees me, it'll get a whole lot worse. The sky will probably split in two.

www.ingramcontent.com/pod-product-compliance
Lightning Source LLC
Chambersburg PA
CBHW030527120726
47904CB00005B/1657